Lucky Strike

Lucky Strike

A Love in El Dorado Romance

Janine Amesta

TULE
PUBLISHING

Dedication

To my fellow Sagittariuses
And to unlikable female characters. Never put out your fire
just because some can't take the heat.

Content Note

Dear Readers,

Never forget that your mental health is important. As a note, this book does contain discussions about parental abandonment, past death of a brother, divorce, depression and poor mental health. There's also strong language and open door love scenes. Even though these characters are put through it, have no fear as a happy ending waits for you on the last page.

Chapter One

KISSING A STRANGE man wasn't on Luna Lanza's to-do list today.

If it had been, perhaps she would have thought twice about getting out of bed this morning—or she would have gotten out of bed faster, depending if the person happened to share the same physical specifications of one Henry Cavill. Yeah, like she'd ever be that lucky.

Not that Luna was looking for kisses. She wasn't. And even if she were, this kiss certainly wouldn't have quenched her thirst. Not that she was thirsty. She wasn't. Even so, it was her first kiss since her breakup with Viggo and returning to her hometown.

The situation surrounding the whole kissing-a-stranger fiasco started when her cousin-in-law, Mia Russo, asked her to be a model for some jewelry images. While Luna was a big fan of selfies and posting to social media, she wasn't the biggest fan of taking posed promotional images. #FakeSmiles #Boring #Ugh

But the photos were for Lanza Fine Jewelry, a shop owned by Luna and her cousin, Ross, a business inherited from their late grandfather. They each had their assigned roles. Ross designed and created the jewelry. Mia, his wife, took pictures. And Luna, when she wasn't using her business degree to do the financial side of the jewelry business, would loan various parts of herself like fingers, wrists, earlobes, and neck for these images and—

Well, she didn't want to get into the whole thing, especially since she was irritable after waking this morning with a fresh batch of cramps. And, without the use of an ax, it was impossible to send individual body parts alone and, therefore, her whole crampy, crabby body was required to meet Mia in Lumsden Park where her cousin-in-law sifted through the contents of her bag, grabbing a camera body and lens.

"Where's this apartment you're going to look at?" her cousin asked.

"There's two. The first one is a cute duplex near Old Town. Then afterward I'll look at Schnell Ridge Apartments. The second is just a backup. I'm already in love with the duplex," she said.

Luna's gaze swept through the park, noticing only a few potential witnesses and, thankfully, most of them were kids. She wore a silky, olive-colored slip dress, because Mia had requested a nice garment with an open neckline that would provide a good canvas backdrop for jewelry displaying. Except Luna wondered if the strappy low-cut bodice with the short hemline was *too* nice and she was feeling more self-conscious than anything else.

At a nearby picnic table was a young man in a faded gray baseball hat. A finger twisted a tawny-brown strand of hair, which had escaped the bottom of his cap. His shoulders hunched as he read a paperback, too enthralled to notice Luna emoting sexy but sweet while in the midst of crabgrass and discarded burger wrappers.

"There's no need to move out so quickly," Mia said, adjusting her glasses. "You know you're welcome to live with Ross and me for as long as you want. No pressure when you're looking today. I never had a sister growing up, so you're the next best thing and I love it. Maybe we can have a scary movie marathon tonight and make gourmet popcorn." The woman offered a bright smile.

This was exactly the problem. Luna would be living *with them*, as though she was a spinster aunt crashing in the guest room. That wasn't much of a consolation prize, especially considering Mia was five months pregnant and they needed the extra space. All Luna wanted, all she'd ever wanted, was a special place of her own.

"Do you want me to go with you?" Mia asked. "I don't mind. We can give each other a code word, so if you don't like the place, I can come up with a great excuse to get us out of there. Like maybe I'm having weird contractions or I'll have an emergency pregnancy craving for a buffalo chicken waffle wrap." Her eyes drifted upward as if considering this. "The second one might be true. Maybe after apartment hunting we can stop for some lunch. I tried one of those waffle wraps the other day when I was taking photos for that new restaurant downtown, Placerville Waffle Company. Have you tried it? We should totally go there."

"I haven't. Maybe another time. I have other errands I need to do."

Mia shrugged, not at all affected by the rejected offer. After making some adjustments to the camera in her hand, she began posing Luna, arranging the rose gold necklace featuring a delicate pine branch, until she was satisfied and the shutter on the camera clicked away.

"Your hair makes me so jealous. Ross has great hair too. Must be something in the family genes. I'm looking for a new hairdresser. The one I've been seeing is not working out and she convinced me to try these bangs. I hate them already." The point was illustrated further when Mia blew out a breath, feathering the flat bangs in question. "Now I have to grow them out and find a new person. I swear, finding your hairdresser soulmate is even more difficult than finding your *actual* soulmate."

"You should see Tessa Lui." As soon as the name passed Luna's lips she regretted it, her mouth snapping shut.

Mia flicked through the images, not noticing her sudden unexplained silence. "Is she downtown? If that's who you see, then I'm definitely in."

"I'll text you her information later." Or conveniently forget. Thoughts about what the hair stylist, also her ex-bestie, might say to Mia, about Luna, put an instant rock in her stomach.

"Aw, you're really the best. I'm so happy you're back in town again and I know Ross loves it too." Her face was so warm and sincere, Luna considered changing her mind about forgetting to send Tessa's information. Perhaps Mia wouldn't mention where the recommendation had come from and, therefore, her opinion about Luna wouldn't be at risk of changing.

Her cousin's smile turned into a frown as she studied the images on the camera's LCD screen. "I wish we could make this a couple photo."

"Since I'm the only one here, I don't think that's going to happen."

Mia tapped a finger against her chin. "Unless we could get someone else."

"I hope you're not thinking Ross because that would be gross and weird—"

"What about that guy over there?"

Luna's gaze followed Mia's pointed finger of destiny, which led to the man at the picnic table in the baseball cap. She hated this plan already, because she didn't like strange men getting involved in her daily activities, nor did she believe in destiny. "Please tell me you're joking."

"What? He's cute and seems nice. I just want a few shots. It's not a big deal."

Luna opened her mouth to protest further because this whole thing was already awkward and humiliating enough, but Mia was on a new mission, making her way toward the man. As a distraction, Luna considered shouting, *Let's get buffalo chicken waffle wraps!* or *If you don't stop at this moment, Mia Russo, you can forget about Tessa and you'll be stuck with horrible bangs forever.* Threats and bribery were all Luna had at the moment.

At the picnic table, her cousin cautiously approached, and the man jerked from his intense book-reading focus with surprise. They were too far away for Luna to understand the conversation, and she stood in place, with her hand on a hip, trying to decipher the interaction through charade skills.

First, Mia swept a hand to her camera, then to Luna, and, lastly, to her pregnant belly. *Really, Mia?* What did being pregnant have anything to do with anything? She doubted the woman would ever go so far as to say, *Hey, see this camera? If you don't take a picture with my depressingly dumped cousin over there, my demon baby will come for your blood while you sleep.* Unlike Luna, Mia didn't have to resort to threats. Plus, her cousin-in-law was too charming and sunny to ever be carrying a demon baby. The kid was an innocent pawn in Mia's plan, and was currently Luna's favorite baby in the world, demon or not.

Mia was more likely to convince someone by saying something sweet, and then she'd flash her solitary dimple. The dimple was the *closer* when it came to sealing the deal. Luna was convinced the dimple was the root of all Mia's power.

Regardless of what was said to the man, it worked, like a charm. No surprise there. Both of them approached her spot in the park. Luna was doubtful about the whole couple photo idea, especially considering it was being thrown together with whatever random park man Mia could persuade into her scheme, cute or not.

From what she could see, he was nearly the complete opposite from Viggo. Her ex-boyfriend was extremely tall, with the body of a linebacker, dark hair, and the bluest eyes ever imagined. Luna didn't believe in love at first sight but wasn't someone like Viggo exactly the type of man she was supposed to fall in love with?

If Viggo was Dolce & Gabbana, the man walking toward her was second-hand Levi's. He was a white guy with brown hair and most definitely wasn't six feet tall. She would guess five feet eight inches at the most with a slighter build than her ex. Both the baseball hat and army-style jacket he wore were weathered at the edges. Unlike her ex though, he had an approachable, easygoing vibe about him, which was probably the reason her cousin had chosen him.

"I'm Mia, by the way," her cousin said to him.

"Sam." His voice, while deep, was unassuming. There was a barely perceptible hitch in his step. "I think we went to the same school."

Mia brightened. "Oh yeah? Sorry, I don't have the best memory when it comes to that kind of thing. Do you know my husband, Ross?"

"Manasse? Yeah, we weren't friends but we had a few classes together." Sam's hat overshadowed most of his face. His exact features were still somewhat of an enigma at this point, except for a jawline covered with a scruff of facial hair.

Since he went to school with Ross and Mia that put him only a few years older than Luna, who was twenty-five. She felt forgotten at this impromptu class reunion, which did a great job of exacerbating her PMS.

"Oh, this is Lulu," Mia said. "She's Ross's younger cousin."

Luna almost chipped a tooth, grinding her jaw. She still hadn't broken Ross from his habit of using the childhood nickname but, even worse, Mia sometimes did as well. She couldn't very well shout, *Luna!* without appearing childish, and it's not as though it mattered since she'd never see this guy again. Instead, she offered a tight smile.

"So, yeah, as I was saying," Mia continued in an extra cheerful tone of voice to cover the lull in conversation, "we just need a few photos of you standing next to Lulu, looking at her like you're her boyfriend or whatever. I won't take too much of your time." The dimple closer made its appearance.

"Okay," Sam replied but he didn't move.

The whole thing was weird, and without thinking Luna blurted, "Are you sure about this, Mia? Look at how he's dressed compared to me. He looks like—" The rest of her sentence dropped off a cliff when she realized she was about to voice her inside thoughts, ones Mia would, no doubt, consider mean. These days, she was trying her best to keep most of her brutally honest opinions locked inside her head.

The other two people waited, as if expecting Luna to finish her sentence. When she didn't, Sam said, "I look like what?" His expression was neutral but she swore there was an amused glint in his eye as if his question was a dare.

Unfortunately for him, Luna always took a dare, regardless of whether it was a good or bad idea. Spoiler alert. It was usually bad. "You look like you're about to meet someone from Craigslist in an abandoned parking lot in order to sell some illegal turtles or something."

Mia gasped. "Lulu!"

Confirmed. Bad idea.

He barked a small laugh as though surprised, her comment giving him permission to give her an up-and-down perusal in return. She was finally being seen but now the judgment was clearly on the other foot. Not that Luna didn't deserve it. She most definitely did.

"Yes?" she asked, daring him in return.

He blinked. "Nothing."

Well...that was disappointing. In truth, he didn't have to say anything because she could guess his opinion about her outfit. She looked like the third-in-charge at a bachelorette party, the one who's secretly jealous of the bride and making out with a stranger after getting too tipsy. This was one more reason she regretted unearthing this dress from the recesses of her closet, because she wasn't that girl—not anymore.

"What are you wearing underneath? I-I mean under the jacket." Mia asked, getting somewhat flustered.

Sam revealed a simple black T-shirt, and Mia declared it fine enough for the photos. As much as Luna wanted to continue voicing her disapproval, it'd be all lies. The guy had great arms and he'd chosen a shirt that fit him well. *Dammit.* Her reluctance in participating in this couple photo plan was already eroding.

"I look nice," Luna said as if to refute his earlier unspoken judgment, sweeping her long, wavy locks across the front of one shoulder.

"Yeah, you *look* nice." His tone implied she only looked the part and wasn't nice at all. Ha! Perhaps the guy had some bite after all. Her interest shifted back to intrigue. Also, Luna wasn't about to argue because she may be a lot of things, but she would never claim to be nice. That adjective was reserved for people like Mia.

Before she could reply, her cousin stepped between them with an "excuse me" and removed his hat, unleashing a mass of wavy, light brown hair. His brows were a shade darker; his left eyebrow was bisected with a scar. And he had the sharpest cheekbones she'd ever seen. God, maybe the finger of destiny was on to something.

She nearly jumped when her cousin-in-law took one of those solid arms of his and posed it around her waist like both of them were bendable dolls. His gaze, no longer shadowed by his hat, lifted to hers and she was hit by the color of warm bourbon making up his irises. Her breath hitched in her chest as she felt his hand flexing where it was fixed on the small of her back.

In the background, Mia clicked the shutter button on her camera but Luna hardly noticed, finding herself fixated by the man beside her. "I'm not always a brat, you know," she murmured. Who knows why it was important for her to tell him this. And, truth be told, she wasn't a brat as much as she was prone to mischief but these two things sometimes looked the same.

His gaze remained fixed on her, starting at her eyes before traveling lower on her face. "Well, we all have to sleep sometime."

His response was dry but was exactly the kind that appealed to her—

Nope. This would not do at all. Luna needed to keep a distance, and since a physical one wasn't possible at the moment, an emotional one would have to do. She sighed and flatly said, "I knew I should have stayed in bed today."

"I knew I should have held out for more than free coffee."

Ah, so that's what was promised to Sam in exchange for his cooperation. Mia's best friend, Natalie, co-owned Pony Expresso, which was the coffee shop next to the jewelry store, and therefore Mia got free drinks all the time. Luna wanted to laugh and she had no idea why. Maybe it was the ridiculousness of the whole situation. "Sucker," she said, giving him a slight hip check.

His reaction to this additional physical contact was releasing a soft grunt. This delighted her, and she considered doing it again.

"Hello? Lulu?"

Luna's focus snapped to Mia, whom she'd forgotten about. "What?"

"I just asked if you could focus in this direction." The woman pointed to the ground near her. "And smile. Sam, you can just keep your head turned to her. Yes. Beautiful. Love it." The camera shutter clicked away. "Sam, turn to me and, Lu, look at him now. Perfect."

Luna tried to refocus and remember this was just a quick photo shoot and wasn't anything else... Sam's profile was nice. His nose was strong and straight, even better than Viggo's. A person only had to get past twenty pounds of hair and an old baseball hat to see it, like uncovering a weathered chest and being completely unaware of what treasures might be inside.

"Lu, maybe you can do a quick..."

"What?" Luna asked.

Her cousin-in-law poked her cheek with a finger, giving herself an additional dimple. "Last pic, I swear."

She rolled her eyes. Mia was impossible. Except, while she should hate everything about this, there was a part of her that didn't hate it at all.

Strange.

As she leaned toward the man, her mouth puckered in preparation to plant a fake kiss on his cheek, Sam said, "Huh?" while rotating his head.

And, because she had the worst luck in the world, their lips met.

Chapter Two

THE LENGTH OF time their mouths were pressed together was between receiving an electric shock and the words, *Oh Shit*, going through Luna's mind. Her eyes popped open and Sam jerked away as if her lips were covered with razor wire instead of lip balm.

"Why the hell did you do that?" he said while at the same time she yelled, "Why'd you turn your head?"

"How'd I know you were going to kiss me?" A hand swiped across his mouth, which did a great job of popping whatever playful bubble she thought they'd been in.

It appeared she had been wrong. Again.

Their exchange from before hadn't been a fun, flirty back-and-forth. He *actually* had been annoyed by her. This was the only explanation for why he reacted as if her lips were the most repulsive thing he'd ever experienced.

Not that she cared, but still. Her skin grew hot as the humiliation set in, and she wanted to die. Then a flash of anger went through her at being put in this situation in the first place.

"Did you not hear Mia? She said to give you a peck on the cheek. It's not like I was doing it for fun. Why in the world would I give some random guy in the park a kiss? I'm done, Mia." When things got too far out of her control, Luna did what she always did: looked for the nearest escape route. Except, when she stepped away, the stiletto heel of one of her shoes caught in the soft dirt, causing her to reel backwards, her arms windmilling like a cartoon character.

In a step, Sam was there, steadying her with a solid arm around the waist. "Whoa. Sorry, I—You just caught me off-guard."

"You don't seem to be off-guard now." She pushed against his chest, her blush approaching a hue that could be considered atomic. He didn't get to play the nice guy now. It was too late. She knew the truth of how he *really* felt. While Luna preferred to stomp away with all the warranted indignation owed to her, this was made more difficult when her heels kept sinking into the soft ground. She managed to propel herself across the park on nothing but spite and aggravation.

Behind her, Mia scrambled to collect her camera bag and rushed to catch her. "God, Lulu. I'm so sor—"

"Luna," she replied through gritted teeth as she continued to hobble across the grass, narrowly avoiding being tripped by a rolling soccer ball from one of the nearby kids. "I don't like it when you guys call me Lulu."

"You're right. I'm sorry."

She brought a hand to a heated cheek. "That was completely embarrassing. I told you I didn't even want to do the couple thing."

"I'm sorry. It was my fault. I got a little caught up in taking pictures. But you're right to be mad at me. Let me make it up to you."

"No." The word came out a little more forcefully than she intended, and Luna stopped at her vehicle in the parking lot, taking a breath to calm herself. She could push against Mia a little but she worried about pushing too much. What if Ross found out? His wife and unborn baby were everything, and Luna couldn't risk losing more than she already had simply because she couldn't always control her mouth. "Sorry, I'm...I'm just PMS-y today."

She rubbed Luna's upper arm. "Oh, yeah, I totally get it." Although Luna had her doubts Mia *did* get it. Had she ever had a day of breaking down in tears and yelling at someone for no good reason? Even with the misfortune of a bad haircut, Mia treated it as an inconvenience, one that would grow its way out and everything would be fine.

Mia's eyes held concern. "Do you want me to get you a tea or something from Pony Expresso? I don't mind."

"No. It's fine. I'll be fine. I have to go to the bank to make a deposit for the store and then I want to run home and change out of these clothes before meeting with the landlady at the duplex." Luna wished she could change now because the hemline felt shorter and shorter all the time and she didn't want to give her potential landlord the same flighty, party-girl impression she'd surely given Sam. Unfortunately, all she had was a pair of old leggings and a ratty tank top she kept in her bug-out bag in the back of her SUV for when the need to escape became too much for her.

"Just call me if you need anything. Don't worry about the photos. You know you have the final word on which one gets picked. If you don't like the ones with Sam, then no problem. You looked gorgeous in all of them by the way."

She pulled Mia into a hug. "All right. I'll check in with you later."

Luna got in her car and drove to the bank. As she waited in line, she allowed the embarrassing photo shoot to replay in her mind. With fifteen minutes of distance from the situation, she concluded it wasn't a big deal and perhaps she had overreacted a touch. Regardless, it was an innocent accident, and no one was to blame. And maybe Sam hadn't hated her and been telling the truth when he said he'd been caught off-guard. Aw, well. It didn't matter.

As she was leaving, she almost bumped into a familiar person.

"Tessa."

Her ex-hairdresser/ex-best friend's dark eyes became wary. "Lulu. How are you?"

"Uh, fine. You?" Luna nervously adjusted the dress strap on one shoulder.

"Good. Your hair looks nice." This could have been a compliment if it wasn't for the complete lack of warmth in the sentence.

"Oh, thank you." Luna flushed. She had driven an hour to get her hair done at a nice salon near Sacramento a few weeks prior.

In high school, Tessa and Luna had been instant best friends. Tessa, with her Thai-American heritage, had warm brown skin, glossy black hair, and was adorable in her petiteness. Luna, with her hodge-podge mixed European blood, was taller and fairer in coloring.

Luna had thought this was a friendship she could always count on, but she had been wrong. Their paths diverged when she went to Chico State and Tessa had stayed behind to get her beautician license and work in her mom's salon. The friendship, which had once been loud and electric, fizzled away like a windblown dandelion. She learned, once again, that she couldn't count on anything, a lesson she'd learn over and over again.

"How's your mom doing?" Luna asked awkwardly.

"Okay," Tessa answered, shifting out of the way of another bank customer. "She keeps talking about retiring."

There was an uncomfortable pause between them, which was something they never had to worry about before. Luna grew nervous, pulling on the ends of her hair. "Are you still seeing Cam?" she asked, referring to Tessa's high school sweetheart.

"We were married last year." Her ex-best friend raised her hand, displaying a simple silver band.

Luna's jaw jarred open at this new information. Tessa hadn't been active on social media for the last few years and their communication had been non-existent. She did her best to recover, feigning cheerfulness. The truth was, there was no reason to expect her ex-friend to invite her to anything, let alone a wedding. Luna didn't have a right to feel snubbed. "Oh, that's great. Congratulations. You should have reached out. You know Ross could have made something special for you."

Tessa dropped her eyes as she adjusted the purse handles resting on her forearm. "The wedding was very low-key and we didn't have a lot of money. We just went to one of those tiny chapels in Tahoe. It was just family and our friends."

"Oh, yeah, that makes sense." But her skin grew hot because she felt the sting of no longer being included in the *'our friends'* group of Tessa's life. Whether she had a right or not, Luna was hurt all the same even while knowing it was her own fault.

The awkward silence returned.

Tessa straightened. "I should really get in line."

"Yeah, of course. I have an appointment I need to get to anyway. It was good catching up with you. Tell Cam and your family hello for me." Luna pushed through the door to escape the uncomfortable interaction.

While crossing the parking lot, she noticed a roundish bulge on top of the front passenger tire of her SUV. It was a cat. It quickly climbed down as she approached, hiding behind the same tire on the pavement. Luna had a soft spot for most animals, but she preferred cats because, personality-wise, they had a lot in common.

She knelt and made soft noises while reaching a hand toward it. "Here, kitty kitty." After some coaxing the small gray and white cat took a timid step forward before making the decision Luna was an okay human being, approaching close enough to rub against her leg.

"You're just a scrawny thing, aren't you, little cat?" She gently stroked along the animal's spine, the bones feeling like delicate twigs. The cat was thin, and probably flea-ridden, and definitely filthy. With her heartstrings properly tugged, Luna decided she couldn't very well leave the cat here. She had time. The cat allowed her to clutch it to her chest and she tucked the animal into her bug-out bag in the back, zipping it enough so the cat's head peeked out.

Luna drove to the local animal shelter to surrender the

cat. It meowed helplessly while pawing at her clothes and arms. Even though it might complicate things, she couldn't help but leave her number in case the animal was never claimed.

By the time Luna turned the key in her car's ignition, she was alarmed to discover the time. She'd taken too long. There was no time to go home and change. Luna had to drive straight to the duplex. Her eyes dropped to the party-girl olive-green slip dress she wore, and she patted it to remove cat hair and grime.

With a nervous energy, she sped to the duplex near Old Town. The 1940s-era split-building was tucked into a hill covered in some kind of vine, looking as picturesque as she had imagined. She loved it and crossed her fingers the landlady would be taken with her, too. From her car, she snapped an image of the place with her phone, uploading it to Instagram with #futurehome #foothillsliving #greendoor before checking her reflection in the visor mirror and reapplying lip gloss. On her walk to the door, she ran a hand across the fabric of her dress while helplessly tugging the neckline up and the hemline down.

When a woman opened the door, Luna's heart jumped in her throat. At first glance she had the mistaken impression it was her mother, who had abandoned four-year-old Luna to be raised by her grandfather when she moved to the other side of the country to start a new life without her. There was a period of time, mostly when she was young, that Luna would have given anything to see her mom. She now felt the opposite and didn't want to have anything to do with Amy. Why should she waste time and energy on someone who obviously didn't care about her?

While the woman at the door shared the same coloring and had similar features, it wasn't her mother. Of course not. Now it was obvious. But the woman grew impatient waiting for her to say something. "Yes?"

"Oh! Uh…hi. I'm Luna Lanza. I-I have an appointment to view the rental." She tried evoking as much of Mia's charm as she could while reaching out her hand with a smile.

The woman shook it with a light touch while doing a slow scan of Luna's outfit, making her even more flustered. "Oh. You're Luna? Fine. I'm Michelle."

In the entryway, glossy wood flooring and white walls greeted her. The living room wasn't big but it had plenty of natural light, built-in bookcases and a beautiful brick fireplace. If Luna was going to live in Placerville, she wouldn't mind doing it in this style. She was already making a mental map for where to put the new, elegant furniture she would later purchase. "The floors are lovely."

"They're original to the house," Michelle said. "We spent a lot of money having them restored. You might want to be careful if you're wearing heels."

She flushed. "Oh, should I remove my shoes?"

The woman breezed through the living room into the kitchen, ignoring her. "We need someone who's going to treat this home with respect. It's been in my family for a long time. Do you know how to properly clean hardwood floors?"

Luna rushed to remove her heels and catch up with the woman, almost tripping over her own feet and bashing a toe into the wall. "Ow. Um, I mean, I've never lived in a place with real hardwood flooring, but I'm sure—"

"We put in all new appliances and expect them to stay in pristine condition and to be cleaned regularly."

"Okay—"

"All the cabinetry is original and very old. Please don't slam the doors or be too rough with the hinges."

Luna carefully shut the cabinet she had been inspecting. "No, I wouldn't."

She was taken through the rest of the home, as the landlady listed one "don't" after another while also making it a point to inform her she wasn't allowed to bring anyone else to live with her "like men or filthy pets". Was Michelle this way with all tenants or was this attitude only geared toward Luna? Her confidence at getting the place was dropping with every passing moment.

Once they had made their way to the front door again, Michelle gave her appearance another thorough inspection. "This is a very old house. Maybe you're looking for something easier, more modern."

"I actually really love old places. They have character." She slipped her shoes back onto her feet.

Michelle opened the door, ushering her to the concrete stoop. "My brother and I just want to make sure we're getting someone who will take care of the home like their own. This is not really a party house, nor do we want it to be."

"I-I'm not really a party girl anymore," she replied, attempting to make a convincing argument for herself.

"You have a blessed day now." And Michelle shut the door in her face, leaving her stunned and dejected.

She trudged to her car, holding her emotions at bay.

How could something she dreamed about be gone in less than ten minutes? She wasn't given a fair chance. Her eyes dropped to her dress and she noticed a dirt smudge in the fabric from when she had clutched the stray cat to her chest earlier.

Dammit.

She raised her chin, pushing everything down, as far as it would go, to the tips of her toes where she wouldn't have to feel anything if she didn't want to.

Someone who looked like her mother would not beat her today.

Besides, she couldn't cry. She had another apartment appointment to go to.

Chapter Three

S AM SUNDERLAND RAN a frustrated hand across his hair, before turning his hat backwards and hunching behind the old, coin-operated dryer, searching for answers as to why it wasn't working. He'd finished replacing the drive belt and yet the drum stubbornly refused to spin.

"Have you tried unplugging it and plugging it back in? Maybe you forgot the second part." This was asked by the precocious eight-year-old named Zabe, who enjoyed following him around as he did repairs around Schnell Ridge Apartments.

He narrowed his eyes at the gangly-limbed kid with sun-kissed skin and pixie-cut blue hair. "Yeah, it's plugged in. I have half a brain." Just in case, he gave a quick glance at the outlet and was relieved to confirm his status as person-with-brain. For good measure, he smacked the metal wall of the appliance to see if this helped. Sam wasn't looking forward to giving his dad, the penny pincher who owned the property, the bad news about the necessary purchase of a new second-hand dryer.

One thing he didn't need was an audience, especially one who made it necessary to curtail colorful expletives after jamming a finger. "It's the middle of the day. Aren't you supposed to be in school?"

Zabe rolled her eyes. "Do you not know about weekends? Besides, I bet I can learn more in half a day than you could learn in a full one."

"That's probably true," Sam muttered beneath his breath. Zabe was smart. She'd probably become a senator or a lawyer instead of a twenty-nine-year-old manager/handyman of a collection of shitty apartments. "Why aren't you inside, wasting time playing Heroes' Calling or something and making other players cry? That has to be more fun than watching me break things."

She tilted her head, lips scrunching together. "What's Heroes' Calling?"

"Are you kidding me? That game was da bomb. My brother and I used to spend our whole summer playing that on Xbox." At the mention of Nate, an emotional rope wrapped itself around his chest and tightened. He ignored it, returning to his task with the dryer instead.

"What's *da bomb*? Is that an old man saying?"

"Get out of here, youth." Sam chucked a red grease rag at her but, with a giggle, she dodged the soft projectile, and it flew past the open laundry room door. Zabe chased after it.

"Hey, Sam?"

"Yeah."

"There's a girl knocking on your door. A *really* pretty girl." Zabe said this last sentence in a teasing, sing-song fashion.

"Ow. Fu—dge." Pulling his head out from the inside of the dryer, he had banged it on the edge, knocking his hat off. He rubbed at the scalp pain before replacing the baseball cap.

"Why would a pretty girl be coming to see you?" Zabe squinted an eye as though this was the most perplexing math problem. Pretty girl plus Sam equals error. Does not compute. Please try again.

The time on his phone sent him scrambling to his feet. "Oh, shit. That has to be the prospective renter for apartment seven."

"Ooooo. You said the s-word."

Dammit. He had been doing so well, too.

As he patted the dirt and cobwebs from his clothes, Zabe leaned out the door with one hand gripping the door frame, keeping her anchored. She waved and hollered, "He's coming, lady. Don't worry. He's just fixing his hair."

He sighed. "Give me a break, Zabe."

She giggled and continued waving her free hand. "He's coming. Any minute now."

He made his way across the yard toward his apartment/office. His right knee was bothering him today, as if someone had replaced his tendons with brand-new rubber bands. Seven years after the accident, most days he was fine but today was not one of those days. As someone who had started college with the intention of going into sports medicine, he was well aware of what exercises and stretches he could do to help the situation, but he also didn't care. As far as he was concerned, the punishment could continue. Busted-ass knee, crap-shack apartment, no younger brother. Play stupid games, win stupid prizes.

The pretty girl, as Zabe described her, had her back to him with a hand placed on one jutted hip. She was focused on the phone held in her other hand. She wore black leggings that hugged every curve on the lower half of her body. The top half was a loose gray tank top but this was partially covered by long wavy brunette locks. If the back part was this tantalizing, he couldn't imagine what the front—

"You." Her gaze zipped to his after turning her head.

"Lulu?"

Full, glossy lips tasting of watermelon stretched into a disapproving flat line. His taste buds still marveled at the burst of flavor that had hit his lips that morning. Sam had instantly regretted reacting so quickly, wishing he had allowed himself to relish the fruity sweetness before wiping it away. This probably made him a sad, desperate single guy but he didn't care.

The point was he'd never met a person who'd instantly set him on edge by their very presence. How was a man supposed to prepare for this? When it came to interacting with a woman such as Lulu, his brain had to go with the worst possible options. Either he'd be a flustered, bumbling buffoon, or someone who was ready to pick a fight. There didn't seem to be anything in between. This was not the impression he'd wanted to make but maybe his luck was changing and he was getting a second opportunity, a chance to do better with her.

Her frown hadn't budged. "I actually prefer the name Luna. Please tell me you're just wandering through and you don't live here."

His brow pressed together because his second chance wasn't off to an encouraging start. "If I did, is it a problem?"

"Well, I've been spending the day assuring myself that I would never see you again, so you being here is only proving that the powers that be thought it would be hilarious to toy with me, which I don't appreciate at all. Today has already been challenging enough." In spite of her words, he detected a brief glint of amusement flashing across her features.

He relaxed, letting his lips curl upward. "Somehow, I'm not surprised you've centered yourself, even in the world of gods. You ever think that maybe they're actually toying with me?"

Her gaze dropped, a smile appearing, and, suddenly, getting back into her good graces no longer felt insurmountable, like a fresh breeze sweeping through the area. Zabe was right. She was really pretty with her dark wavy locks and bright hazel eyes, like the personification of the first bright days of fall.

"Either way, that's probably a good enough reason for us to avoid each other," she said.

He kicked a loose rock on the ground, before meeting her eyes again. "Sounds like a lost cause then."

"Completely lost. So, you just move along wherever you were going so I can continue with my business."

"Sam's the apartment manager here, and he knows how to fix anything. And, trust me, there's *a lot* that needs fixing, so you want him around." Zabe crossed her arms in a typical defense stance, ready to do battle on his behalf.

Sam scratched his eyebrow. "Okay, thanks, Zabe. I can take it from here." He refocused on the woman. "I suppose you're the Luna Lanza who's here to look at apartment seven."

"Yup."

"Let me just grab the key."

When Sam returned from his office, Zabe was bouncing on her heels, chatting happily with Luna. "And then Nicholas Papadakis, his family was from Greece, in number two, lives next to me and my dad. He has a Chihuahua named Luna too. Wouldn't it be great to have two Lunas living here? But if you're looking for a place that's da bomb, it's *definitely* not here. It doesn't have a pool or anything. Do you think you can talk Sam into putting in a pool? He'd probably listen to someone pretty like you."

"All right, Zabe, I'm sure your dad wants you to be doing something productive like...I don't know. Reading? Let me show this apartment in peace."

The kid waved after exclaiming she couldn't wait for Luna to be her new neighbor, before scampering away.

"Da bomb?" Luna asked as they climbed the staircase.

He cringed because he already felt less than cool without having to be shown up by an eight-year-old. "Not sure where she picked that up. No one talks like that anymore."

"She also asked if I was going to make cookies like Ms. Carol. She was trying to convince me that this is an apartment building rule."

A smile touched his lips. Ms. Carol's oatmeal cookies had always been a welcome gift on his doorstep. He didn't have much in his life to look forward to but sitting on the steps, inhaling ten cookies at a time, while chatting with the older woman, was one of those simple pleasures he missed. "Ms. Carol used to have apartment seven but she died."

He realized his mistake when Luna paused on the stairs, her eyes large. "Excuse me?"

"I—N-no. Not like—" He couldn't get his mouth to

cooperate other than to release a series of stammers. His fingers interlaced on top of his ballcap-covered head. *Goddammit.* He should have let Zabe give the apartment tour. She may be a know-it-all Chatty Cathy but she at least knew better than to mention tenants dying. Yup, bumbling buffoon mode came right on schedule. He tried to save the situation and his dignity. "She didn't die *in* the apartment. She was visiting family in San Francisco when it happened."

Her moss-and-gold-colored eyes studied him for a few moments before continuing her climb to the second level. Sam was never so off-kilter in his life, gripping the metal stair railing tighter as he followed her. If he wasn't careful, this was going to be the park situation all over again, and he couldn't let that happen, not if they were going to be neighbors.

The Schnell Ridge apartment building was basic in its rectangular shape, and its landscaping was almost non-existent. Built during the 1990s, it claimed two levels, with twelve apartments total. All apartment entrances were on the outside with a balcony-type walkway on the second level.

Number seven was the one above his, and Sam had occupied apartment one since graduating from high school. After spending his youth, being obsessed with *The Fast and the Furious* type of street racing, along with his brother, he'd finally buckled down and decided on going to college. The plan was then for him to hand the keys over to Nate, who wanted to go into the family business of property management. Of course, the accident changed everything. With Nate's death, Sam never finished his sports medicine degree and was still here at Schnell Ridge Apartments all these years later. When he and Luna reached the door to apartment seven, he slipped the key into the deadbolt. It took some jiggling for the bolt to unlock. "I...uh...think the door frame may have settled a bit and is a little tight is all." He jammed his shoulder into the door to pop it and then caught it before the knob slammed into the wall.

"I can try and fix that for you," Sam said, rubbing the shoulder that had acted as a battering ram moments before.

He let her enter first, making the conscious decision to keep the door open. At least the place was clean. The tan-colored carpet was freshly vacuumed and there was a light scent of Pine-Sol and fresh paint in the air.

Luna's face, though, revealed a slight frown. "Well...it looks like an apartment."

"Yup, exactly as advertised." He shoved his hands in his pockets before following her into the small galley-style kitchen beside an equally small spot for a dining room table. There were a couple cracks at the edge of the beige checkered linoleum.

An apartment was the best way to describe the living conditions at Schnell Ridge because the place had all the personality of a basic cheese sandwich. His own place shared the same specifications as did the remaining ten apartments. Regardless, he wasn't sure what she expected, nor did he understand the disappointment flashing across her face. It was clean, in relatively good working order, and had enough room to throw down a mattress. What else was needed?

"The appliances are included," he mentioned when Luna inspected the fridge.

He fiddled with a kitchen drawer and the knob popped

off in his hand. *Dammit.* He shrugged sheepishly as he tossed it onto the counter. "The screw must have been loose in the back, maybe it's stripped. I can put in another one."

Luna flicked on the kitchen faucet which started fine, but then the water hit the basin with enough force to send a spray of liquid in her direction. She squeaked in shock.

He rushed to shut the faucet off. "Sorry. I...uh, it's just the aerator. Probably needs a new one or maybe it wasn't screwed in all the way. I—Are you okay?"

Luna wiped a sheen of droplets from her neck and he couldn't help noticing one single drop as it did a graceful glide from her neck to the dip at the center of her collarbone.

"I'm starting to wonder if this place is booby-trapped."

She was half right. For Sam, the apartment building had become all trap, no booby. This wasn't ending anytime soon as his day was turning into one embarrassing moment after the next. So much for making a charming second impression thanks to this cursed apartment complex.

He screwed the aerator onto the end of the faucet. "Sorry. This place keeps you on your guard."

Those clear hazel eyes flicked to him with a slight smile on her lips. "That certainly explains this morning. This place must take *all* your guard."

"Yeah, maybe," was all he could say because whatever she did to him was happening again. All he could focus on were her lips, his mind replaying how soft she felt, and how she tasted of watermelons. Around her, he didn't seem to have any guard at all. Even worse, she appeared to be the type of woman who'd push all sorts of buttons that didn't need to be pushed. Half of him hoped she hated the apartment to save him the agony of ever having to deal with her.

"I'm going to look at the rest of the place," Luna said.

"Yeah, sure." He occupied himself with the kitchen faucet, turning it on. The water flowed with a steady stream, the issue resolved. He'd focus on fixing one problem at a time.

"The place comes with one parking spot," he said, kicking himself for resorting to the same boring bullet-point information that had been posted on the apartment listing. Didn't he have one interesting thing he could say? There had to be something... Oh, he had it! Sam cleared his throat. "The guy in apartment eight is pretty quiet. Lives by himself." Quiet neighbors were a plus, right? "He's a firefighter."

Damn, Sam. He could almost feel Nate smacking him on the head. *Why not continue telling this very attractive woman more about the handsome bachelor neighbor with hero-size muscles? Might as well introduce her to Firefighter Ryan right now.* Between the two brothers, Nate had been the one with the smoother charm game. Sam was out of practice these days.

"He's gone a lot though, so he's...not around much," he finished, cringing once more. Ghost Nate had to be shaking his head in disgust.

"Mm-hmm," was all Luna said before moving into one of the two bedrooms. The zipping sound of Venetian blinds ascending came from the room. The window offered a glorious view of the trunk of a large sequoia tree and not much else. The mirror closet doors slid open followed by a bang.

Luna gasped. "Oh God! A little help."

Sam rushed into the bedroom and found her wrestling

with one of the closet doors that had slipped from the track. He jumped into action, his hands pressing against the mirror to take the weight from her. It took a moment to realize Luna was trapped between him and the door, his body pressed against her back. Without heels, she could tuck her head under his chin, which was something he missed experiencing or perhaps he only missed having a warm body in general to melt into.

Except, this wasn't appropriate behavior toward a potential tenant. "Sorry." He shifted the weight to one arm, allowing her to escape. Heat traveled across the surface of his skin as he popped the closet door into place. "Maybe the track is cracked. I can replace that."

God, what a fucking disaster, he thought, following her into the living room. Second chances were clearly wasted on him because making an impression of someone who was smooth and charming wasn't something in his wheelhouse.

Even while wearing a tank top featuring a roaring lion, instead of a silky green dress, Luna was far out of his league—not that he had much of a league these days. It wasn't how she dressed but rather her posture, how she moved and talked, as if she aspired to the position of queen someday. She didn't belong in a crap-shack apartment on Schnell Ridge Road.

"Would that be okay?" Luna asked.

Uuuuuuuh. What?

She'd been talking to him, and he'd been completely preoccupied with his own thoughts. He focused on the carpet, his hat hiding the view as if giving her mystery request careful consideration. His mind raced through common apartment inquiries. Was this about a pet? The building allowed small animals. Perhaps the tank top was a hint. Luna strutting around with a pet lion was a queen move. Although, she probably had some pampered designer dog named Peaches or something. How bad could it be? He decided to take the risk rather than admit he'd been so flustered and distracted he hadn't been listening.

"Sure," he said. This was the correct answer since her face lit with a high-wattage smile. Sam had never been so happy agreeing to some unknown thing in his life. Maybe charm was in his wheelhouse after all.

"Great. I'll fill out an application then," she said.

"I'll get one from the office. Just so you know, there's an extra deposit for a pet."

Her expression slipped to surprise. "Oh. Okay. Good to know." Her smile returned. "Maybe I'll get one."

Fuuuuuuuuck.

What did he just agree to?

Chapter Four

LUNA HAD GONE through a gamut of emotions today. Annoyed, embarrassed, crabby, sad, hopeful, dejected, crabby again, surprised, disappointed. Current emotion: conflicted. One thing she didn't want to do was go into work. Instead, she stopped at the coffee shop, Pony Expresso, where she knew she'd find Mia.

As she predicted, her cousin-in-law was there with her best friend, Natalie, who was overseeing some remodeling going on in the shop.

"Ah, es mi prima favorita. Hola, Luna! ¿Quieres algo de beber?"

"What?" Luna asked over construction noise.

Both Mia and Natalie were Latina, but Natalie was full Mexican-American while Mia was biracial. Mia had told Luna she hadn't grown up with much of a Mexican influence and was trying to reclaim her heritage. Learning to speak Spanish was one of those ways. Luna suggested she spend a few months in a Spanish-speaking country—oh, like Spain!—as a better way to learn a language rather than gossiping with Natalie, but Mia had shrugged her shoulders, and said something cheesy like, *It's really hard to kiss Ross from Spain.*

Mia repeated her question in English. "Do you want something to drink? Nat and I want to hear all about the apartments, don't we?"

"Yup. Spill it." Natalie pulled her glossy dark locks into a high ponytail, her soft brown skin practically glowing in beautiful perfection. Both women, in the same exact way, leaned against the tabletop as though Luna was about to reveal the most interesting story in the world. They were clearly the bestest of friends, allowing a new emotion to infiltrate Luna's heart: jealousy.

She plopped onto one of the chairs at their table. "It was fine."

The other women shot each other a glance. Besides Spanish they also had whole conversations through facial expressions. Mia sipped the iced tea in her hand.

She put off going into detail by pulling out her phone and dialing the animal shelter. "Hi, I dropped off a gray and white cat earlier. I was just wondering how the cat was doing and if she's been claimed yet."

"Not yet," a woman on the other end replied. "She's been examined and besides being pretty hungry, seems to be doing well."

This information did give Luna some relief. Although she found it weird Sam had coincidentally mentioned a pet. When she inspected her shirt after leaving the apartment, she found a single, inconspicuous cat hair. Wow, he was good. That was some forensic science shit or something.

After disconnecting the call, Luna scrolled through her Instagram feed on her phone. When she raised her eyes, they were still watching her. "What?"

"You're getting a cat?" her cousin-in-law asked.

"I don't know. I'm thinking about it, if the owner doesn't show up."

Mia took another sip. "So, how were the places you looked at?"

"I said it was fine, Mia. I don't want to talk about it."

"Makes sense to me. Who wants to talk about fine?"

Her instinct was to snap back at her cousin, but taking her frustration out on Mia could bite her in the ass with Ross and she wasn't about to take the risk. Instead, her frustration came out in the form of tears, which was equally annoying. Luna pressed a hand to her face to hide them. She hated crying and demanded her eyes stop producing tears immediately, because there was nothing more embarrassing than crying in the middle of Natalie's coffee shop with the random electrician walking past.

Her cousin didn't say a word but rubbed a soothing hand across her back. It felt good and awkward at the same time. Luna had never depended on anyone's shoulder to lean against when she was sad, even after being dumped. Here she was, tempted to seek comfort in Mia's gentle strength and use her shirt as a handkerchief as much as she preferred stamping her emotions into a deep, dark well.

Natalie briefly left before returning with a box of tissues. "Here, you can borrow Mia's Kleenex."

Natalie wasn't kidding. On the outside of the tissue box were the words *Mia's Big Box of Tear Tissues Boohoo!* written in black sharpie along with several drawings of rudimentary crying faces with tears exploding from their eyes.

She helped herself to a tissue, blotting her eyes in an attempt to keep her makeup intact. "You have your own box of tissues?" she asked Mia. She wasn't sure she'd ever seen her cousin cry except from the occasional coffee commercial these days.

"She cries all the time," Natalie said. "She was bawling her eyes out yesterday over a TikTok video."

"It was a big shirtless muscle guy who had a puppy in one arm and a baby in the other. There must be something wrong with your heart, Natalie."

Her best friend snorted. "I wasn't thinking about my heart when I was watching. Did you see that guy? So, what happened?" She produced a hard peppermint candy from her pocket, popping it in her mouth.

"I didn't get the duplex. I know it's a silly thing to cry over..." Even as she said the words she choked with tears again. It wasn't simply being rejected but rather how the landlady made her feel, as if she wasn't good enough.

Mia rubbed her back again. "It's not silly. It's okay to feel bad when you're disappointed. I know how excited you were about that place."

"Screw them," Natalie said. "You'll find something better."

"And then I went to the other apartment and it's just so..." Luna waved her hands in a way to convey how utterly mediocre Schnell Ridge was "...not what I wanted. I signed a lease anyway, but only because I asked if I could do superficial home improvements to the place to fix it more to my liking and he said okay—Oh! And *he* was there?"

"Who?" Natalie asked.

She leaned forward to make her point clearer to Mia.

"The guy, *you know*, from the park."

"What guy from the park?" Mia's eyes brightened as she caught on. "Ooooooh. The guy you kissed?"

"Wait? Who's this guy?" her friend asked.

She jabbed a finger in the direction of the actual guilty party. "Mia made me do it."

Natalie laughed. "Really, M? I thought we made a deal that you weren't going to do that anymore, that your bizarre powers of persuasion were only to be used for good, like convincing Ross to let us borrow jewelry for special occasions."

Mia's mouth gaped. "It was an accident! And I meant to *act* like you were going to kiss him on the cheek, not actually do it. I wasn't trying to get Luna to make out with the guy."

"Whoa, what? You made out with this guy? Good for you."

"*No*, I didn't make out with him. It was a quick peck and not anything to make a big deal—"

"I got a picture," her cousin said to Natalie, her eyebrows doing a playful wiggle under those terrible bangs.

"Mia Russo! You better delete that photo right now or you can forget about getting information to a new hairdresser."

A sweet smile and slight lift of a shoulder was the response, a picture of amusement. "You actually look really cute in it, but I'll delete it if you want."

Luna shut her mouth as she considered this. What if she really did look cute in it? She should at least take a peek, right? And, perhaps, she could take another look at her future landlord, in the interest of becoming more familiar with a guy. Shouldn't she be on friendly terms with him since he was going to let her improve her new apartment? It made sense to her. And what was the harm?

"Can I at least take a look? Come on, Luna." Natalie gave her a nudge.

"Fine. Let's take a look but I'll probably hate it." She feigned a sigh and crossed her arms as if in complete resignation instead of being curious.

"Yay!" Mia retrieved her bag from the floor. She pulled out her camera, flicking through the images. "Aw, I love it." She leaned toward her friend first, sharing the image.

"Okay, I will admit it's a pretty good photo," Natalie said.

Luna jumped from her chair, her interest now piqued, coming around the table. She squeezed between the two women to get a view of the camera screen. Sure enough, the impromptu moment of shock was caught by the camera. Luna's puckered lips made contact with Sam's, her body leaning into him, her left leg slightly lifted in a typical romance kiss pose. Even more surprising, one of her hands had fisted Sam's T-shirt. Luna didn't remember doing any of this. Her eyes were closed, looking completely serene and relaxed. On the other side, Sam's eyes reflected clear shock as if this simple kiss was the biggest surprise of his life. The image had a modern Norman Rockwell aspect to it, an unexpected slice of life. If it wasn't Luna and Sam sharing this embrace, she would have agreed it was sweet, funny, and photo-frame-worthy.

But it *was* Luna and Sam, and she couldn't forget how he made her feel like repulsive trash afterwards. Sure, he didn't treat her like that at the apartment complex. In fact, if she didn't know any better, there might have been a spark of interest from him, but she'd been wrong the first time. It was better not to take the chance of looking foolish again. In the end, there was no other option than to delete the image because there was no point in keeping it.

"So, the guy is your new neighbor?" Natalie asked.

"Apparently, my actual next-door neighbor is a firefighter."

"Really? That is a perk," Mia said. "Maybe he could take some couple photos with you next time."

"Are you kidding? I'm done with your bright ideas. Anyway, Sam's the apartment manager. Can you believe that?"

"Wow, what are the odds?" her cousin said. "Well, at least Sam seemed nice. And he takes good pictures. Am I deleting this or not?"

"You can do whatever you want," Luna responded, but she took one more glance in case Mia did delete it. She made an internal note of how Sam had pressed his hand to the small of her back. Luna could still feel the warmth, as though his touch had left a mark.

"Sam? Wait, let me see that photo again." Natalie leaned closer to Mia to study it. "Is this apartment a Sunderland property?"

"Yeah. Why?"

"I lived in one of their apartments when I first moved out. It was owned by his parents. They had a managing company I'd go through, so I didn't really deal with them. But I remember Sam. He and his brother used to race their cars on the street near the apartment complex. It was irritating as hell. We even called the cops once or twice. We got kids playing on that street. We didn't need arrogant, reckless white boys using the street as a racing track."

Mia adjusted her glasses. "What? Are you sure? He seemed nice." She flicked to another image, one where Sam was facing the camera.

"Yeah, that's Sam Sunderland. I'd know that asshole alliteration anywhere. Those boys were trouble. There was a car accident a few years ago. I don't remember the details except that Sam was supposedly really drunk and his younger brother was killed."

"Good Lord." Mia covered her mouth with a hand.

Luna was also shocked but, most of all, it instantly changed the way she saw him. Ross's parents were killed by a drunk driver, and there was no way she'd ever be friends with someone who went through life making bad decisions and ruining lives like her cousin's. To even consider it could be a betrayal, and Ross was the most important person in her life, the only person she had left. She'd already felt she'd wronged her cousin by flirting with Sam, even though she hadn't known any of this. One thing was certain—she couldn't afford to keep being wrong about her future landlord.

While Luna was originally disappointed to be getting a Schnell Ridge apartment instead of the Old Town duplex, she tried to assure herself it wasn't settling if she was able to take something boring and basic and make it less so. Luna could be creative and resourceful when it came to decorating and she had planned to hang curtains on the windows or put things on the wall. But now she didn't care what Sam thought about any of her ideas or whether she was on friendly terms with him. And who was he to lay down any sort of rule anyway? Him being a stickler for rules had to be the ultimate hypocrisy.

His endearing awkwardness, dry delivery, sharp cheekbones, and warm brown eyes no longer held any currency for her.

She was going to do what she wanted to get the apartment of her dreams.

No one cared what Sam Sunderland thought, least of all her.

"Delete the picture," Luna said to Mia.

Chapter Five

"I WANT TO move away, Sammy."

Sam had come to his mother's house to repair the side of the fence that had blown over during the last windstorm. Not that the weathered old boards needed much help as many of them were rotted through. It was only a matter of time. Still, one didn't come for fence repair only to be hit with such a surprising declaration from their mother.

He set down some of the fence planks before saying, "What do you mean you want to move away? Why?"

His mother, who was a petite woman with gray streaks running through her auburn hair and steel-colored eyes, crossed her arms as if expecting a fight. "What, so your father can move away, but I have to be stuck in this?"

This being his childhood home, which had been a little neglected the last few years, inside and out, and it wasn't just the fence. After the accident, and his parents' divorce, his father moved down to San Diego, got remarried, and seemed to have moved beyond Sam and his mother. Except for the property his father owned in the El Dorado area and holidays, Sam and him didn't have much to talk about these days.

"Where do you want to move?" Sam asked.

"I just want to get a little cabin in the woods near Tahoe." When she noticed her son wasn't going to fight her, the crossed arms dropped, her posture softening. "It's just this place is too big. It doesn't work for me anymore."

"Okay," was all he replied.

"So, you'll help me fix up the place to sell it?"

"Yeah." He'd give his mother whatever she wanted even if it meant she'd be leaving him, same as his father. He owed her that much and he tried to assure himself that a little cabin near Lake Tahoe wasn't too far away, unlike San Diego. He couldn't fix the emotional turmoil but having something substantial, like fixing a house…well, this was something he could do. He'd put his own feelings on the matter aside and do whatever he could to help his mom sell her house.

Sam continued with the fence as he started to make a mental checklist of what this project would entail, and as bad as a blown fence was, it was easy compared to what could be on the inside of the house.

"You want something to drink?" His mom offered him a glass of ice water.

He stretched his back, removed his hat, and took a long greedy drink from the glass. It wasn't quite summer yet, but it was already warm.

"You're not going to get everything you need for the new fence using your motorcycle, are you?" his mother asked.

Sam let out a small chuckle. "You don't think I could balance the boards across my lap?"

A frown stretched across her lips, demonstrating she didn't find his teasing at all amusing.

"Don't worry. I'll rent a truck or something," he assured her.

"I hate that thing. Why don't you get yourself something else to drive?"

"Because I like it. Don't worry, I'm being careful." He wouldn't tell her the truth. He only had one rule. No rides given, no rides taken. His bike guaranteed there would only be one rider and, therefore, he'd never have to be responsible for someone else. That was good enough for him.

"You should at least get yourself a haircut," his mother said, eyeing his hair.

He raked his hands roughly through his thick locks before replacing his ballcap on his head. "I just haven't had time."

"What do you mean? What have you been busy doing?"

"I don't know. Apartment stuff and now I'm trying to fix up a house to sell. I'm busy." And going to a barber or even a Supercuts was never on his list of priorities.

"How's everything going at the apartments?" his mom asked.

"Okay. Signed a new tenant for apartment seven."

"Oh yeah? What are they like?"

Whatever his thoughts were about Luna, he wasn't going to discuss them with his mother. "It's one person. She seems okay." He concentrated on stacking the discarded boards into a neat pile.

"What does she do?"

"Works in one of the shops downtown, a jewelry store."

"She's single?"

"I don't know. That's not a question asked on an apartment application, and it's not any of my business."

"It wouldn't hurt for you to find someone nice."

Sam found the conversation surprising. His mother wasn't one to ever encourage him into a relationship. She'd always let her sons manage their own lives, choice of vehicles aside. Her line of conversation was surprising because, ever since Nate's death and the divorce, his mother had retreated even further from commenting on Sam's life. He never realized how much he missed being pushed by someone.

"Oh, I bought a new raccoon. I think it's almost exactly like Nate's."

Sam nearly choked on his water. "Mom—"

"Don't you mom me. I can spend my money how I want, Sammy."

When Nate was three years old, his favorite stuffed animal was a blue raccoon a relative bought for his birthday. He used to take it with him everywhere, until the fur was matted and threadbare. The neck on the raccoon became so weak, the head could no longer be supported and flopped around. But then the toy disappeared, probably thrown away when it had become more rag than toy.

After the accident, his mother became obsessed with trying to find it, insisting she would have never gotten rid of it. But the stuffed toy was never found. Of course, if she came across another raccoon, blue or not, she had to have it.

This was the thing that worried Sam the most about getting the house in shape for the housing market. These days, he didn't spend a lot of time inside his childhood home and it wasn't simply because of the tough memories of Nate, although it was a little of that as well.

When he entered her home later that afternoon with the beginnings of a fix-it list on his phone, he felt the sharp inhalation of breath enter his lungs at being faced with an impossible mountain of a situation. This was not one or two raccoon stuffed dolls but hundreds of items, many of them sharing the common theme of having some kind of raccoon motif, but it didn't stop there.

His mother had never been the best housekeeper when he was growing up, always prone to collect things, but it was clear things had gotten a lot worse as he toed a stack of large black garbage bags. The garbage bags were definitely new since the last time he'd been inside the home.

"Do you want me to toss out these trash bags for you, Mom?" He was hoping against hope the task was as easy as that.

His mother, though, came rushing into the room. "Don't touch those. I'm getting organized."

Sam swallowed his disappointment, and his mom must have read his face because she said in a small voice, "You're going to help me get that little cabin in Tahoe, right, Sammy?"

He hadn't known when he became more of an adult in their relationship but, lately, he had the need to pull himself up and be the strong one for her to lean against. He offered her a reassuring smile and said, "Yeah, of course." Putting his arm around her shoulder, he rested his face against the top of her hair. "Don't worry. We'll fix the place up and sell it."

There was a part of Sam that doubted his words, that maybe he wouldn't be able to overcome a problem this big on his own. But he no longer had Nate, and his father was unwilling to get involved, so it only left Sam. He didn't have a choice; he had to help her. Doing whatever he could to sell her home and get that little forest cabin would be his new goal.

He had to do it.

He owed her.

Chapter Six

L UNA WOKE THE morning of moving day to the smell of grilling onions in the air. The biggest thing she'd miss about living with Ross would be his cooking. Weekend breakfasts were about to get a lot more pitiful.

She'd also miss her little snuggle buddy, Hermes the terrier mix, who was currently snoring like an old man and curled alongside her stomach. She would have taken the old three-legged dog with her to the new place, (she saw him first which, technically, meant he was hers), but Ross would one hundred percent fight her. Her cousin may pretend to be a huge grump, but his insides were jam-packed with marshmallow fluff.

"'Bout time you got up," Ross said, standing at the stove and sautéing something in a skillet when she finally made her way into the kitchen. Mia stood beside him, cutting fruit into a bowl.

Luna checked the kitchen clock. "It's only seven. I will never understand why you need to get up so early. I'm sure Mia didn't want to. Let the pregnant lady sleep."

In response, Mia crossed her eyes and stuck her tongue to the side. Luna snorted a laugh. When Ross glanced at his wife, her expression quickly shifted to neutral pleasantness.

"You know I'm always happy to help you, Rosso."

"Uh-huh," he replied, sounding unconvinced. He pulled Mia to him, kissing her temple in a disgusting display of sugary-sweet affection.

Luna wasn't going to miss this. Not that she wasn't happy for Ross. He deserved to find love as much as anyone. But everything Ross had was what Luna imagined she'd have at this point. She'd certainly thought she'd had it with Viggo, and all this served as a reminder to how wrong she'd been about that man as well.

"I'm almost done. Why don't you take the fruit and relax at the table," Ross said to his wife. "Can you grab some plates, Lu?"

With a groan, Luna retrieved dishes from a cupboard. It was clear she wasn't the princess in this house.

"Are you excited about the new place, Luna?" Mia asked.

She shrugged. Luna wasn't sure how excited she could be moving into Schnell Ridge. The best thing about it was she'd have complete privacy and a whole place to do whatever she could imagine. It wasn't everything, but it was something. "I guess."

"I don't know why I have to help you move again. I already did this once," Ross said.

"I remember packing up the car myself when I left for Chico, so I'm not quite sure what you're remembering. Becoming a dad has turned your brain into mush."

"Come here." Ross grabbed her in a big hug, rubbing his prickled jawline against her cheek, exfoliating her face like sandpaper.

"Ross! Stop! You're going to scratch up my skin." She

pushed him away. Yup, the man was ninety-five percent marshmallow fluff these days.

"Do you need help packing or moving?" Mia asked as she fished a strawberry from the bowl.

"No," Ross replied. "I can do it. I don't want you carrying boxes up a bunch of stairs."

"Good Lord, Ross." Mia rolled her eyes. "Stop acting like I'm going to break."

"It's not like there's a lot to move anyway. Lulu only has two pieces of furniture and a bunch of clothes."

"Ugh! Stop calling me Lulu." She popped a piece of cheese from Ross's cutting board into her mouth. "And I have more than that, but I do need to go furniture shopping."

"Going shopping could be fun," Mia responded with a hopeful smile.

"Oh. I'm not actually going to real furniture stores. I'll probably just scrounge around at thrift stores—"

Ross gave her a subtle nudge with his elbow and his expression read, *Come on. Throw a bone.*

"But you can come with me if you want, Mia." Luna stuck her tongue at Ross while holding a plate for him as he slid an omelet onto it.

"THIS SHOULD BE the last of it," Ross said, dropping a heavy box onto one of the stacks in her new living room. He rested the upper half of his body on a pillar of cardboard. "God, Lu. Next time get an apartment on ground level. I'm beat."

"It probably would have gone faster if you let Mia help. Although, it's kinda nice hanging out just you and me. It's like old times. Maybe you want to go furniture shopping with me. I'll let you treat me to a milkshake afterwards."

"Stop it. You don't need to be a brat."

Luna's jaw dropped at the offense. "I'm not. I was just joking. God. You take everything so seriously."

Ross ran a hand across his jaw. "You know Mia gets excited to hang out with you, but you always treat it like such a chore. This isn't high school anymore. You can hang out with people who weren't in the cool kids' clique."

"Excuse me. I am not like that. It's just…"

It was more that Mia was sweet and nice most of the time, making Luna aware of her own deficiencies. Mia was good and good things happened to her. She was happy with Ross and starting a family. Luna, as hard as she tried, didn't consider herself naturally good and therefore that's why people left her, like her mom, and Tessa, and Viggo.

"Mia's great and all," Luna started. "But sometimes I miss how it used to be when it was just you and me. I came back to Placerville, and everything was different, you know."

Ross sighed. "Everything is always going to be different. You just adapt and keep moving forward the best you can. Isn't that why we're moving you into a new place? This is a beginning for you. Just like Mia was a beginning for me and with the baby coming… Well, you can't ever go back. Only forward."

She did know, even if he didn't say it. Once the baby came, she'd get even less Ross than she had now. Maybe Luna should start adjusting her expectations, and put her energy into something else, like fixing up her apartment.

She let the tension ease from her body. "Okay, Ross. You're right. I'll send Mia a text."

"All right, come here." Ross opened his arms.

"Ew, no. You're probably all sweaty."

"No, I'm not. I promise. Give your cousin a hug." His arms beckoned her.

"Fine." Luna surrendered to his embrace, and he held her tight...almost too tight. Like a death grip. "Ross?" She realized the whole thing had been a trap once her hands reached his back, discovering his T-shirt soaked through with sweat. "Ross! Gross! Get off me, weirdo!"

She pushed him away. "You're disgusting. I don't know how Mia stands you."

He grinned. "Oh, trust me. Mia loves me hard."

"Ew. And now you know why I was so eager to move out. Good riddance to both of you. If it wasn't for a very cute baby on the way, you'd probably never see me again. Thanks for the help."

"You know I'd always help you."

"And I know you don't really think I'm a brat."

Ross brought his pointer finger and thumb together until there was a small gap between them. "You're a little bit of a brat. I just don't want you getting into trouble because of it."

Her bottom lip pushed into a pout as she feigned hurt. "I don't know what you mean. When have I ever gotten myself into trouble that I couldn't get out of?"

"Uh-huh. Well, you got the confidence at least, I'll give you that." He tapped the stack of boxes supporting him. "All right, I need to take a shower. I stink. You definitely

shouldn't hug me. Let me know if you need anything else."
He took his leave.

The apartment was quiet.

She was alone.

Chapter Seven

ONE OF THE latches was loose on Sam's toolbox. When he lifted it, the bottom flipped apart, sending his tools scattering across the pavement.

"Goddammit."

"Oooooh, Sam." Zabe clucked her tongue while shaking her head. "You have a language problem." She bent beside him, helping him collect the fallen items. "Anyway, as I was saying, I'm going to ask Nicholas if I can dog walk for him sometimes. Do you think it'll be enough for my dad to see that I can take care of a dog?"

It was best for Sam to stay as far away from this debate as possible. Jason was the one who paid the rent, but, on the other hand, Zabe was his little buddy. It was a lose-lose situation. "I don't know. But it would be a nice thing to do for Nicholas."

Nicholas was an elderly man who never stopped coughing when he took a walk around the patio. As far as Sam was aware, the man didn't have any family, at least none that visited him. Nor did the retired engineer seem to do much. It was as though Nicholas was waiting for life to be done with him. Sam worried this was a premonition into his own future and made sure to spend a few moments talking with him whenever the older gentleman milled around the patio with Luna the Chihuahua.

"I want the biggest dog I can get. Would that be a German shepherd?"

Uh-oh. Perhaps Sam should step in. "Why would you want to squeeze a giant dog into a tiny apartment? If you get a dog that's Luna's size then the apartment is going to feel huge to them, as if they're living in a mansion."

With the toolbox packed, Sam climbed the stairs with Zabe following behind him. The bathroom faucet in apartment number eight needed fixing.

"Huh. I never thought about that before. In that case, what's the smallest dog I can get? Oh, the new girl moved in last weekend—Luna Number Two. Did you see?"

"Yup." Sam couldn't help but notice every time she moved around. He was already growing familiar with her daily routine.

"Oh! She's at the window. Hello, Luna!" Zabe waved enthusiastically.

There she was, as clear as can be, which was surprising because the dining room window, where Luna was perched on a stepladder inside her apartment, was extra clean instead of the usual layer of dust. Yup, still pretty. She gave a wave to Zabe but ignored Sam completely.

"What's she doing?"

The kid had asked a good question. He stood at the top of the stairs, head tilting. Was she putting in new blinds? The old plastic Venetians were gone and she had a drill in her hand, installing something on the inside of the window frame.

This was not okay.

His job, keeping this place cobbled together, was already hard enough. The last thing he needed was to fix someone's shitty DIY project. These days, Pinterest made everyone think they could accomplish any home project with a hammer and glue gun.

Forgetting about his task in apartment eight, Sam marched to the closed dining room window and tapped on the glass. "Hey! You can't do that."

Luna jumped in surprise at his presence being so close. Her delicate eyebrows pressed together. "I'm sorry?"

There was no way she couldn't hear him. It wasn't as though the cheap windows were sound-proof. "You can't do that." He jabbed a finger in the direction of the shade.

"Oh, don't worry. I already did the one in the living room. They're actually quite easy to put in." She pointed to the living room window and sure enough there was a woven shade there as well.

"Oh wow! I love the color of her wall. Can I do that, Sam?" Zabe asked, peering into the apartment beside him.

Sparkling windows be damned. Sam flipped his hat around before pressing his own face to the glass, using a hand to block the glare from the sun. The dining room wall was peacock blue with a large modern framed artwork of yellow and white ombré hung in the center of the wall. The beige cracked linoleum was missing because there appeared to be grayish wood or laminate flooring going from the dining room through the kitchen.

"Excuse me," Luna said with a hand on her hip. "Do you normally invade your tenants' privacy by peering through their windows?"

"Are you kidding me right now? We need to talk. Come to the door."

"Why?"

Sam's agitation grew. "Because I don't want to be shouting through the window!"

"Then stop shouting!" Her own irritation sparked from her eyes.

What right did she have in being annoyed? He didn't care how pretty she was, she'd crossed a line. "Are you going to let me in or not?"

"How about not. According to California law, you have to give me at least twenty-four hours' notice before entering the premises and I don't remember getting any notice."

"Oh, now you're going to be a stickler for rules? Here's your own news flash. According to the lease, you can't make these types of renovations to the apartment."

"It actually doesn't say that." She sat on the stepladder with her arms crossed like a queen on her throne and he was the fumbling subject before her. How did this even happen? He was the landlord here, not her.

"Do I need to get the lease for you?" His jaw worked overtime grinding his molars together because he had enough on his plate without dealing with a spoiled brat who was probably used to getting away with things.

"Fine. Go ahead. I'll be waiting right here to witness your humiliation. I'm sure it won't be the first time."

He didn't like how confident she appeared. His gut told him this wasn't good at all.

Luna's eyes narrowed. "I don't even know why this is

suddenly an issue. We had a whole conversation about this during the walk-through. Are you telling me you don't remember agreeing to this? Or do you make agreements only to back out later?"

"What fu—" He glanced at Zabe who was enthralled with the whole conversation. The only thing missing was a bowl of popcorn in her hands. "What agreement?"

"I asked you if I would be allowed to make improvements to the place as long as I covered the costs. You said okay. I even crossed out the section on the lease and we initialed it and you never said anything. Why did you agree if it's a problem?"

"I—" All the blood drained from Sam's face. His father was going to kill him. He'd screwed up once again. "Can you please come to the door so we can discuss this before you do anything else?"

She smiled but it was more dangerous than friendly, like a cat who happened across a mouse. "Oh I'm just getting started, buddy." And the shade slammed shut.

"Well, damn," Zabe said.

The understatement of the year.

Chapter Eight

"YOU'RE PUTTING ME on," Mia said as they strolled through the furniture section of St. Vincent's Thrift Store.

"Nope. And then I closed the shade on him. I'm kinda sad I had to miss the expression on his face." When she thought about it, lying in bed at night, she couldn't help but laugh because she found the whole situation amusing in the best possible way. One point for her, zero for Sam. It served him right.

"I don't think I'd ever be brave enough to do something like that." Yeah, because Mia didn't have to. She had a dimple and a golden way with words. "You're not afraid he's going to evict you?"

Sure, she was worried. Her courage didn't stick around forever. Her gutsy guts only made an appearance in the first place because he wasn't being fair going back on his word, and it made her angry. It wasn't as though Luna was being sneaky—except for the part where she wasn't giving him a list of all of her planned renovations for the place. She'd been completely up-front about the apartment from the beginning. His agreement with her plans had been the one thing that appealed to her about moving into Schnell Ridge

Apartments. For him to act as if she'd tricked him was completely offensive.

The fact that the man was now pleading ignorance, as if the whole conversation had taken place in a dream, was a complete mystery. If Sam lacked the imagination on what a creative person could do with a blank canvas, that was on him.

Luna did not lack an imagination. In truth, it had been the opposite. Having free rein to express herself was both thrilling and the type of distraction she needed. Working at the jewelry store didn't occupy her mind as much as it had before and there was a lot of downtime. She kept herself busy by making notes on her phone and saving pictures to a Pinterest board with affordable things she could do. Luna also started using her Instagram to take progress pictures of her work. #HomeSweetApartment #DIYstyle #FixitGirl. Surprisingly, her photos were generating more activity than normal, and from complete strangers, which inspired her to do more. It was almost a blessing she didn't get the perfect duplex as this whole activity was stretching her creativity (and her budget) in a way that challenged and interested her. As Luna had told Sam a few days prior, she was just getting started.

"I'm not sure you're going to find any treasures here today," Mia said as they reached the end of the aisle.

That's when Luna saw it. Tucked in a corner, beneath a stack of decorative pillows, was a small kitchen table with two mustard yellow chairs. Once the pillows were removed, a wooden mid-century-style table was revealed in all its glory. "Oh my God," she said. "This is it."

Mia checked the tag. "Sixty dollars. I thought you said your budget was fifty."

Yes, but the budget was for a standard table. When it came to *the perfect* table, there was always some wiggle room. This one would contrast nicely against a peacock blue wall and fit with her modern style. "Mia, I *need* this table. You brought Ross's truck right? This isn't going to fit in the back of mine."

"Yeah."

"Okay, wait here. Don't let anyone take it. Sit on it if you need to." Luna departed to find help. Apparently, she didn't have to do anything because as soon as the cashier was notified, Mia was on her way with a man carrying the table over his head. She smiled and chatted while rubbing her pregnant belly. Then her wonderful cousin procured an extra discount from the cashier due to a wobbly leg needing new screws. Perhaps inviting Mia shopping was a good idea after all.

When they arrived at Schnell Ridge apartments, they met at the truck bed. "I should call Ross to see if he can slip out of the store for a bit to help carry this upstairs," Luna said. The items weren't heavy, but she also didn't want Ross yelling at her for letting Mia carry furniture to the second level.

"Or we can ask your landman." Luna loved Mia for changing Sam's title as there was nothing lordly about the guy.

"No. Definitely not. I don't want him inside my apartment."

"Honestly, I think you and I can handle it. We'll take the

table together and then each of us can grab a chair. We'll be done in ten minutes. It'll take Ross that long just to leave the workshop."

"Are you sure? I don't want to get in trouble."

Mia laughed. "I don't either. That's why it's our secret. Plus, if I'm expected to push a baby out of my body then I should be strong enough to lift half of a small table and climb a few stairs." A mischievous spark lit her eyes, and Luna wondered if there was a different side of her cousin-in-law that she hadn't noticed before.

"Okay," she relented. "But we'll have to be quiet. I don't want Sam to see us. He can't come inside my apartment."

Luna climbed into the truck bed and lowered the table and two chairs to Mia, who put them on the ground. Each of them took a side of the round table with Luna being the one to walk backwards. She could probably manage to lug the furniture to the second level on her own but it certainly would have been more awkward without Mia's help.

They were at the halfway point of the staircase when Sam departed the laundry room. The women froze, both hoping Sam's lowered baseball cap would block them from view. Luna made a silent shush with her mouth and that's when Mia began pressing her lips together in an effort to keep from giggling. Great. Now the other woman was fighting against a laugh attack.

Sam stopped when he spotted Ross's truck with the two yellow chairs beside it. His head swiveled in their direction when Mia couldn't hold the giggles any longer and released a snort laugh.

"Mia!" Luna said.

The apartment manager opened his mouth, but Luna jumped in before he could say anything. "We got it. Don't need any help. Thanks."

With their cover blown, they continued climbing the stairs not caring if they were making noises and they certainly were because Mia couldn't stop laughing. Luna never pegged her cousin-in-law as a person to get the giggles at inopportune moments but here they were.

"God, Mia. What is so funny?" she asked as they carried the table inside.

"I don't know. I just find it hilarious we're sneaking furniture in. I mean, what exactly did you think was going to happen? Did you think Sam was going to say, *no, you can't have a kitchen table*? I just found it funny."

"I told you, I don't want him helping me. The less I have to deal with the man, the better." Luna was surprised to find the mustard-colored chairs waiting on the second level walkway. He must have carried them for her anyway.

"Nice!" Mia said. "I like it when things magically appear."

They each grabbed a chair and put them in the dining nook on either side of the table and it was perfect.

"I love it. I admit, I wasn't sure about this table when you found it, but I'm in awe of your vision. You were right. It looks great in here," Mia said, but she was soon interrupted by a tiny *meow*. "Oh my heart. You got her?"

The little gray and white cat approached with caution, wearing a fluorescent pink collar. Luna scooped the animal from the floor, cuddling the tiny furball to her chest. The feline purred, rubbing her head against Luna's chin. "I did.

I've named her Duchess and she's the sweetest thing."

Mia stroked the animal's head. "She's a gorgeous cat. Perfect pet for your perfect little home. You have a great eye, Lu. I know this is all a work in progress, but I love what you're doing. It feels like you. Maybe you could help me decorate the nursery."

Luna was struck by Mia's request and was sure she misunderstood her. "You want my help?"

"Of course. You're really good with this, and it's making me feel a bit overwhelmed right now. I like how you just fearlessly throw yourself into something, and I need that."

"Okay," Luna replied. She didn't trust herself to say anything else. Mia wanting her around, inviting her to take an active part in her and future demon baby's life, that had to mean something. She hoped it wasn't due to encouragement from Ross. She wanted Mia to mean her words, to be able to trust the sentiment was real. Because if Mia liked her, it meant she had to be doing something right. It was both daunting and terrifying, and she *really* hoped she didn't screw this up.

Mia smiled, her dimple making an appearance. She then bit her lip to prevent giggling.

"You're thinking about sneaking furniture again, aren't you?"

"I am. Next time we have to try to sneak something past Ross for fun."

Yeah, Luna enjoyed this side of her. "What are you doing next weekend?"

"I'm not sure," Mia replied.

"Maybe you can help me look for a living room sofa and

we can also see if we can find things for the nursery."

"And get waffle wraps for lunch?"

"Sure."

"Yeah, sounds like fun."

Her cousin-in-law grinned.

Maybe things were starting to turn around for Luna.

Chapter Nine

S AM PARKED HIS motorcycle, having finished the fence repairs for his mother, and was ready for a shower. He removed his helmet, swapping it for the baseball hat. Walking past Luna's white SUV, he noticed her struggling with what appeared to be a rolled area rug.

"Need any help?" he asked because it was his natural instinct to jump in to help, even for a woman who mysteriously seemed to hate him now.

Her shoulders stiffened but her eyes remained locked on her task, avoiding him. He wouldn't be surprised if she had forgotten his face altogether.

"Nope."

He was confused as to what had changed between them. How quickly she shifted from a woman he'd like to know better to a pain-in-his-ass tenant. Sam's lesson? Never get distracted again while in conversation with her. He'd have to stay on constant guard whenever she was about.

While previous conversations, before she moved in, hadn't exactly been amiable, it still felt as if there had been something between them. Dare he believe it was almost flirty. But he'd obviously been mistaken or else something had shifted, and he didn't understand why. He wondered if it was because she no longer found him useful, getting the apartment on her terms, and now she was free to treat him with contempt. Any hope he had for a second chance with her had shriveled and died.

Sam wasn't happy about the situation inside apartment seven, but he wasn't going to make any more fuss about it than necessary. No way was his dad going to learn about the renovations. His current plan was to fix everything whenever she moved away. He'd paint the walls, return the Venetian blinds to the windows, and his dad, in San Diego, would never be the wiser as his visits were sporadic at best.

He leaned against the staircase railing, crossing his arms, because watching a stubborn woman struggle with a rug, after refusing help, was about all the entertainment he had these days. Why was she attempting to do this by herself? Was she planning to drag the rug across the dirty patio and up the staircase? The rug was too long, going across the whole length of the interior of her SUV. Even Sam wouldn't try carrying it alone.

She released a growl in frustration, roughly grabbing her hair and yanking the strands into a tight ponytail. When she noticed him leaning against the railing, one hand locked onto a hip.

"Seriously? You're just going to stand there and watch me? You don't have anything else to do?" She was in clear spitfire mode.

"Not really."

She retrieved her phone from her pocket, pushed a few buttons, and held it to her ear. "Come on, Ross. Pick up," she said while pacing.

One of the apartment doors opened. He glanced over his shoulder.

"Excuse me, do you think—" but Luna stopped herself. It was Nicholas with his dog.

"What was that?" the old man shouted, also being hard of hearing.

"Never mind." Her shoulders sagged.

"What?" Nicholas asked again.

"Never mind!" she yelled, and the older gent shuffled away, his hacked cough following them.

Luna hopped her butt onto the lowered tailgate of the SUV, crossing her legs and leaning a bent elbow against the rug as though trying to appear casual and not at all frustrated.

"Do you want—" Sam started to say.

"No," she replied.

"Are you always this stubborn? Isn't this all a little dramatic?" he asked while scratching his eyebrow.

She glared in response. "I don't like doing anything that isn't a little dramatic."

"Okay then." At least she was honest.

He removed his hat to run a hand across his hair before putting it on again. At this point, he was confused. Even if she did hate him, why refuse the help? He was offering to carry a rug, not take her out to dinner. He supposed she meant to keep him out of her apartment as much as she could, as though his presence could taint the whole place.

"Look, I've already seen the wall and the shades and the floor. And I'm going to be in your apartment at some time or another. What if there's something I need to fix?"

"I'll take care of it."

His brow lowered. "Yeah, that's not how any of this works. You're not supposed to take care of it. That's my job. What do you think I do around here?"

"That's probably why it's better if I just deal with it myself."

Sam swallowed a bitter growl. It wasn't his fault the apartment complex was falling apart. Considering what he had to work with, and his father's refusal to invest much money into the place, he thought he did a pretty good job. "Then there's apartment inspections, cleaning out the filters for the central air, that sort of thing."

She didn't respond, picking at the rug backing with a fingernail.

"Anyway, I'm just saying, me inside your place is only a matter of time." Was that creepy? He wasn't trying to be. Oh well. He didn't need all this grief, especially because Luna and her area rug weren't his job nor his problem.

Sam was done playing this game. "If you don't want my help, fine." He headed to his own place.

"Sam."

He turned toward her, and her jaw was still locked in stubbornness.

"Okay," was all she said.

"Okay what?" After everything, this wasn't going to cut it. The queen would have to lower herself a bit more for his help.

She closed her eyes and released a breath. "Help me?"

"Wow, the adversity you must have had to overcome to ask that," he deadpanned.

Her eyes rolled in reply, which didn't seem to be the appropriate reaction for someone in her situation.

"On second thought, I don't think I will."

Her mouth popped open. "After all that, you're not going to help me? You're such an asshole."

Sam took the steps necessary to come close enough to see the green flecks in her hazel eyes. This was done to keep them from shouting at each other across the yard, and, yes, he was also irritated. "I'm an asshole? I offer help out of the goodness of my heart, which you treat with disgust. And then, when you begrudgingly do want my help, I'm supposed to come running? No, thanks."

Luna's features scrunched into extreme displeasure and her fists tightened as though she was about to burst. She'd probably never experienced a guy not bent at the waist for her. In a quick move, her arm shot out and snatched his hat, whipping it behind her back. Even she appeared somewhat shocked at the action before her expression switched to defiance. "I don't get my rug, you don't get your hat."

"Are you kidding me? You're going to hold my hat ransom? Just five minutes ago, you hated the idea of me touching your rug!"

"Well, now I want you to touch my rug!" Her cheeks grew ruddy, her eyes bright.

"I wouldn't touch your rug even if there was a million dollars rolled up inside. Knowing you, there's probably a dead body in there," he replied through gritted teeth.

"If there's going to be any body in my rug, it'll be yours."

"Hand the hat over."

"No!"

It was clear neither one of them had worked out the end game to this childish situation, but he could be just as stubborn as her and he wasn't about to let her win. He pulled nearer, nose-to-nose. "Gimme my hat, Luna."

"No."

His next move was making a scramble to reach behind her and grab it himself. "Gimme my—Ow!"

Luna had transferred the hat to her other hand and was now smacking him on the shoulder with it as he leaned into her. It didn't hurt as much as it was shocking. It also wasn't fair to beat a man with his own hat.

She was able to get in a few whacks before he managed to grab it. "What the *hell* is wrong with you?"

"I just want you to help me!"

"I don't get you at all. Does this approach normally work for you? Because it doesn't work for me at all."

"No. But I'm not Mia."

"What?" he replied, shoving the hat onto his head.

"Mia can get anyone to do anything."

Sam released a bitter huff. "All you had to do was be nice."

Her face fell into defeat. "I'm not even sure I'm a nice person. Do you think I'm nice?"

"Not particularly."

A death glare zeroed in on him. "Well, I don't think you're nice either."

"Great. I'm glad we got that settled. So from one not-nice person to another, do you want me to help you lug this rug up to your apartment?"

She studied him. It had to be the longest amount of time

her gaze had ever spent in his direction, and he wished he could see into her brain. "Yes. Please."

"Okay, then. How about you get in your car and push. I'll pull."

Luna scrambled across the inside of her SUV. The rug was larger and heavier than Sam had expected. There was no way Luna would have been able to get this thing upstairs by herself.

"How did you get this in your car in the first place?" he asked.

"The guy selling it on Facebook Marketplace helped me."

"Wait. You bought this rug from some guy on Facebook, and went to his house by yourself?"

"No, don't be ridiculous." She had the gall to be offended. "I went to his storage facility outside of town."

Sam stopped pulling. "Let me see if I've got this straight. You met some random guy from Facebook at his storage facility, in the middle of nowhere, alone?"

"When you put it like that—"

"What other way is there to put it?" It was fortunate she wasn't his responsibility because he wasn't sure his nerves would be able to handle it. As it was, he was annoyed enough by the whole situation, probably because he was concerned he'd have to soon begin the process of searching for a new tenant for her apartment. Sam made a note to check the storage garage for more boring white paint, because he might be redoing the place sooner than expected if this woman kept taking chances like this.

"I can take care of myself. I keep bear spray in my glove

box and have taken self-defense classes. Just to point out the obvious, I wasn't murdered, and I got a great rug for seventy-five bucks. I think it was worth the risk."

All he could do was grumble in response.

With each of them on separate ends, they ascended the stairs to the second level, with Luna clearly straining the whole way but it served her right. The first thing to hit him inside her place was the scent. It smelled like cinnamon and fall and warm cozy blankets. Number seven previously only smelled this good when Ms. Carol made her oatmeal cookies.

Not only did it smell inviting, but the apartment's style was completely different. He allowed himself to do a slow perusal of the place. There was the peacock blue wall, soft natural-color woven shades, and the new flooring in the dining/kitchen area, but the longest wall in the living room had a large art-deco-style graphic going across it in gold and white. Honeycomb shelving and artwork covered the opposite wall. There was also elegant furniture and tall houseplants filling the place, giving it a modern style out of something like *Interior Design* magazine. He couldn't even complain about sloppy handiwork because it would be a lie. There was a new light fixture over the dining room table instead of the old brass globe one. She was doing electrical work? He found himself gritting his teeth again.

"You look mad," Luna said, appearing unsure instead of cocky.

"Where do you want this thing?" Sam was irritated but he wasn't in the mood to get into another argument with her; once a day was enough. At this point, he had to finish the task and leave before he ripped the skin from his bones due to frustration at his fix-it list for this apartment growing larger.

"You can put it here. It's staying in the living room." They dropped the rug on the beige carpet, and she rushed to shut her bedroom door as though worried he was going to snoop every corner of her apartment. "You don't have to stay. I'll just roll it to where I need it."

"I'll help you move the furniture."

"I don't need—"

"Let's just get this over with and then I'll be out of here."

She stared at him as if she was as perplexed by him as he was by her. Silence was her concession as they moved the furniture in order to put the new rug in position. After she used scissors to cut the binding, the oversized rug was allowed to unfurl across the carpet, revealing plush cream-colored long shaggy fibers.

"This is a used rug? It looks brand new."

She smiled, looking pleased, and it softened her features. "Right? Such a bargain for seventy-five dollars. The guy said it was only used once."

He cocked his head, pondering this information. "Why would you buy a rug to only use it once?"

"I don't know, and I don't care. My gain."

They each took an end of the larger sofa, moving it into its original spot. "Maybe it's..." but he stopped the sentence before going any further.

One of her eyebrows quirked. "What?"

Sam shrugged a shoulder in a sheepish display. "Maybe it's a porn rug."

"Excuse me? What does that even mean?"

He scratched his neck. "They bought the rug for some amateur porn shoot."

"It's *not* a porn rug."

Sam pressed his lips together and raised his brow in a display of skepticism.

She crossed her arms. "You seem to know a lot about the set décor of amateur porn. Maybe the ones you're watching aren't doing a good job of holding your interest."

The more exasperated she got, the harder it was not to let a smile slip from his face. He dropped his eyes to the soft rug in question before sneaking a glance at her. "What'd the guy look like?"

Her mouth opened to respond before she shut it again, her face flushing with color. "I...don't remember."

Sam lifted the glass and gold metal coffee table, returning it to its position on the rug. "I'm not sure if I believe that. I bet you're really good with faces."

It was clear Luna was torn between taking the compliment and not giving him the satisfaction. "It's not a porn rug," she insisted.

"What'd he look like, Luna?"

"Just some middle-aged white guy."

"And?"

"And nothing. You're not going to make me feel bad about the great deal—"

"Is that a stain?"

"What!" She bent to have a closer inspection of the shag he pointed to with the tip of one work boot. There wasn't any stain, but it was too fun not to rile her. When she straightened again, he couldn't help but smirk at her expense. Grinning, she snatched his hat and gently whacked him in the arm with it. "Bastard."

Luna returned the baseball cap to his possession but eyed him with a humored glint. "Thank you for helping me with the rug." When she was like this, as if things were okay between them, he could almost forget about the time five minutes ago she made him want to tear his own skin off.

"You're welcome." His eyes drew across her face. Sam couldn't help noticing the freckle beside her right eye—it drew his attention like the North Star. It was as though every time he studied her, he couldn't help finding a new aspect to appreciate. It was annoying as hell, especially since he couldn't forget there was another Luna, one who apparently hated him. He had to keep reminding himself she was just another tenant, nothing else.

He cleared his throat. "I hope this is the end of what you're planning to do to the place."

Her chin lifted in stubborn determination. "No. Not even close."

"Luna—"

"I told you I wanted a nice apartment and I'm going to have it. You agreed to it." Her eyes sparked, ready for a fight, the hardness returning much to his disappointment.

"I don't give a fuck what you do in here, but I also don't want to get fired!"

She threw him an odd look. "Is this not a Sunderland Property? Doesn't your family own the place?"

He tensed. "My dad. But it doesn't matter. To him, it's all business and he wouldn't give two shits about firing my ass." As much as Schnell Ridge apartments could sometimes be an inescapable cage to Sam, it wasn't a cage he was eager to leave. What else was he supposed to do? Go back to school? Take up sports medicine like nothing had ever happened? He wasn't that same person anymore. "He left, and the only thing he cares about is that I'm not sitting here screwing it up, losing him money."

Her expression shifted again, her lips stretching into a frown, her eyes attempting to see the absolute truth of him. As much as he didn't want her anger, he didn't want her pity. Sam stuffed his hands into his pockets. "Look, how about this. Whatever you're going to do, you let me know. If it's something I want to help with, you let me. It's not that I think you can't do these things—clearly you can. I would just feel better to be involved and knowing it's going to be done right. I don't want you to get hurt."

She blinked as though surprised, tilting her head as she thought about it. "You're not going to stop me?"

"You don't seem like the type of woman I can stop."

This pleased her, the mischievous glint returning to her eyes, and his traitorous chest warmed at the sight of it. "So, I can do anything?"

"Within reason. We're going to have a problem if you start knocking down walls. But the deal is you have to be honest and up-front with me. Sneaking around, going behind my back, both you and your new rug will get evicted."

"Fine, but let's say I want to paint the kitchen cabinets. You'd be okay with that?" Luna waited with raised eyebrows, probably trying to see if he would renege on the deal directly after making it. The reality was, he already regretted everything.

Paint the cabinets? What the hell? They were perfectly fine except for the occasional handle popping off. The wooden cabinets were functional, and what else did a person need them to be? God, he hated that she was making him use the same line of reasoning as his father. When did he stop being fun? Scratch that. He and his knee knew exactly when he stopped.

"Why do you need to paint them?" he asked.

"Because it would make the kitchen look brighter and updated."

"Okay, I said within reason."

"How is that not within reason? I'm not replacing the cabinets. They'll essentially be the same but better."

Sam groaned. He was going to hate everything about this. "Fine, but only if I'm allowed to help. And no more risking your life for rugs."

The confident look on her face made it appear as if she was taking all the victory points. "Deal."

This could be the worst deal he'd ever made.

Why did it make him feel so good?

Chapter Ten

L UNA WAS UNSURE about this whole apartment renovation arrangement as she preferred doing her own thing without opinions from other people. She was eager about the painting part, not about hanging out with her landman, who probably had a lot of unwanted opinions and was also a person she was trying not to become familiar with. Ross would have been her preferred painting partner. Even Mia would have been okay. Even so, she wasn't about to fight Sam, especially considering she hadn't planned to paint the cabinets in the first place, nor did she think Sam would agree. But he had, and she was going to take advantage of the situation.

And why not? Cabinets painted, with new hardware added, were going to make her kitchen brand new. Plus, with the white subway tiles she'd installed as a backsplash, it would transform everything. She'd already taken a picture of the "before" and couldn't wait to share the "after". The commendations she was receiving on her social media these days were giving her a buzz like no other. #GirlGettinItDone #ApartmentFlip #MakingLandlordsCry

Luna laid protective plastic across the floor and countertops, and was putting blue painter's tape on the wall when a knock came at the door. She jumped off the stepladder to answer, but the door was having an issue again.

"It's stuck!" she yelled.

"I'm going to push," Sam said on the other side.

She turned the knob, giving it a strong yank. The door popped open with Sam almost knocking her to the ground as his body collided with hers. His hands grasped her hips, keeping her upright. "Shit. Sorry. Did I hurt you?"

Luna couldn't do more than shake her head as his hands dragged across her arms, taking the same path as those warm brown eyes, as he inspected her. His calloused skin was not even close to the smooth hands of Viggo, but Sam moved with reassuring purpose.

"You okay?" he asked.

"Yeah." Luna pulled from his arms, and shook away the feeling of—

She didn't feel anything. Why would she? It was ridiculous. But nothing or not, she shook it off anyway.

"I'll take another stab at the door frame. Sorry about that." He took a step away, his face flushing, and adjusted his hat. He clearly didn't feel anything either because, again, ridiculous.

"I have everything in the kitchen." She hoped to distract from the awkwardness and return them to the task. Her paint and brushes were waiting on the countertop.

He stepped outside, returning with his own can of paint.

"Oh, I already got..." she started. Luna couldn't imagine what color he'd selected when she had already chosen the dream shade that was dove gray.

"Primer."

"What?"

"I told you that if we were going to do this, it would be done right. It's best to do a coat of primer on the wood before the paint."

He strolled into her kitchen but stopped, peering through the plastic. "You tiled a backsplash?" The muscles in his jaw flexed in a way that was becoming quite familiar.

She was beginning to take a lot of pride in her ability to draw so much ire from the apartment manager. It meant she did a good job. On the other hand, if they were going to work together, perhaps it was time to let him in on her secret.

"It's stick-on."

"Sorry?"

"I didn't actually tile it. It peels off."

Maybe he didn't believe her because he pulled the plastic away in order to inspect it closer. To his expert eye, it had to be obvious now, but from a distance, and for her purposes, she was quite happy with the results.

He pointed to the floor. "And this?"

"It's floating. The linoleum is underneath."

"But the wall…" He nodded to the peacock-colored wall in question.

"Peelable wallpaper. In the living room, they're stick-on wall decals for the design. They can both be removed without any damage."

His eyes rose to the new overhead light fixture in the dining room.

"An oversize shade with fabric glued to the bottom. It's stuck to the ceiling with sticky Velcro since the shade isn't heavy. The original light is underneath, although I removed the glass cover," she said with pride.

"And the window shades?"

"Oh, those I definitely put in the right way. I figured if I'm allowed to put holes in the wall for shelving and pictures, then what's a couple extra holes for proper window treatment." She waited for him to praise her ability at being creative.

It was disappointing when a frown appeared instead. "Why would you waste your money like that?"

A flare of irritation surged inside her. He was one more person who didn't get her and expected some kind of justification when she simply wanted to do what she wanted. "Why do you care?"

"And why the hell are you making me paint the cabinets?"

"I'm not making you do anything. You insisted." Luna swept her hair into a ponytail.

"I—What?"

"I'm perfectly capable of painting the cabinets on my own."

"You know what I mean. If you're so smart with all these workarounds, why are we painting the cabinets?"

"You said I could do anything, and I wanted to see if you meant it."

Sam's eyes turned in the direction of rustling and found Duchess pawing the plastic on the floor. "You have a cat?" There was another tick along his jawline.

Darn it! She forgot to shut the cat in her bedroom like the last time he was here.

"You said I could have a pet. I just got her. She's really good and not destructive and I just need…" Luna allowed the sentence to die because it almost ended with, *I just need something so I feel less lonely.* A sentence like that might cause some emotions to slip out. Instead, she tucked those feelings back in place. "And you said I could."

"I said you would have to pay a deposit. You can't keep sneaking around me."

"All right, fine. I'm sorry."

A grumpy expression settled across his face. "You'll have to keep the cat locked in the bedroom while we're doing this because I don't want to take any chances it gets in—Is that what you're wearing to paint?"

She placed her hand on a hip. Was he going to pick on everything? "What's wrong with it?" Luna sported the lion graphic tank top because it was old. She didn't care if it became completely splattered in his presence. She also wore a pair of distressed denim shorts. She considered the ensemble the ideal painting outfit, and if Instagram hearts were a metric of opinion, she wasn't wrong. Luna didn't know what type of outfit he saw, but he must have forgotten the question since his gaze did a lazy drag across the length of her bare legs. "Or maybe you don't find anything wrong at all."

Brown eyes snapped to hers, the tips of his ears turning red. "It's going to get paint on it."

"Again, why do you care?"

Sam didn't have any answer. His threadbare vintage Nirvana tee and paint-splattered jeans left no question as to whether or not he was prepared to paint.

Luna retrieved Duchess, locking her in the bedroom.

When she returned, he was setting up. "There's not a lot of room. Do you mind if I'm on top?" he asked, while setting out paintbrushes and rollers.

"On top? On top of what?" What the hell was he talking about and why did it send her heart racing?

"We can only fit one ladder. I'll do the top cabinets and you can do the bottom."

"Oh. Okay." Well, obviously. What else could he possibly have meant?

It's not as though she was expecting Sam to do all the painting himself. When he had said *help*, he meant the literal definition of it. She wasn't complaining but it was a small kitchen, which meant they'd be in close proximity for most of the day. This wasn't a good idea since she'd promised herself never to be friends with him. The more they interacted, the harder it was to remember this. Although giving him a hard time about things and seeing his jaw muscles twitch in agitation was also fun.

He used a screwdriver and straight muscle to pop the lid on the can of primer. When his bicep flexed, Luna concluded she wouldn't mind if his T-shirt contained a few more holes. If his muscles stressed the seams, snapping the thread in its wake, it might make this afternoon worth getting out of bed for. Unaware of her handyman-related fantasies, Sam climbed the ladder, removing the blue painter's tape from around the cabinets, crumpling the tape into balls and tossing them to the floor.

"Hey, what are you doing?" Luna had spent a lot of time taping in order to demonstrate her preparedness, and he was failing to recognize any of it.

"The tape will make you lazy and your edges will come out worse because you'll slop paint on and it'll seep under the tape. Maybe we need a painting lesson."

Never mind. Keeping her promise to never be friends with him would be easy because, *rude.*

"Excuse me. I know how to paint." What else was there besides putting paint on a brush and then connecting it to the cabinet? Was he about to drop some *Karate Kid* knowledge? Using this as a reason to sidle behind her, take her painting hand in his calloused one, and demonstrate how to *brush on, brush off* in upward, downward strokes. Lots and lots of upward and downward strokes. Would he still be on top? *Gah!*

She should open a window. The summer heat trapped in her apartment was melting her brain.

"Luna?"

"What?" she said too loud, being startled from a day…dream? A day-mare? Which, of course, was a night-mare during daytime hours. She hadn't decided which one. It was time to stop these damn handyman fantasies. They weren't even creative.

He stared at her, his arm raised while in the process of putting the first coat of primer on the cabinet, allowing his T-shirt to ride up and revealing skin along his lower torso. Luna forced steady eye contact with him, while scraping her fingers through the end of her ponytail and trying to keep her heartbeat even.

"I'm trying to show you how to do this and you're not paying attention."

"I was thinking about something…for work." That was

convincing, right? Her throat may have been a touch parched, and she snatched a water bottle from the counter, guzzling from it. It didn't help that she found skilled, competent men appealing. How was she expected to survive this afternoon of painting? This was definitely a bad idea.

He patiently waited for her to finish drinking before trying again. "As I was saying, put some paint on your brush, but use the edge of the cup to wipe most of the paint off. You just want a little bit. When you paint, don't start directly on the edge, but a little ways away from it. Then swoop closer to the wall letting the edge of the brush angle out. And you'll get a nice clean edge. No tape needed."

"Okay."

Based on his flat facial expression, Sam was unconvinced. "Can I see you do it?"

She didn't want to be put under a microscope at this moment, not until she was more in control of herself. "I said I got it."

"I'm not signing you off on edge duties until I see you in action."

She glared at him. "You're not the boss of me! This is my kitchen." How he managed to always push her buttons was a complete mystery.

"Wrong. This kitchen and the cabinets belong to Sunderland. Now get up here and start edging." He jumped from the stepladder with a thud, which wasn't remotely impressive, and pushed the brush and cup into her hand.

She released a long groan to make it clear how much she hated him, his ballcap, and his silly paint lessons that were not even close to being as sexy as her *Karate Kid* fantasies.

Luna climbed the ladder, dunked her brush in the primer, and removed it.

"That's too much paint."

She wiped the brush on the lip of the cup.

"That's still too much."

If there was one thing she hated, it was being told what to do. She considered shouting, *Forget it! I'll just stick with the old wooden cabinets*, to get rid of him. But, with her heart set on dove gray cabinets, she bit her lip to keep her temper at bay. He was probably doing this on purpose, and she wasn't about to let him win.

Before she could attempt to get the appropriate amount of paint on her brush, Sam stepped on the ladder, took her hand, and gently guided it until the brush was wiped to his satisfaction. Her breath snagged in her chest. The close-proximity thing was happening, which she didn't want... Or did want? *Dammit*. She couldn't remember.

"A little goes a long way." His face was raised to hers and his arms were on either side of the ladder, boxing her in.

Luna wondered about the scar on his left eyebrow. Was that from a childhood incident? From the car accident? There was a small desire on her part to smooth her finger along it.

"Are you worried?" he asked.

"About what?" Her voice was soft, almost breathless.

"That you won't be able to do it."

No one was allowed to doubt her and the spark inside reignited. "I bet I can do it better than you." She took the wooden end of the paintbrush, putting it beneath the bill of his hat, and flipped the cap from his head causing the headgear to plop on the floor.

"Why do you keep abusing my hat?"

"I don't know. Maybe you look better without it."

The natural upturn at the center of his brow lifted even higher at this, his forehead wrinkling in a cute, sympathetic way. If she knew this was a possibility, she would have thought twice about removing his hat. Luna realized her mistake too late.

"Do I look as good as the porn rug guy?" he asked in a slow, easy fashion.

"At least that guy didn't boss me around."

"Maybe you need to be bossed around a little."

"I may need a lot of things, but I don't need them from you," she replied.

"And, yet, every time you need help, I seem to be here."

"Only because you're always poking your nose where it doesn't belong. I can handle everything on my own just fine."

Sam shook his head. "You are the most stubborn woman I've ever met."

"I don't find it surprising to learn that you have a severely limited social life."

"I guess not all of us can be royalty."

"Well, that's obviously true." She made a point of eyeing his grungy paint clothes that looked pretty good on him, but he didn't need to know that.

He barked out a laugh. "Well, guess what, Queenie? Right now I'm going to stand here and watch you edge. And you're not going to stop edging until I'm completely satisfied. Got it?"

She almost swallowed her tongue. He was insufferable and arrogant and…and completely making her hot…with anger, of course. She wanted to smother him with her mouth. At a complete loss of words, Luna let out a frustrated growl, before flipping around and stomping her way to the top of the ladder. Sam remained at the bottom, holding the sides. She was conscious of the fact that his face had never been so close to her ass before and her body was a few degrees from catching on fire. Having to do anything in this kind of environment was impossibly unfair.

Luna managed to place her brush on a cabinet, painting the same way as he did. For all the noise he made about painting the correct way, it was easy and her primer line was neat and precise. Huh. Guess painter's tape wasn't necessary after all.

"You're left-handed?" he asked.

"Yeah. So?"

"Nothing."

She swiped a hand above the area as though it was a big reveal. "Happy?"

"It's fine."

Liar. Her paint line was more than fine. She pushed her way past him down the ladder, handing off the paint cup and brush. No longer being confined between the ladder and his body, she already felt more in control. Flipping her ponytail over her shoulder, she said, "Now I'm going to watch *you* edge all day, but don't expect any gratification. I'm certainly not as easy to please."

"I don't find it surprising to learn you have impossibly high standards."

"Standards. I just have standards. If you see them as high, that's probably a *you* problem."

"You remember that conversation we had when you asked me if I thought you were nice?"

"Yup."

"This afternoon isn't changing my mind," he said.

"Mine either."

"Fine. Maybe we can just work in silence then."

"That's the first thing you've said today that I actually like," she replied.

He made a slow climb on the ladder but snapped his fingers once he reached the top. "Hat." His hand was outstretched like he didn't have any doubts she'd obey him.

Luna gritted her teeth as she scooped the baseball hat from the floor and flung it to him.

In a single graceful motion, he snatched the cap from the air, and slid it backwards on his head. "I don't care what you think about my hat," he responded, which irritated her even more.

For thirty minutes they worked in silence and, while it was peaceful, she grew tired of it. It was too quiet. Almost like Sam was ignoring her. If anything, it should be the other way around. She should be ignoring him. Whatever this was, it wasn't right, and he didn't deserve the peace of mind.

"Have you done this type of thing for any of the other apartments?" she asked.

"No." Sam kept his eyes on his work. "No one else has any problem following the rules."

Luna glared from where she sat crossed-legged on the floor. "You could have said no during the walk-through. I don't know why you're acting like all of this was sprung on you out of nowhere. When I said I wanted to do some renovations to the place, what exactly did you imagine that would entail?"

"I wasn't exactly..." His words didn't go any further.

"You weren't exactly what?"

"I wasn't exactly paying attention." This was spoken as an annoyed confession.

Luna stopped painting, confusion descending upon her. "You weren't paying attention? What the hell does that mean?"

"It means I was distracted. Okay?"

She wasn't sure what to make of this statement at all. Was Sam saying *she* was the one distracting him? If this was the case, it amused her a great deal. Luna chewed on her bottom lip to keep from smiling. "Interesting," she replied.

He glanced at her from his spot on the ladder, his lips stretching into a line. "I was having problems with the dryer in the laundry room right before you showed up. I couldn't figure out what was wrong with it and it was bothering me. That's all."

"Ah, yes, the dryer. I can see how that could be...*distracting*." She made sure to enunciate every syllable of the word. When his cheeks flared with color, she slid a knowing smile to him, noticing his Adam's apple bob. Yes, this was way more entertaining than painting in silence.

"So, now that you know how the miscommunication happened, maybe you can cut me a break and let this cabinet job be the last project you do."

"Maybe. But it'll probably inspire me to do more." She

poured more paint into her cup, and stood beside the ladder, watching him work. "I like my apartments like I like my men."

"Someone who only looks good on the surface?" he grumbled. "I'm sure you have a lot in common with that."

Luna was going to reply with the words *modern and stylish* but his comment irritated her and she was no longer amused. Without thinking, she dunked her finger into the paint, stood on the bottom step, and smeared primer from his cheekbone to his chin.

Sam's eyes bugged when he noticed her pointer finger covered in paint. "What the hell did you do that for?" His own hand went to his cheek, smearing the paint on his skin.

"I feel like that's been a long time coming for you."

He glared. "You've got something on your face, Queenie." And he tracked his paint-covered fingers down the center of her face, from brow, along the ridge of her nose, but he paused when reaching her bottom lip.

With any other painting partner, she would have pulled away, shouted, taken her revenge by dumping her cup of paint on his head. But she didn't. Luna took it. Because like Sam, this had to be a long time coming for her as well.

Deep down inside, Luna knew she was a brat. She didn't care because the further away she could keep someone, the less reason for her to be vulnerable. It was easier, less risky. She was already exhausted trying to stay on Mia's good side. But, for everyone else, it was okay if they didn't like her because if they did, then she'd have to worry about when they'd stop liking her. As a result, she was someone who provoked. Someone who liked getting under people's skin.

Someone who took pleasure when others were—

"Distracted?" she asked in a soft voice, her eyes unwavering.

His darkened gaze focused on her mouth as his finger slowly tipped off her lip. But the hand didn't move far. In fact, his fingers flexed over her chin as if he ached to make physical contact again.

It was at that moment where Luna forgot about provoking, where she held her breath.

Tap! Tap! Tap!

Both Sam and Luna jumped.

Outside the dining room window, Zabe had a huge grin on her face and was waving. "Hey! Can I help you guys paint?"

Luna stepped off the ladder and away from doing something she'd regret.

Chapter Eleven

THANKING HIS LUCKY stars.

That's exactly what Sam was doing. Thanking his goddamn lucky stars.

Zabe tapping on apartment seven's window was the wisest thing to happen to him all day. The kid's appearance saved him from making the biggest mistake one could make while hanging out with the most perplexing, aggravating woman in his life.

Luna stood at the kitchen sink, using a damp paper towel to remove paint from her skin.

"Did Sam drop his paintbrush and smack you in the face with it?" Zabe asked.

It was even worse than an accidental fumble with a paintbrush. It had been his hand. He had touched her, marked her, as she had done with him. And, in that moment, he had wanted to keep touching her, all of her. Even when she wore a simple tank top and frayed denim shorts with her hair swept into a messy ponytail, she still was the most intriguing woman he'd ever known.

"Something like that," Luna replied.

Zabe gave his leg a light smack. "Sam! Why would you do that to her?"

He said nothing in response but pointed to his paint-smeared jawline as if this was all the explanation required. Luna had started everything. He tried his best to avoid being drawn into her provocations. Every interaction felt the same as verbal clickbait. Before her, he preferred keeping his head down and moving through his day without causing trouble for anyone. He was done being the brash, smartass version of himself—at least, he'd thought he was. Except, Luna had a way of revitalizing it, like a zombie version of Past Sam. Every time she pushed, he couldn't stop himself from pushing back.

"You dropped the paintbrush on yourself and then on poor Luna?" Zabe asked.

He opened his mouth to correct her, but Luna responded first. "Yup. That's exactly what happened. Who knew he was so clumsy, right?"

"Oh, Sam is always getting hurt doing this stuff. In fact, just last week—"

"Okay, I don't think we need to get into all that," he said. He missed the blissful half hour of total silence he'd had. That was actually relaxing. This was not. He didn't want to spend another weekend in close proximity with Luna. It was dangerous to his self-control, which already felt as threadbare as his painting clothes. Sam had no choice but to get the cabinets done today, no matter how long it took.

The kid bounced on her heels, full of excitement. "But I'm not clumsy. I'm really good. I can help, right?"

"Does your dad know you're up here?" he asked.

"He's still sleeping. He had to work a double shift at the hospital yesterday." She grinned at Luna. "He's a nurse, so that means he helps save people's lives. He doesn't have a girlfriend. Do you like nurses?"

"What happened to Bethany?" Not that Sam cared about Jason's love life. The petite redhead had seemed nice, although perhaps she didn't give Zabe enough attention. Other than that, she was perfectly fine for Jason. The tenant downstairs wouldn't appreciate his kid trying to set him up with random people in the apartment complex. Besides, Luna didn't have red hair. Sure, the strands on her head were a glossy, rich tapestry of luxurious mahogany, but this still had to put her in the category of *not Jason's type*. Again, not that Sam cared.

Zabe gave a casual shrug. "I don't know. Dad just said Bethany was moving on. I didn't really like her. One time I came home early from hanging out at my friend Noel's house and she was—"

"I'm sure your dad doesn't want you gossiping about his love life."

"If I had something to do, I probably wouldn't talk so much."

"You can help me," Luna said. "We don't have any extra brushes but you can hold my paint cup for me and keep me company since Sam doesn't like talking with me."

"Why not?"

"I don't know. He thinks I'm annoying or something."

Sam shook his head as he continued his task. That was one way to describe Luna. Annoying, stubborn, fussy, lovely, and—Lovely? Wait…he meant *lousy*. Yes, lousy was more accurate.

"Can I tell you about Bethany?"

"Zabe," Sam warned with a sigh.

He caught Luna bringing a finger to her pursed lips. Zabe squeezed her hands to her mouth and attempted to suppress a squeak. Sam spent the following hour switching between painting and rolling his eyes as Luna and Zabe stage-whispered gossip to each other, but at least they were managing to leave him alone and he could focus. The faster he finished, the sooner he could leave.

"Do you think you can help me fix up my room?" Zabe asked Luna at one point. "My dad is always too tired to help me."

"What about your mom?"

The girl shrugged. Sam didn't know the whole story but he did know her mom wasn't in the picture anymore. "She lives somewhere else."

Luna immediately set her painting stuff aside and broke out her phone. "We can create a board of what you like. Do you have a favorite color? Of course you do. Who doesn't have a favorite color?"

Sam for one. However, he suddenly found himself drawn to colors like peacock blue these days. He should have said something to discourage any more renovations, especially when it was spreading into other apartments, but he didn't have the heart, not when both Zabe and Luna were energized by this topic. The brightness of the moment glittered with their excitement and joy. For once, he'd rather wrap himself up in it for a little while instead of squashing it.

"I like the name Zabe. Is that your birth name?" Luna asked.

"Elizabeth. I like Zabe better. Do you have a nickname?"

"I was raised by my grandfather who used to call me Lu-lu, but he died several years ago and it…kind of makes me miss him so I'd rather go by my real name: Luna. Although, if I'd known I'd be living in an apartment building with a dog also named Luna, I might have gone with my middle name Rose. Let me tell you there's nothing worse than listening to your neighbor yell, *Come on, Luna. Go potty, Luna.*"

The girl cackled at this, and he couldn't resist smiling as well.

"Do you have a nickname, Sam?" Zabe asked, drawing him into their private club.

"Sam is my nickname. It's short for—"

"No! Let me guess." The kid scrunched her face in thought. "Sammiches?" A hand covered her mouth as she giggled and threw a humored glance in Luna's direction.

"Don't be ridiculous. Who would name their baby Sammiches?" Luna said. "I know. It's probably Samderland Sunderland." Now they were snort laughing at his expense.

"Samuel Oscar Sunderland. I was my parents' first kid and they were terrified. They thought if they gave me the initials S.O.S. the nurses would pick up on it and give them extra help."

"What's S.O.S.?" Zabe asked.

"It's a distress signal. If a ship is in trouble, they used to tap out S.O.S. in Morse code to let people know they needed help." He tapped the code on the vent hood.

"Wow, Sam! It's like your parents gave you your own bat signal," she replied. "If Luna needs you, she can just tap on the floor, and you'll come running, right?" Zabe demonstrated this by tapping three quick taps followed by three slower taps and then another three quick taps on the laminate flooring. "Oh, Sam, please come rescue me," she said in a high, breathless, damsel-in-distress voice before getting the giggles.

Luna rolled her eyes, which saved him the trouble of having to do it himself.

"Calling me on the phone would work faster and I can probably only help if it's a clogged drain or something," he replied. Sam could remember her retort from earlier in the afternoon. *I may need a lot of things, but I don't need them from you.* Exactly. He got the message loud and clear.

Soon after, Zabe was called to dinner by her dad and silence descended on apartment seven once again. He missed the buffering Zabe had provided and how she drew out a different side of Luna, one that gave the exact type of attention the kid needed. She treated Zabe's wants with importance and as if they were not at all silly.

"I'm ordering a pizza. What kind of toppings do you like?" she said, breaking through the quietness.

"I'm fine."

"That's not what your stomach says."

Dammit. He was hoping she hadn't noticed the embarrassing grumbles running rampant through his belly for the last hour.

"I'm also hungry and need a break. Besides, you're helping me do all this work and it's taking a lot longer than I thought, so I can at least spring for some food."

Was she showing appreciation? He was shocked. "Whatever you want is fine."

"In that case, I'm getting the gut buster deluxe because I'm starving." She busied herself, tapping on her phone and putting in an order.

Thirty minutes later, the pizza arrived. "Break time," Luna said as she put the box on the small two-person dining table and grabbed a couple bottles of water.

Sam slowly ambled down the ladder. His arms were tired, and his back was sore, but it was nothing compared to the nerves he was hit with at the thought of sharing a meal with her. After he took a seat in one of the mustard yellow chairs, a new awkwardness filled the space between them.

"Pizza has to be the most perfect food in the world." Luna had one leg bent and propped on her chair. Her slice of pizza was held at eye level and she studied it as if it was topped with jewels instead of a large variety of meat and veggies. "Can you think of any other food where it's basically, let's just throw every ingredient together? All toppings are welcomed. And, even if we disagree about a certain tropical fruit, well, that's what personal pizzas are for. As the unofficial queen, here is my royal decree for today. Pizza is the United Nations of food. It could probably bring about world peace if we let it."

"I can't find anything wrong with your pizza philosophy, so you might be onto something."

She lifted the remaining half of her slice like a glass of champagne. "To a piece of pizza peace and to my beautiful new kitchen. Amen." Luna took an enormous bite following her elegant toast, appearing quite pleased with herself.

He looked over his shoulder to inspect their progress. While he'd been staring at the cabinets most of the day, he had yet to really see what they were accomplishing. The countertops were still cheap, white laminate, same as before, but with the faux tiled backsplash and the surrounding cabinets now painted a light gray, it was different. Better.

He returned his attention to the woman behind the improvements. "Can I ask you a question and still maintain pizza peace?"

"I guess you're about to find out." Her tone made it hard to detect if she was warning him or daring him. Either way he couldn't resist.

Sam held his hands in a surrender pose. "I'm just curious why you're doing all this. Why not save your money for an actual house and then you can do all the improvements you want without any restrictions?" He wasn't trying to anger her. Sam was genuinely curious. It didn't matter if apartment seven was suddenly more inviting than the crap shack it had been before, he still considered the improvements to be a waste.

Luna took a deep breath. "I'm an accountant. I deal with numbers. A few months ago, I decided to do the math and see how long it would take for me to save for a house deposit. The answer? Twenty years. And this isn't some wild exaggeration. I think the exact number was twenty years and seven months. And that's if I'm lucky, and house prices don't skyrocket, which they probably will. Of course, I could continue to live in my tiny childhood bedroom, in the same house my cousin lives in, but you saw Mia. She's going to need a nursery soon. Besides, I don't want to wait. After spending all day working in a tiny office, I just want to come home to some kind of sanctuary. So maybe it is a waste of time and money, but it gives me one tiny happy thing to enjoy. I can look forward to coming home *now* instead of in twenty years. Maybe that makes me ridiculous and frivolous, but I also don't care."

Luna's sharp chin lifted, her eyes determined as though daring him to fight her, to call her ridiculous to her face. He couldn't though because it made sense to him. Her words made him think about his mother and how she wanted that tiny cabin in the woods. The current house hadn't been a sanctuary for anyone for a long time and, even if it was hard on him, he wanted that for her.

Sam cleared his throat. "No, you're right. It isn't ridiculous. So does this mean you're going to be my upstairs neighbor for at least twenty years?" Knowing she might be sticking around for the long term gave him a warm, floaty feeling inside.

She ate some pizza while considering his question, leaning her cheek into the palm of her hand. "Well, at least until I find another charming duplex rental that fits within my budget. Those don't come up too often. I want some place that's bright and cozy and has built-in shelves, a brick fireplace, and an adorable kitchen." Her eyes dropped to her dinner, and she picked at the crust on her pizza. "I found a place like that, but I didn't get it. It had a green door and everything. All I want is a cute little place with a green door."

The doors at Schnell Ridge had always been dirt-streaked white. Although Luna appeared to have put some elbow grease into cleaning hers and it was now a brighter shade than the surrounding ones.

"Why a green door?"

"I like how it looks. Did you know the color of your door actually means something? A green door symbolizes prosperity and, considering where I've started, where I've been most of my life, having a cute place with a green door would feel like I'd actually made it somewhere."

"I hope you get your green door someday," he said.

Her clear hazel eyes studied him, as if attempting to detect any sarcasm. She wouldn't find any. If anyone had the determination to get the door color of her choice, Sam had no doubt it would be Luna.

"Me too." Luna smiled and it was genuine before switching to one tinged in mischief. "I don't suppose I can paint my door green."

He almost choked on his pizza. Why didn't he see that coming? "You don't know this, but I secretly gave you a choice between the door or the cabinets and you picked cabinets. Now that we're almost done, it's too late to change your mind."

"Ah well. I guess it would look pretty funny for the building to have only one green door. Besides, with how faded the rest of the outside paint job is, the building has to be due for a refresh soon. Maybe I'll petition the neighbors to get us all green doors."

"I wouldn't hold my breath if I were you." He wasn't. Not with his dad.

"Does management ever do work on the outside?"

"What do you mean?" he asked. What work was there to do? There was the concrete patio, a small patch of mostly living grass and then the parking lot.

"Oh, it's just that the patio area, even the laundry room,

is so dusty."

"Obviously. They're exposed to the outside. And guess what? Outside is dirty." Okay, maybe Sam was somewhat embarrassed about the laundry room. The door was always propped open, letting in all kinds of dirt. But who exactly expected a clean patio? Certainly not the residents of Schnell Ridge.

"And you have those barrel planters around the patio but they're just filled with old dirt. I know it's all surface beauty to you, but just cleaning off the patio, utilizing the planters with some seasonal summer flowers is something simple to make the place feel more homey. Don't you think?"

"Nope." Sam slid the bill of his hat lower on his face. "I've already wasted a whole day painting your cabinets. I don't need any more projects added to my list, especially from you. I don't know the first thing about plants." He swept a hand in the direction of her kitchen. "This is all the homey you're going to get, Queenie."

Chapter Twelve

"WELCOME TO MY home," Zabe said in a formal tone after answering the door. Luna was sure she would follow this with a curtsy or bow, but instead the kid grabbed her hand and pulled her inside.

"This is my beanbag!" she said, falling into it. "Oh, and this is my dad." The kid stood up and then plopped on the sofa beside him.

Zabe's father looked up from his laptop and nodded an acknowledgement with a "Hey, how are you?" as though Luna being in his home was not strange at all. But perhaps the girl's explanation of: "This is Luna number two and she's going to make my room da bomb," was enough of an introduction.

The kid then ran into the kitchen. "Oh, I have your payment." Luna had previously joked that she wasn't sure Zabe could afford her room-styling fee, before telling her she loved nothing better than a really good peanut butter and jelly sandwich.

Sure enough, this is what Zabe bounded out with, carrying it on a plate. "This is the best PB and J sandwich I've ever made. I even used a cookie cutter we had. See? It's shaped like a pumpkin. I make good sandwiches, right,

Dad?"

Her dad assured her she did with an approving "Mm-hmm."

Luna followed her to the bedroom with a bag of tricks, and plopped on the carpet next to Zabe while scrolling through a Pinterest board on her phone and munching on her sandwich. While the girl had pinned a few elaborate pictures, she'd also pinned a lot of images of dogs. Luna wasn't sure what Zabe wanted more: a new room or a pet. Many things on the girl's Pinterest board weren't possible even if Sam gave her free rein. While Luna was willing to be risky when it came to her landlord and her living situation, she wasn't foolish enough to take chances where Zabe and her father were concerned.

Instead, it was better to get creative, like gluing brown fringe on a lamp shade because it represented a Yorkshire terrier's fur. Or cutting a bunch of spots out of black sticky-back felt and putting it on the wall for a dalmatian pattern. Then Luna rearranged the furniture for a better flow. Zabe didn't care as she kept declaring her room was *definitely more amazing than it was before.*

Luna loved to be appreciated, so she had a blast and took before and after pictures for social media, letting Zabe choose the hashtags. *#SeeingSpots #GirlPower #Dogs*. That last one was a little generic but this was a compromise when the kid originally wanted *#doggystyle*. Regardless, Luna left the apartment satisfied, and it made her think about all the times when she had been a kid and wanted to redecorate her and Ross's childhood home. At the time, her grandfather was less than enthusiastic about the idea and she never had any money for it.

Schnell Ridge was the first time she'd been able to really express herself in her living space. Ross had jewelry; she had this. Speaking of which, she needed to get to work. While her cousin would allow her to come in late, he didn't like her to miss the whole day even if there wasn't anything pressing for her at the moment.

Luna arrived at Lanza's Fine Jewelry and, as she predicted, it was quiet. In fact, the only people on the shop floor were Aanya Pujari, the semi-retired, part-time saleswoman, and Mia who was excitedly talking about baby stuff.

"Oh, Luna," Mia said at her entering the shop. "I was wondering where you were. I brought you your favorite, an iced caramel macchiato."

The price for Luna claiming her surprise drink was getting swept into a side hug.

"Luna is helping me put together the nursery," her cousin-in-law said brightly to Aanya.

"She does have good taste," the older woman agreed, which made Luna feel even better. Things were definitely looking up for her.

"Do you know the baby's sex yet?" Luna asked.

In response to this Mia pressed her lips together.

"Wait. Do you know? Mia Russo, I swear to God, you'd better tell me. You know I hate secrets." She considered what kind of persuasion was appropriate to use on a pregnant woman—probably something involving buffalo chicken waffle wraps.

"We just found out at our appointment yesterday." Her cousin-in-law could hardly contain herself. "A girl."

The women squealed together in happiness.

"Do you still want a colorful nursery?" Luna asked.

"Yes. I want to do something that incorporates a Mexican art aesthetic." She pulled out her phone and retrieved an image of white fabric that had large embroidered birds made up of bright blocks of color and bordered with black. With this, Luna was hit with a flicker of inspiration.

"Can you send me that image? I'll start putting together a Pinterest board for us to serve as our inspiration. What if we repainted the walls white but we had these pops of color as artwork, similar to these birds? And the accent color can be gold, like using gold and black frames." It was all coming together for her and the excitement was becoming contagious if Mia's face was any indication.

"Now you're reading my mind. I love it. I knew you'd be great at this."

"How did Ross take the news?" Aanya asked.

"Honestly, he's so excited about having a kid, I think he would have been just as happy if the doctor told him, *Congrats, your kid is a block of cheese.* But we're thinking Victoria for the name, after your grandfather." Mia rubbed Luna's arm.

"You're not going to name her after your mom?" She was surprised the baby was being named after Victor, especially since Mia had been close with her mom when she was alive.

Her cousin put her hand over her stomach. "She just feels like a little Tori."

"Have you told the judge?" Aanya asked.

"I talked to him last night," Mia replied. "I have a feeling he's going to be one of those grandfathers who has a million pictures on his phone and shares them with everyone. I am apologizing to the city of Placerville now and to Ross because my dad will probably be over a lot more now that he's semi-retired."

The judge was Mia's gruff, stern father. Luna preferred it when he wasn't around as she didn't like the guy very much since he'd never treated Ross as well as he should. Him visiting all the time was one more reason she was glad she didn't live there anymore. She could visit the tiny family and spoil the baby but she'd have her own wonderful sanctuary to return to.

"Have you thought about a baby shower?" Aanya asked.

"Natalie wants to give me one but so does my mom's family that lives in Sacramento."

"There's no reason you can't have two showers."

"Well, I might have to. I don't want to disappoint anyone."

The truth was, Luna should have been first in line to give a shower but eager-beaver Natalie had jumped in, not that she had a big enough place to host such an event. Regardless, Luna was disappointed it wouldn't be her.

"Will you go with me to my family one in Sacramento, Lu? You don't have to if you don't want to, but you're family and it would be fun to make the drive with you."

Ha! Take that, Natalie—Unless, of course, Mia had already asked her and was turned down. "Is Natalie busy that day?"

"Oh, I don't know. I didn't ask. Do you not want to go?"

Luna smiled, a warmth passing through her at being chosen. "No, I'll go. We can discuss nursery designs and stuff."

This drew another side hug from Mia. Luckily, the phone rang, giving her a reason to pull away as a lot of affection made her uncomfortable, as if she couldn't believe she deserved it. "I'll get it." She went behind the glass cabinets, snatching the wireless phone on the fourth ring. "Lanza Fine Jewelry."

The other end was silent.

"Hello?" she said.

A throat was cleared on the other end. "Hi. Is this Luna?"

Luna picked at her chipped nail polish. They needed a redo after the projects she'd been doing lately. "Yes, it is."

"Luna, how are you? This is Amy—"

Her heart jumped. She hit the disconnect button, fumbling with the phone before returning it to its charging dock.

"Is everything okay?" Aanya asked, her face filled with concern.

No. No, it wasn't. Her heart raced with anxiety.

"That was my mom." And the last person she'd ever want to talk to.

Chapter Thirteen

S AM'S AFTERNOON ACTIVITY had been entirely accidental. He'd been inside the Schnell Ridge Apartments onsite storage garage searching for... Well, he couldn't quite remember what he'd been looking for. Regardless, he discovered something previously forgotten tucked in a corner.

"What are you doing back there?" Zabe asked.

"Stay out there. I don't want you to get hurt," he said.

There was a time, in the early days of Schnell Ridge Apartments, when it was considered a promising and glittering apartment building. (Okay, it was never considered either of those, but it was more than the rundown place it was today.) This was when his parents managed the place together, and, because it was their first investment property, there was a bit more effort put in for the upkeep. Everything had held such promise.

Back then, it was he who used to follow his father around as he made repairs and showed him how to do things. Sometimes Nate would tag along too, but it was mostly Sam and his father. He had considered his dad a very important man who could fix anything and owned a mansion-size collection of impressive apartments.

Like the apartment building itself, the Sunderland family was rundown and less sparkling these days. His father's interest, since he'd moved to San Diego, was non-existent except for making sure the properties continued to bring in income. In fact, if the conversation didn't pertain to apartment business, there didn't seem to be much for father and son to talk about.

"You know we have these old planters just lying around," Sam had mentioned in their most recent phone call.

"Are you just going to toss them?" his father asked. "Maybe try posting them on Craigslist and see if anyone would buy them. People will buy all kinds of things."

"No, I-I was thinking maybe I can...maybe plant something in them."

"You garden?"

"No. I don't know. If, uh, there was a little money for some—"

"You don't know what you're doing, so you'd just kill them and..." The sentence died as though his father couldn't bring himself to finish it. He quickly added, "You know what. Maybe just do some research on the whole Craigslist idea so we don't waste money."

Sam didn't answer and an awkward silence sat between them.

"Am I wrong?" his father asked.

"No." He dropped the topic and the call soon ended. He didn't think his dad was bad, but he had checked out and didn't want to invest anymore into Schnell Ridge, neither financially nor emotionally. Not that Sam blamed him.

Coming across the old patio table and chairs set in the

storage garage, the same one his mom had picked out years ago, he realized that the apartment building still had a few surprises to offer. Using them when the weather was good didn't require much effort nor would his dad take any issue since it wouldn't cost any money. In fact, it would be a nice thing to do for the residents, especially for someone like Nicholas, who would appreciate having a place to sit while letting his Chihuahua roam the grassy spot. So, really, he was doing it for Nicholas more than he was doing it for anyone else. There was no point in having a nice patio set for it to simply go unused in the storage garage.

"Here, Zabe, why don't you make yourself useful and carry these cushions for me."

"Ew, they're really dirty." She took the cushion corners between pinched fingers holding them away from her body. "Are you throwing these away?"

"They're still good. I just need to spray everything down."

"With disinfectant? Like at a hospital? My dad taught me about biological hazards and this thing is probably covered in them."

"What? No. I'll spray it with the hose. It's just a little bit of dust."

Next, he handed her the standing umbrella, and carried out the four metal chairs and a matching metal and glass table. The jet mode on the hose washed away most of the grime. Even with the faded fabric, it looked good. While he was outside doing the work, he might as well spray down the patio. It would take him less than ten minutes and it wasn't a big deal, plus it was fun to tease Zabe with the hose water.

"Wow! I wouldn't say this is as good as having a pool, but I can sit out here and read instead of being stuck inside," she said as they were tying on the cushions to the seats.

"Uh-huh," he replied.

"Why do you keep looking at Luna's apartment?"

His head snapped to her. "What? I'm not."

"Oooooh, Sam." Zabe wiggled her eyebrows. "Do you want to kiss Luna?" The kid shut her eyes, squeezing her mouth to form kissy lips before giggling.

"No. Knock it off." He brought the bill of his hat lower. Besides he had kissed her, or rather she'd kissed him, and the whole thing had been a tease. It had been over before it began. He didn't even get to reciprocate or revel in the feel and taste of her lips or pull her body flush with his and run his fingers through the silky locks at the nape of her neck—

Not that he had thought too much about it or wanted to kiss her which, of course, he didn't. The whole thing was a pointless exercise of imagination.

"It doesn't matter anyway. She doesn't like me," he said after a moment.

"Why wouldn't she like you?" Zabe was at a complete loss. This was unsurprising considering she got along with everyone. "Is it because you said she's annoying?"

"I never said that." Luna *was* annoying. But Sam had never said the word aloud and, therefore, he was allowed to defend himself against such an outrageous accusation. She had merely guessed his opinion and it happened to have been the correct one. But that wasn't the same thing at all.

"My dad says you shouldn't assume anything. Maybe this is a situation where she thinks you don't like her, and you think she doesn't like you, but in the end you're both wrong. I don't know. I'm just an eight-year-old kid. What do I know about this stuff?"

This did make him stop to process her words, but he soon shook his head. "Even if I did like her, I wouldn't know what to do about it."

Sam's past relationships were not ones he considered to be serious or long-term. Most of them had started when he and his brother had gone drinking at local parties. Liquid courage, Nate's help, and his own horniness had been the primary forces in jump-starting those relationships. It was all different now, and he had no interest in attempting to revive a horny, reckless version of his past self.

Zabe raised one confused eyebrow. "When I like a girl at school, I learn what she likes. But again, I'm eight. You're an adult. You shouldn't have to learn this from me."

Sam continued thinking on the issue after she departed to go shopping with her dad. He sat in one of the patio chairs and pondered all of it, before jumping up to pace. He took another seat, worried his hands together before springing from his chair again. He couldn't decide between pacing or sitting or doing anything at all.

Lacing his fingers over his head, his eyes rose to apartment seven.

Forget it.

Time to return to his own place or at least do something else. Zabe was right. She was eight years old. What did she know? Figuring Luna out wasn't going to be that simple. He knew she preferred nice things, which already put him out of his depth.

As soon as he hit his apartment doormat, he whipped off his hat, ran his hands through his hair before plunking the cap low on his head. *Hell with it.* Flipping around he smacked into a warm body.

"Oof! See? This is why wearing that thing is a hazard," Luna said.

"Sorry. Did I hurt you?" He wanted to touch her, make sure she was okay from their collision, but he resisted. Her appearing like a wish fulfilled was enough. She was dressed in shorts and a bright pink crop top but wore a pair of black Converse, putting her height at perfect. She had to tilt her chin to make eye contact with him or, if he stepped closer, her head would fit snugly along his neck and his arms could wrap themselves around the warm band of skin shown above her waistband.

He licked his dry lips. "Did you need something?"

"Actually, I do. I picked up an old mirror that I want to take apart so I can repaint and reuse the frame but the latches holding the mirror to the frame are giving me issues. I'm afraid I might break the mirror and get glass everywhere." She paused here as if her request was obvious to anyone and didn't require any further explanation.

Silence seemed to be the best response when it came to dealing with her, and his mouth remained shut, his eyes fixed, not jumping in to ease her ego.

After a moment her eyes dropped while she adjusted one of her black bra straps that had slipped from her shoulder. He couldn't stop his gaze from tracking the movement. "I thought maybe you might be able to pry the backing off for me. Can you help me? Please?"

Sam swallowed before replying, "Okay."

"The patio furniture is a nice addition," she said as they walked past.

He waited for follow-up critique, where she'd comment on the age of the furniture or mention the faded fabric. Her restraint in saying neither was an impressive feat. It allowed an added boost to his effort and maybe walking through a million cobwebs had been worth it—not that it mattered because, again, he had done it for Nicholas, not Luna.

But the feeling of pride was nothing compared to when he faced her kitchen. Sure, he'd been there when they had finished painting late last weekend, but she had added new handles to all the cabinets and there wasn't painter's tape and plastic everywhere. Even with the older black appliances, the kitchen had transformed into something belonging to an apartment going for twice the rental amount. According to him, it was a pretty nice sanctuary.

The mirror was on her table, placed in the middle of a laid-out newspaper. One latch was slightly lifted, showing where she had made some effort herself.

"You don't want the mirror part?" He took her flathead screwdriver in hand, wedging it under a latch. With brute strength he was able to pop the metal backing.

"No, it has a crack in it already and it's all mottled looking. It's basically trash, but the frame is in decent shape and unique. I picked it up from one of the antique stores in Old Town for three dollars. I'm going to repaint the frame bright red as wall decor for Mia's nursery."

He nodded his head, continuing to work the other latches until the mirror was freed from its frame. Clearly, Luna had a vision and Sam didn't need to understand it. He'd seen enough to realize she knew what she was doing. He was fine being the muscle, perhaps he even enjoyed the idea of being the brawn to her brain.

"Anything else?" he asked when finished. The task had been completed way too fast for his liking.

"Nope, that's it. Thank you."

Sam should leave. His feet should move to the door, and he should leave. He didn't though. Instead, he adjusted his hat and shifted his weight. "I…uh…" He cleared his throat. "I-I was thinking about what you said about the patio and maybe the tenants would like to have a nice place outside for the summer. But, like I said before, I don't know anything about plants or what looks nice and you're really good at that…at knowing what looks nice, I mean." Was she going to help him out here instead of torturing him by letting him fumble with his words?

"What exactly are you asking for?" She was as direct as always.

"I looked it up and there's a garden center nearby. I was…hoping you might go with me to help pick out some stuff."

Luna brightened. "Really?"

"Yeah."

His idea of fun was not spending an afternoon perusing plants but, if it meant being with Luna, he was all for it. The way she was studying him produced a tiny kick inside his stomach. Perhaps Zabe, in her eight-year-old wisdom, had it correct. Maybe she didn't hate him. His feelings on the matter were conflicted to say the least but he couldn't help being intrigued by the pretty brunette. Any attention he got never seemed to be enough. Something in him ached for more, even if it meant he had to keep putting himself on the line.

"When do you want to go?"

He scratched his eyebrow. "Um, I'm free today."

"Okay."

As they departed her apartment, Sam was shocked at how easy the whole thing had been. He had assumed she would say no to any of his requests, but she hadn't.

Luna slid a glance at him as they descended the stairs. "Are you just asking me because you need a car?"

"What?" he replied.

"What would your plan have been if I had said no? I'm just imagining you trying to bring a bunch of petunias home on the back of your motorcycle."

"Oh." Actually, he hadn't considered this at all. He didn't have any concrete plan when he invented Operation: Plants for the Patio. "I'd...probably borrow my mom's car," he lied.

She retrieved her key fob and unlocked her vehicle as he continued to his bike.

"Where are you going?" she asked, confused.

"You can just follow me there." Sam put on his motorcycle helmet.

"You can ride with me. It's silly to not go in one vehicle. I assure you I'm a very good driver." Her eyes narrowed, perplexed, as though she couldn't decide whether or not to take offense.

"I just like riding the bike. It has nothing to do with

you."

Luna didn't appear convinced but after a moment she replied, "Fine," and got into the driver's seat of her SUV.

Today Sam was breaking from some of his normal habits, but he couldn't break all of them.

Chapter Fourteen

"WHAT ABOUT THIS one?" Sam lifted a large hydrangea. Five minutes of wandering plant aisles proved to Luna he hadn't been lying. His knowledge of gardening was next to nothing, but, as amusing as she found this, she didn't point it out. Why damage his confidence when he was clearly trying?

"That one likes shade. The patio gets a lot of sun and it'll be too hot in the summer for something like that."

He returned the hydrangea to the shelf as though quite disappointed with himself as he shoved his hands in his pockets.

Luna worked hard to keep reminding herself the guy was an asshole. He was an asshole because—Well, it wasn't easy to pinpoint an exact reason. Sure, he didn't put up with her shit but neither did Ross, and she didn't consider her cousin to be an asshole. Sam's questionable status as an asshole had her completely puzzled and she was starting to wonder if perhaps he wasn't one at all.

And yet…

And yet, there had been a clear lapse of judgment from the guy, some disregard for life, either his or other people's. How else could one explain his less than stellar history? He was a drunk driver. Did this somehow explain why he wouldn't ride with her? Was he forbidden by law? It didn't make sense to ban him as a passenger and allow him to maintain his license to drive around town on his death-cycle. Luna may be a mischievous brat, but he couldn't be a good person either.

And yet...

And yet, for not being a good person, he didn't seem completely bad either. Even with his ridiculous motorcycle, sketchy reputation, and poor personal style, he wasn't what she would describe as a dangerous bad boy. He wasn't. It was as if something deeper ran below the surface.

He had cleaned the patio, dragged out some furniture, was inspecting plants as if he was a scientist studying a new species, and he had done it all for her. This didn't mark the behavior of an asshole. If Luna hadn't any prior knowledge of the guy, she would have considered Sam a nice, decent person. Some part of her wished she had remained ignorant because maybe they could have had something fun between them. What she wouldn't give to enjoy that instead of feeling guilty that Ross deserved better loyalty from her.

It was all quite perplexing, which frustrated Luna. It was so much easier when things were clear cut, black and white, right and wrong.

"So, what are you thinking?" he asked.

Shoot. She was supposed to be contemplating plants. Plants, plants, plants. The problem was Luna wasn't much of an expert herself except for the few times she attempted a container garden on her grandfather's deck.

"There's three planters, right?" she replied.

"Yeah."

"We don't have to do all of them the same." She pulled on the ends of her hair as she pondered it. "What if each one is different? We can do a decorative container of flowers, one with a variety of tomatoes, and one can be an herb garden. Part pretty, part practical. Tenants who cook a lot will love it."

"But no roses, right?" His expression read teasing. He'd first gravitated toward the plants he recognized until Luna informed him they wouldn't be good for containers.

"Do you have a thing for roses or something? Is there a secret rose gardener under that old baseball hat, dying to get out?"

"I don't know. I just thought maybe every once in a while I could pick some to bring to my mom." He fiddled with the leaves of a plant.

The guy was an asshole. The guy was an asshole. The guy was an asshole. Did she believe it yet? He wasn't making this easy at all.

"Does your mom live in the area?"

"Yeah, for now. What about your family?"

Luna regretted bringing up the topic. She was trying to avoid thinking about her so-called mother ringing the store. She had been making Ross and Aanya answer the phones, and, every time it rang, her heart leaped into her throat as she wondered if Amy's voice would be on the other end. Every time the shop bell jingled, it could be Amy who walked through the door. The only place Luna could relax these days was at home, and she hated the idea her absent mother made her want to hide in a cave for some peace of mind.

After all this time, why would she contact Luna now? For most of her life, she'd been in the same location. It's not as though Amy had misplaced her daughter. When Luna's grandfather, Victor, got sick, he'd called her, interrupting her nice life with her new family in South Carolina, but she hadn't come. She also hadn't come when Victor died. Nor did she come when Luna and Ross had been struggling to run the jewelry store on their own.

Was Amy planning on swooping in after they'd finally figured out their lives and were doing fine? It was too late. If Luna were to cry in regards to her mother, the tears would be bitter with salt and vinegar, and it had been a long time since that had happened. She was a dry well of sympathy because her mother had made it clear that Luna was never a priority, contacting her a few times over the years, making promises of visits or plane tickets, only to disappear and devastate Luna all over again. Why should she risk any more of her heart when it was already fractured?

Sam had asked her a question about her family, and she decided to keep it simple. "There's no one. It's just me and Ross...and now Mia," she replied lightly, using the herb shelf to focus her attention. "Do you have a favorite herb?"

"I never thought about it before. I don't really cook much."

"I think my favorite might be basil. You can be eating the most generic, plain spaghetti in the world but you throw a little bit of chiffonade basil on top and suddenly you have an elegant meal."

"Chiffonade?"

She snipped a leaf from a plant with her nails. "It's when you roll up the leaf and trim it into long thin strips." Luna brought the leaf to her nose, shutting her eyes while inhaling. "I love it, and it's also great on pizza. But, going back to my original pizza philosophy, I don't think there's anything that can't work as a pizza topping and fresh basil leaves make everything better."

She offered the leaf to him, but instead of simply breathing in the scent, he gently took her wrist and brought all of her closer.

"Do you like it?" Luna asked, suddenly finding herself under the intense gaze of those hickory-brown eyes, the same ones drifting across her face as he brought her hand with the basil leaf to his nose. His hand was large and warm, and her heart rate increased erratically.

"Yes," he said in a low tone.

"Asshole." The single word was released from her lips on a soft breath.

"What?" He dropped her wrist as if snapping from a spell.

Shit. Was her reminder said aloud? "I didn't—"

"Did you just call me an asshole?"

"No, I wasn't..." Or was she? At the moment, she was confused and wasn't sure what to say. "I-I didn't mean that."

His brow knitted together. "I can't figure you out at all."

"Why do you need to figure me out?"

"For one thing, you live above me. It would be nice to know how we could stay on relatively friendly terms or at least how I can avoid being called an asshole all the time."

"You could actually avoid being an asshole. I'm sure that

helps."

"Is that what you really think?"

She studied him. His cheekbones were so sharp. Even with the facial hair, she wanted to know what his face was like to touch, not the quick swipe she'd done with the primer paint, but rather to place her hand on his cheek and connect with him. "No."

"No, what?"

"No, I don't think you're an asshole." He could be deceiving her, keeping that side of himself in check for whatever nefarious reason, but her gut couldn't believe it was true. In this, she didn't want to be wrong. "But you don't know anything about plants," she retorted because she couldn't help it. Distance was safer.

Regardless of her intention, he smiled and it hit her in the gut. "I didn't think I was keeping that a secret. In fact, I told you that in your apartment."

"Oh. That's right. You did."

"So, what do you think, Luna?" Sam was doing that thing where it seemed as if his eyes were taking note of every feature of her face.

She could have sworn the neurons in her brain were moving in a more sluggish, rambling manner than normal because she'd already lost the thread of this conversation. "Think about what?"

"About being on friendlier terms."

Could she ever be on friendly terms with someone like Sam? Knowing what she knew about him? He was quite different from what she had expected. With his naturally sympathetic expression, it made everything harder to sort.

"What's your favorite thing to eat?" she asked, putting him off.

"Watermelon," Sam replied without any hesitation.

"Really?" Of all the food in the world, she was surprised at this answer. Watermelon had to be an inferior thing to eat when pizza existed. It wasn't even the sexiest fruit. No one got excited about dipping watermelon into chocolate.

He nodded. "Yeah."

His eyes were so dark and intense, Luna swallowed, licking her lips. Sam tracked the movement with his gaze. Watermelon. Her lip balm. How did he...? She flushed. Not one single part of him was touching her, and the heat from him reached her nonetheless. Except her mind was in charge, not her body. She was strong enough to resist making any bad decisions, especially in regards to him. "Watermelon might be the only thing not allowed on pizza."

"You're willing to risk world peace over watermelon? I thought the queen was more open-minded than that."

"There's a reason world peace hasn't been achieved yet. It's nearly impossible to please everyone."

"What about just one person then?"

As hard as it was, Luna turned away from him, busying herself with the herbs on the shelf, picking a selection of hardy ones, those that didn't mind the unrelenting glare of sunlight, unlike herself. "I'm not very nice, remember?"

"Neither am I."

She stopped to inspect a pot of rosemary. "I suppose..." Luna breathed. "I suppose if you weren't an asshole, I could be less of a brat."

"It'd definitely be a step in the right direction."

"I might only be capable of doing a step here and there."

"Okay," he said.

"You know, watermelon and basil can go together with a little feta cheese. Have you ever tried it?"

"No. Sounds too sophisticated for someone like me. Have you?"

"I had it once with Vig—someone I used to hang out with. It's good. I think that's enough herbs to get us started. Maybe we should look at the flowers next."

"Okay."

She started to push the shopping cart, but he stopped her with a hand covering hers. "I got it. You lead and I'll follow."

Luna made note of his cheekbones again. They were sharp enough to cut right through her bullshit and she liked that.

As they passed an endcap, she grabbed a small bubblegum pink pot holding a miniature rose bush blooming with dozens of sunrise-orange buds. She placed it in the cart with the herbs. A single brow raised on Sam's forehead.

"For you to give to your mom," she said before continuing to shop.

Chapter Fifteen

With Schnell Ridge Apartments having a nicer patio, Sam spent some of his downtime there. He liked chatting with Nicholas, who enjoyed having a place to sit. He originally worried the plants would die under his care, as his father predicted, or he'd forget to water them. Instead, he grew to enjoy taking care of the little garden and checking the tomato plants for new growth and buds. Nicholas, a proficient cook, assured him that summer garden tomatoes were the best thing on earth. The older man even mentioned picking up a small grill for an outdoor cookout. Sam wondered why he didn't do all this sooner and thought maybe he'd take an interest in cooking as well.

When Sam went to his mother's house to do work on the house, he presented her with the small pot of miniature roses chosen by Luna. For a moment, her eyes became the bright, glittering pieces of silver again instead of heavy rain clouds.

"You got this for me, Sammy?" She hugged the plant to her chest and brought the buds to her nose. It hadn't been easy riding his motorcycle with the pot wedged between his thighs, moving slow enough to prevent the wind from snapping the delicate branches or whipping off all the petals, but it had been worth it to see his mom smile for once when greeting him.

"You seem different today," his mother said as he took out tools and gloves from the storage compartment on the back of his bike. "You're doing good?"

"Yeah, I'm doing okay." He raked his hands through his hair before putting on his baseball hat, feeling optimistic for once.

"You still need a haircut." She clucked her tongue in disapproval.

He walked with her up the porch toward the front door of her house. "You ever done any gardening?" Sam never remembered her doing it, but maybe she'd surprise him.

His mother's expression reflected confusion. "Gardening? One plant isn't going to make me a master gardener, Sam. I'm pretty sure I don't have a green thumb."

"I brought out the old patio set, you know, the one with the red and yellow flowers. We put plants in the barrels, like herbs and tomatoes. If you're ever out by the apartments, maybe you can stop by sometime to see."

The patio setup wasn't much to get excited about but at least it was different. He didn't realize how much he craved something new until after it happened. It would also be nice to visit with his mom on the little patio and she could see what he'd done. Perhaps Nicholas would come out to chat and Luna might—

Okay, he was getting ahead of himself. One patio set and a few plants didn't make a block party. It was just...maybe Luna had been right about some things. Making small, seemingly surface beauty changes, while it didn't fix everything, did make things less grim, warmer, like her. These were fixes that were manageable instead of frustrating or overwhelming.

He wanted to be with Luna more. Would it be weird if he bought more barrel planters? She'd likely see through his scheme. Or he could wait until she approached him for another apartment improvement project. Her brain appeared to always be buzzing with ideas so it wouldn't be too long.

While he had assumed Luna would be a prissy sort of person, she surprised him by being a woman who didn't mind getting her hands dirty in order to accomplish her goal, whether it be painting cabinets, helping Zabe rearrange her bedroom, or sitting beside him on the patio and using bare hands to sift through soil. If Luna was a flower, she wouldn't be any of the carefully cultured ones found at the nursery. Instead, she'd be like the pretty, untamed wildflowers scattering across the slopes along the California mountain highways. She was fearless, confident, as though there wasn't any part of her she'd allowed to be contained. He didn't even mind when she teased him by tipping the bill of his hat downward, blocking his face. With the sun highlighting her hair and warming her skin, there wasn't any part of her he didn't find mesmerizing.

"I'm sure it all looks very nice, Sammy," his mother said, interrupting his thoughts.

"The tenants seem to like it."

His mom studied him. "The new tenant is working out okay? I believe you said she was a young lady living by herself."

"Yeah. She settled in okay." *Settled* was putting it mildly compared to the truth of what Luna had done to her apartment, but he wasn't about to reveal the whole thing. His mother wouldn't care since she had removed herself from property business, but Sam wasn't willing to take any chances of word getting to his dad.

"What's her name?"

"Luna."

"Is she pretty?"

He shook his head. "Mom. She's a tenant. That seems like asking for trouble." Doing anything with Luna would be asking for trouble whether she was a tenant or not.

As he stood in his mother's kitchen, instead of being overwhelmed by the overcrowded countertops and kitchen table, he tried to see it in a different light. "What if—what if after we clear the area in here we could maybe paint the cabinets, put up a backsplash, paint that wall blue over there," he suggested, pointing to a dining room wall that was barely visible due to an oversized china cabinet.

"Blue?" his mom said, appearing skeptical.

"You don't like blue?"

"It's a little garish, don't you think. Who's painting walls blue?"

He laughed because perhaps Luna was a wizard. She'd had him convinced blue walls were not only possible but superior. "Okay. What color would you like that wall to be?"

Her skepticism slipped away as she studied the area before asking. "What do you think about lavender?"

"What is that? Like purple?" He was unsure about purple. He wished he had Luna's expertise, but they did not have the type of relationship where he was comfortable bringing her into all this. At this point, he was lucky to be on speaking terms with her.

"Maybe a light purplish gray," his mother responded.

He wrapped his arm around her shoulder. "Okay. You help me get this kitchen cleaned up and we'll paint it lavender."

Sam returned to Schnell Ridge later that afternoon feeling more hopeful than he had in a while.

It was the weekend and there was more activity around the apartment building as people were coming and going. Nicholas sat in a patio chair with his dog sniffing nearby.

"Go potty, Luna," the old man said while his body hacked its way through a cough.

Sam took one of the other chairs. "How are you today?"

"Doing as well as can be. You?"

"Fine. Just got back from helping my mom."

Zabe bounded from her apartment with her dad, Jason, following behind.

"Oh, Luna! Hi, puppy." Zabe kneeled to the Chihuahua who nervously wagged her tail, unsure about Zabe's exuberance but dealing with it nonetheless. "See, Dad. If we get a dog, Luna will have someone to play with. Please, Dad. Pleeeeease."

Jason glanced at the two men at the patio table before shaking his head and sighing. "We can talk about it later. We don't want to be late for the rides at the fair."

"Oh, yeah! We're going to the fair. Are you going, Sam?"

Was it that time of year already? Sam had almost forgotten Placerville had a summer fair. When he and Nate were kids, going to the fair was *the* event during summer vacation. His parents would hand them a limited number of ride tickets, his mom slipping him an extra twenty dollars for snacks, and the boys would wander off to get into small-time trouble, usually hiding inside one area of the fun house to scare younger kids. At least until the person working the place rooted them out.

That could have been a century ago. Going to the fair-grounds was out of character for present-day Sam. He wasn't even sure what he'd do there. These days, he'd probably be more at home socializing with the old man working the fun house and booting troublemaker kids.

"No, not today," he replied to Zabe.

The door shutting on the second level drew all their attention. It was Luna departing in a flowy, red summer dress, her brunette locks falling in soft waves, looking like a dream. Zabe ran to the stairs. "Luna! Hi! Did you know the fair opened today? Are you going?"

"I am."

The girl gasped. "Really?"

Sam had the exact same internal reaction. She always held herself so elegantly, even when walking down the stairs of Schnell Ridge Apartments. It was surprising to imagine she'd go to a dusty county fair with things like petting zoos and funnel cakes, and mingling with the commoners.

"Yup," Luna said. "My cousins are going and invited me along."

"My dad said I can play some games. Maybe I'll win one of those giant bears. They're so big they'll take up my whole bed. Have you ever won one before? Maybe we can hang out at the fair. Can I sit between you and Luna on the rides, Dad? Please. She's so fun to hang out with and doesn't have a boyfriend."

Jason, a giant, burly man, actually blushed, pulling his daughter into his grasp. "Some of us are a little overly excited today." He wrapped his big arms around his daughter. "Luna is going to hang out with other people, honey. I'm afraid you're stuck with your old dad."

"You never know. Maybe I'll see you there." Luna gave Zabe a wink before switching her focus to Sam and sliding on a pair of sunglasses. He may have forgotten how to breathe. If she had said anything else following this, he didn't hear. Before he realized it, she was strolling to her car, completely oblivious to the gazes following her.

"She's pretty, right, Dad? When I asked Sam, he just said, *She's all right.*" Zabe did an imitation of Sam, making him sound like a depressed ogre, which wasn't how he said it at all. At the time, he'd been inside a bathroom cabinet, trying to unscrew a drain in order to rescue a tenant's earring. He was more distracted than anything else, and dealing with old pipes would make anyone sound like a depressed ogre even if they weren't.

Regardless, he didn't like how Jason continued staring after Luna and absent-mindedly saying "Uh-huh" to Zabe's question regarding their neighbor's level of attractiveness. Sam couldn't decide if *Uh-huh* was a better or worse answer than *She's all right.* Who was he kidding? *His* was definitely worse. Jason, at least, had been married for a period to Zabe's mom before the divorce, and he'd also been with Bethany for at least a year. The guy had to have a higher level of charm than Sam. And now Jason was going to the fair where he'd run into Luna, win her heart with a giant stuffed bear, and then Jason, Luna, Zabe, and the giant stuffed bear would be one big, happy family, while the biggest thing in his life was attempting to keep a tomato plant alive.

"You okay?" Nicholas asked.

Sam blinked, emerging from his imaginative spiral. "Yeah." Jason and Zabe were gone. "Everyone left?"

"For the fair. Come here, Luna." The old man grunted as his body folded to lift the Chihuahua to his lap. He stroked the dog's head, who shivered while staring with dark, bulging eyes at Sam.

"You've ever been married before?" Sam wasn't sure what made him ask such a personal question. While they'd had plenty of conversations before, the range of topics were the innocuous type, but he was curious about the man who had lived at Schnell Ridge longer than he had.

"What was that?"

"Ever been married?" Sam asked louder.

"Me? No. My father died when I was young, and I had to take care of my mother."

"Was she sick?"

"No, she, my mother, just always wanted to lean on someone. She depended on me to do everything for her, to always be there. So that was my life for a long time. Working and taking care of my mother. She died, oh, let's see, over fifteen years ago now. That's all I knew. I didn't want to take care of anyone else. But when I was ready to finally go out— let me tell you something. Sometimes you put your life on pause for so long, you can't remember how to unpause it. And then it feels too late."

Sam couldn't respond after that. He removed his hat,

fiddling with the brim, Nicholas's words striking him deep because he understood what the older man meant. Sam himself had been stuck in pause mode.

"You should go to the fair," Nicholas said after a moment.

"Oh. No, I don't—"

"Why not?"

"It's really for kids."

"Is it? That pretty lady from upstairs doesn't look like any kid."

No, she definitely did not. Sam slipped his hat into place. "She's probably having fun with her family." Or being impressed with Jason's skills at winning giant bears.

"Let me tell you something, young man, no one is going to unpause your life for you. Only you can do that."

Soon after, Sam decided to take a motorcycle ride, not heading to any place in particular. Perhaps Nicholas had a point. He had to make some kind of effort instead of being stuck all the time and, after being at his mom's home, he wanted to hold on to the feeling of optimism a little longer. Like magic, he found himself at the fairground parking field, as if his motorcycle had conspired with Nicholas and made sure there wasn't any other place he could end up.

He might as well wander around and see how much things had changed since he and Nate were kids. The problem was, he couldn't see much from outside the ticket booth. What the hell. He might as well get a ticket and stroll through.

"Just one adult?" the teenage ticket worker asked.

There may have been a hint of judgment in the question,

but Sam nodded.

"That'll be twenty?"

"What? Is that just for me?"

The teenager pointed to the billboard with the listed prices. "Twenty for one adult, sir."

Sam was about to pull a *back in my day* in regards to ticket prices but now he was getting a *sir* which made him feel even older. Instead, he grumbled while pulling the cash from his wallet and sliding it begrudgingly to the ticket seller.

No one ever said unpausing one's life would be cheap.

Chapter Sixteen

"KNOCK IT OFF, Lulu," Ross said after getting pelted in the forehead with another piece of popcorn.

It wasn't as though she hadn't warned the man. Every time he made some sweet physical display of affection toward Mia, popcorn. The rules were simple, and also unspoken because she may have forgotten to tell him. It was more amusing when he didn't know the rules. Her older cousin wasn't great at getting the hint since she'd nailed him with popcorn three times, this last time when he'd swept the hair behind Mia's right ear and leaned in to whisper something secretive, which released the dimple.

The fair was already a disappointing bore. For one thing, Mia couldn't go on any rides and Ross wouldn't go on rides without her. The whole outing was transitioning into an uneventful experience except for the food. Fair food was always worth it, even if it meant being exposed to sappy physical displays of affection.

Luna scrolled through the comments on her Instagram where she had posted an earlier selfie while wearing the new crimson summer dress with the ruffled off-shoulder sleeves. She should get a big sun hat and—

"Oh. Hi, Sam," Mia said.

Her eyes snapped from her device. Sam? What the hell was he doing here? She thought maybe she'd run into Zabe and her father but Sam was a surprise, one which could add more interest to the day besides pelting her cousin with popcorn.

Mia swept a hand toward her husband. "This is—"

"Ross," Sam said. "I remember you from school. How's it going? Congratulations on…" He lost his words and instead waved an awkward gesture toward Mia's belly.

Her cousin laughed. "Thanks. How's everything going with you?"

"Fine. Hey, Luna." He gave her a shy glance.

Ross raised his brow, entertained by the situation, but she refused to give him any mind at all because there wasn't any to give. Whatever her cousin thought, he was wrong. One thing was certain, Mia hadn't told Ross anything about Sam, otherwise, she'd imagine he'd be a lot less friendly toward her landlord. Her cousin wasn't one to get into fights, but he was capable of holding an obvious grudge.

"I didn't know you were coming to the fair," she replied, her fingers playing with the end of her hair, feeling nervous all of a sudden.

"Oh, yeah, I like to at least check out some of the exhibits."

"Really?" she asked.

"Yup, I come to this one every year. Lots of great…uh, submissions." His thumb jerked to the large, white exhibitor's tent beside them.

"The Great American Quilt Exhibit?" Luna read from the event poster outside.

"Uh." He peered through the tent doors and then at the surrounding area, appearing lost. "Maybe I'm turned around. I thought it was the woodworking one?"

"We haven't been there yet," Mia said brightly. "We can all go there together."

Sam eyed Luna again who remained silent. She knew it was risky. Ross might find out about Sam's past, but it wasn't as though *she* had invited the guy to spend time with them. That had been Mia. Plus, it would make everything obviously awkward to dismiss the guy, when all he was doing was hanging out. Who was she to say where he could and couldn't go? It wasn't as if she was committing to a relationship with him, so there was no reason to tell Ross anything. It was just that she'd rather be a wheel in a group of four rather than three. Nothing more.

"Okay," was all he replied to Mia's invitation, and she tried to suppress any emotions resembling glee to this.

Before they moved from their spot, Ross plucked the popcorn from Luna's hands much to her surprise. "I think it might be my turn to hold that." Her cousin's dark eyes held a playful glint.

Dammit. Ross was more perceptive than she realized but he'd be holding on to every single kernel because he didn't know about Luna's determination to keep the guy at arm's length. Except, she'd sort of promised to be less of a brat toward Sam when they were at the nursery and this didn't happen without some effort.

"So," Luna said, "you go to these exhibits every year?"

"Well, maybe not every year." He stuffed his hands in his pockets, his head tilting to the ground. "But it's nice to see what talented people can do."

"Now you sound like Mia." As they strolled through the crowded exhibits, she noticed her cousins weren't paying attention as to whether or not Luna and Sam were keeping pace but, with popcorn war in full force, maybe that was a good thing.

"I haven't been to the fair in a few years myself, but Mia has a few photos submitted at the photography exhibit."

"Did she win anything?"

"She got a few first-place ribbons. Not that this is a great shock. Mia pretty much succeeds at everything she does. But they are good."

He was studying her more than the exhibits. "If they accepted submissions for creative home decorating, I'm sure you'd win a few ribbons. Zabe hasn't stopped talking about her new room. You did good."

She was glad her cousins weren't nearby because his words produced a warm glow within her. It was probably the sweetest thing anyone had ever said to her and she couldn't help but respond with a smile. At this rate, she might be willing to drop her bad habit of tormenting his poor hat. Not fighting with Sam was already having some benefits.

She gave his shoulder a playful bump as they stood before an elaborately carved fireplace mantel. "You're a handy guy, right?"

He leaned closer. "Sorry, it's a little loud in here. Did you say handy or handsy?"

"Are you handsy? Is this how you know so much about my rug?"

"I noticed you didn't reveal the true history about your

rug until after I had my hands all over it."

Luna choked on a laugh. "You wish you were that lucky. You barely touched it. In the meantime, I gave it a deep clean and have been immersing myself in the soft luxury of my rug all by myself and it's been amazing."

"It can't possibly be that satisfying."

She slid him a wry glance. "Oh, it definitely is. You have no idea how good it feels. Sometimes I have to stop myself from groaning in pleasure when I sink my fingers into it, especially when I remember you're right below me. I don't want to make you jealous since you're unlikely to ever experience my rug for yourself."

Sam's Adam apple bobbed in a swallow. "I can't remember. Am I the handsy one or are you?"

"I never said you were handsy. I said *handy*. I was just wondering if you can make anything like this?" She nodded in the direction of the elaborate wooden fireplace mantel.

"Are you getting more ideas?"

"Maybe. I'd love an apartment with a cozy fireplace."

"You have that rug. What do you need a fireplace for? Besides, I'm not sure how that would work in an apartment. But to answer your question, I'm not able to hand carve elaborate designs out of wood, but I'm okay building basic things, especially if I have specs. I don't really do it too much though, before you let your imagination run wild all over your rug."

Luna pushed her lip into a pout, enjoying how much he took from her, as though he'd take anything she gave him. "Why are you always ruining my fun?"

"I'm not sure you really understand what my job is. I'm

not supposed to be your personal contractor. Do you think I'm looking for extra projects?"

"What are you looking for?"

His amused expression melted away as he took in her face. "I'm not sure."

"Well, if you don't know, I don't know how you can expect me to."

Those brown eyes locked on to hers and they were full of seriousness, tinged in sadness. For the first time, she wished there was a way to smooth away his unseen pain, as if it was as easy as using her fingers to massage his brow into a more carefree expression. This wasn't like her at all, not normally. She'd never described herself as touchy-feely. But there was something deep and hidden inside him and she could almost sense it reaching out to her.

Luna broke eye contact, searching instead for Mia and Ross. They were nowhere to be found. "Dammit. Looks like I've been abandoned once again. Story of my life."

"Do you need to find them?" he asked.

She returned her focus to him, pondering his question. She hadn't been having a blast before Sam converged on their path. Things got more interesting when he was around, and she didn't see any harm in it. Why not? Her heart raced at the thought of doing something a little reckless. She couldn't be good all the time. "They can text me if they're looking for me. I'd love to go on a few rides, maybe play some games. Are you interested?"

A warm smile kicked up the edges of his lips, completely transforming his face into something more light and boyish. He didn't have the suave handsomeness of Viggo but Sam's smile tugged on something in her chest. It was as though this simple expression unlocked another layer of attractiveness, taking her by complete surprise, one she didn't even know was there. Her breath snagged within her lungs on this unexpected gleam of sunshine.

"Sure," he said.

"I DON'T THINK it's possible to win one of those giant bears."

"You were the one who was convinced that your high school baseball career was somehow an advantage to beating a rigged game." Although, she hadn't minded watching him try and fail. His lean body was surprisingly graceful in his attempts to impress her, and she'd never laughed so hard in her life.

"If the games were fair, we'd be sitting on a mountain of giant bears," Sam said.

"What's your obsession with these bears? I'd have to lug that thing home, and it'd take up half my apartment. No, thanks. Besides, I have Mister Mustache, which I won on my own. I'm quite happy with it." She brandished a tiny plush, mustached hot dog toy she earned after going head-to-head against Sam at the Basketball Shot booth.

"Okay, in my defense, my hoop was right next to the speaker and it was distracting with the carnival worker blasting cutting insults directly into my ear."

"There wasn't a speaker next to you at the ring toss. In fact, the kid working that booth was too busy looking at his phone to even pay attention to us."

"My wrist is still sore after having to paint someone's cabinets. I think it affected my ring-tossing abilities."

"High Striker?"

"I don't think they used the standard-issue mallets. It felt a little light."

"Okay, but what about knocking down the milk bottles with the baseball? If any game should be your forte, it should have been that one. Especially after I had to hear the story about how you pitched the winning game for some high school championship."

"I struck out the best player. Did I mention that part?"

"Unfortunately, yes. And, yet, you still missed."

"You blew in my ear!"

She threw her head back and laughed. "Did I? I don't remember that part."

With Sam's lack of six foot height, messing with him had been exceedingly easy. She couldn't resist standing on tip toes to gently blow a stream of air along his ear. It had been worth it when his wild pitch almost struck the carnival worker. He did better with the following pitches but his concentration was shot and he walked away with wounded pride, and she was thoroughly diverted.

He pulled the bill of his hat lower. "This day has done nothing but demolish my ego over and over again."

"Aw, here. I think you need Mister Mustache more than me." The tip of her finger went to the bill of his hat, pushing it upward.

"I don't want your consolation prize," he said, his face grumpy, but there was a ghost of a smile on his lips.

"Then we'll have to think of something else to make you feel better. Let's see. Oh, let's go on the Ferris wheel." Without thinking she grasped his hand and forearm, but was stopped when he remained fixed in place.

"What's wrong?" she asked.

He stared at her clinging hands and she immediately let go, realizing that grabbing him had been a little too natural. She shouldn't have done it.

"Sorry, maybe I'm the handsy one after all. Do you not want to go?"

Sam blinked, snapping from whatever internal musings he'd been having. "No, I do. Anything you want to do. You lead, I'll follow."

And that's exactly where she led him because when had riding a Ferris wheel ever been a bad idea?

Chapter Seventeen

THE LAST TIME Sam had been on the Ferris wheel was with Nate. He was thirteen years old at the time, which meant his brother was eleven. They had thrown popcorn from the top, egging each other about who could get the best shot. Extra points if it landed in someone's hair and the victim continued walking without noticing their new snack-related hair accessory. He once overheard his grandfather refer to the Sunderland brothers as the "little bastards" and he hadn't been wrong.

Sixteen years later, Sam found himself sitting next to trouble again, but this one was an entirely different kind. Instead of him causing the mischief, he was the one who was in the cross hairs of danger. He could barely keep his breath even or his hopes low.

Here was this beautiful woman who laughed fully, flirted freely, and made him feel there was still light to be had in his life. And she had touched him, taken his arm in her smaller, softer hands, and his heart had almost stopped beating. The logical part of his brain kept warning him to lower his expectations, that nothing would ever come from this. All of it became nothing more than white noise whenever her bright hazel eyes met his.

"See?" she said. "Now aren't you glad we didn't win a giant bear? Think about how crowded this seat would have been."

This was true. There was not enough room on the bench for Sam, Luna, and a giant stuffed bear. Although, perhaps it would have been nice to have a reasonable excuse to be shoved together. As it was, there was a good six inches of space between them, and six inches might as well have been six miles—as far away as Luna was from him at the moment.

Their bench started and stopped at intervals as the carnival worker swapped older riders with new ones, slowly making its way higher, not yet reaching the ride's pinnacle of height.

"Oh, look, there's Ross and Mia. Oh my God, that butthead is eating all my popcorn."

He scooted closer to peer over the edge and saw where she was pointing.

"Ross! Hey, Ross!" she shouted until the couple lifted their heads in response. "You jerkwad. You owe me more popcorn."

On the ground, Ross shook his head, before flipping popcorn in the air and catching it in his mouth.

"He's really lucky I'm on a Ferris wheel and there's nothing I can do about it. I need to plan my revenge," she said.

"Should I regret getting on this ride with you?"

She turned to him, a wicked glint flitting across her features as she looked at his hat. "I don't know what you're afraid of, Samderland Sunderland."

He quickly removed his baseball cap, putting it on the seat as far away from her as possible.

Her eyes glittered, her smile growing more dangerous. "Are you worried about your hat or something?"

"When I was younger, my dad took my brother and I to a River Cats game in Sacramento. Just going there was a treat because my dad didn't like taking time off from work. He also doesn't enjoy spending money. Any food or snacks we wanted were packed with us from home and we ate in the parking lot or snuck it in because buying food at any sort of stadium or event was considered a rip-off. Imagine our surprise when, at the end of the game, my dad bought us each a baseball hat. It wasn't even one of our birthdays or anything. It would be upsetting if my hat somehow got flicked off at the top of the Ferris wheel by someone who didn't realize the sentimental value of it."

Luna's amused expression didn't falter. "Well, looky here. Seems like we got ourselves a poor little rich boy. You know what I was doing when I was a kid? Working in the jewelry shop. I've never been to a live game in my life. Getting your hat could be some kind of consolation prize and, unlike you, I take them when I can get them."

Her arm shot out, reaching for the hat on the seat, but his hand snapped around her wrist, locking her limb across his lap. Laughter bubbled out of her as if her joy was overflowing and their bench seat rocked on its axis. Her new position was close enough for him to smell a delicious note of floral coming from her skin or to touch the freckle beside her eye. Luna was giddy and breathing hard when her eyes dipped to his mouth, her teeth dragging her pouty bottom lip inward. All he could think about was watermelon. He was convinced that one small taste would be enough to satisfy him. Sam's pulse stuttered as his head dropped, waiting for her to push him away. But she didn't move, not even when he dragged a finger from her beauty mark to her cheekbone.

They had reached the top of the Ferris wheel and would soon start to move at full speed, but currently the moment had frozen around them, the rest of the fair noise melting away. The late afternoon sun was setting, giving Luna's skin a warm rosy glow.

"I'm curious what kissing you would be like," he said lightly.

"You forget we've already kissed. I wasn't impressed."

A slight smile tipped the corners of his mouth. "My ego has taken enough hits today. I'm not sure I can let that slide without at least trying to redeem myself."

"Unfortunately for you, I'm a huge believer in first impressions. I'm not sure how second chances fit in there."

"I hear lasting impressions are better than first ones."

"I don't like being wrong."

"Get used to it, Queenie." With her being a breath away, he couldn't resist. When his lips connected with hers, his stomach dropped, either from their basket swooping down as the Ferris wheel reached speed or because her lips were so soft he might never recover. He pressed and pulled from her lips gently, releasing her arm.

Internally, he pleaded. *Please. Touch me.*

And then he felt it.

The featherlight sensation as her fingers brushed his throat and spread along his jawline. His own hand claimed the nape of her neck to pull her closer, deepening their kiss, a zing of electricity awakening every nerve ending inside his body. He took note of the sweet burst of watermelon, the heat of her tongue brushing his, and how full her lip was when he nibbled on it. Whatever senses were to be had, she filled all of them.

He pulled away as their ride was coming to an end. Luna, though prettily flushed with pink, kiss-swollen lips, appeared to be in a state of shock. She didn't say anything, no clever, smartass comments or biting critiques. Instead, she took the carnival worker's hand to disembark the ride and stiffly walked away. Sam wasn't sure what to make of her reaction.

He jumped from the bench only to be called by the carnival worker for forgetting his hat. He did a quick pivot, to grab it from the man's hands, tweaking something in his knee. With a slight limp, he tried to catch her. She wasn't waiting around for him.

"Luna," he called. If Sam had to apologize, he would. He'd do his best to forget about how, in the moment, her lips had answered him with their own needy pull or how her nails had scraped along his jawline. It would crush him to apologize but he would take his consolation prize and go home, if that's what she wanted.

She jerked to a halt, nearly running into another couple. "Tessa," she said.

"Oh, hi, Luna," replied a petite, pretty Asian woman with a large sun hat who held the hand of a lanky man with pale skin and blazing red hair.

"Hey, Cam. Are you guys enjoying the fair?" Luna's hands busied themselves by pulling on the ends of her hair that had been swept across her shoulder.

The couple glanced at each other before Tessa replied, "Yeah, it's fine. I'm surprised you're here though. You always snubbed your nose at fairs in high school."

Luna released a nervous laugh. "Oh. Well…I'm actually here with Ross and Mia. She's…uh, a photographer and I-I wanted to support her work at the exhibit. Have you seen it? It's good."

Tessa's eyes scanned the surrounding area. "Really?" Her dark eyes landed on Sam who had stopped short of Luna. "Is that what you call whatever you were doing on that Ferris wheel? Because I don't see your cousin anywhere."

Luna's face slightly turned to him, revealing her profile, but her eyes remained glued to the ground and her cheeks burned bright with color. "No, I…this is just my landlord. We ran into each other. We aren't here together. I…I just got separated from Ross and Mia and ran into Sam. It's funny actually—"

"Whatever you say. Keep being supportive, I guess. We should get going." They walked away without a goodbye.

Luna remained in the same spot, head tilted downward, clutching Mister Mustache.

Sam moved closer. Whatever light and happiness had existed before had completely vanished. The weather of Luna's mood had shifted as her shoulders slumped. "Luna—"

"I need to find Ross and Mia. They're probably wondering where I am." She pulled her phone from her bag and attempted to text before fumbling and dropping the hot dog toy to the ground. "Shit."

Sam bent to retrieve it, holding the toy out to her.

"Thank you." She avoided eye contact, her voice slight.

"On second thought, maybe you should give it to Zabe. She'd probably really like it."

"I'm sorry."

Her eyes finally flicked in his direction for a moment, but he caught a glossy shine in them. "What for?"

"For the kiss." Because it was clear she'd never claim him as anyone other than *just* her landlord.

She gave a sniff. "Oh, that." Luna returned her attention to the phone as though they had been talking about ancient history. She cleared her throat, her words coming stronger, colder. "Whatever. I hope your curiosity was met."

"Yeah, same to you."

It was as though a light switch had flicked, and Luna's old attitude seeped to the surface. She wasn't looking at him but he caught her rolling her eyes. "Well, it's not like I even really kissed you."

His forehead drew together in confusion. "What?"

"I didn't kiss you back because you're not someone who I would kiss."

"Ah, yes, clearly. So, that was just my imagination then?" He didn't know what upside-down world he'd found himself in, whether she truly regretted the kiss, or it had something to do with her friend, or if she was a snob and was embarrassed. Maybe it was possible all three things were true.

But even if Luna was out of his league, and she certainly was, he refused to pretend it didn't happen at all. She *had* kissed him. If she regretted everything, that was her problem. Until this moment, he hadn't regretted any of it. In fact, he had hoped to kiss her again.

"I have no idea what you imagined. I just know I

wouldn't kiss you back." She didn't even have the decency to make eye contact, stroking his irritation.

"I don't know what game you're playing, but I know when I've been kissed, and you were a full participant. In fact, I think you really liked it. But, for whatever reason, you can't accept it and it's short-circuiting your brain."

"Excuse me?" A fiery gaze hit him.

"You heard me. I bet if I pull you into my arms right now, you'd kiss me again." Not that Sam was going to try. Judging by her current expression, there was an equal chance she'd bite his nose clean off his face, but he was so annoyed at this point, he wanted to make her angry in return.

She stepped closer, her finger jabbing his chest. "I didn't kiss you then and I will never kiss you. I have standards—"

"Screw your standards."

Luna looked him dead in the eye, the gaze completely absent of any mischief or humor. A cold chill spread through his internal organs as though they sensed that this particular expression preceded something bad with her. "Look, pal, you could win the lottery tomorrow, buy a mansion, an expensive sports car, get the best haircut money could buy and, even then, you still won't meet my bare-minimum standards. You wanna know why? It's because I know your history. I know about the accident and that your drunk driving killed your own brother. And there isn't anything you can do in your life that will ever change that. That is why nothing will ever happen between us and why I would *never* kiss you."

Sam stood there, unblinking, and took it.

He took every word of vitriol as though she was a dragon incinerating him to bone and ash from the firestorm pouring from her mouth.

He took it because he didn't deserve kisses, or to have a speck of light in his life, or to have someone see him as anything other than the bad person he was.

And the price one paid for taking a small moment of pretending otherwise? Absolute incineration.

Chapter Eighteen

B ECAUSE LUNA STILL spent a lot of time working the sales floor at the jewelry store, covering when Aanya wasn't there, it gave her a lot of time to think. She hated that it was slow, because then she had to reflect on what happened the day before at the fairgrounds. Her reaction to a lot of things wasn't something she was particularly proud of.

She'd learned a long time ago to hold a little bit of herself back. Never give someone a hundred percent. People may say they wanted honesty, but they rarely wanted the brutal variety. Her brutal honesty was instead kept locked in her skull most of the time, a place where it couldn't get her into trouble. Because when Luna removed an arrow from her quiver, she couldn't help but aim straight for the center of someone's heart.

Honesty: Viggo had, at most, eighty percent of Luna.

Brutal honesty: Eighty percent had been wasted on him. Besides his looks, there'd been nothing special about him, but Luna wanted, more than believed, that there had been something lasting between them. When he'd accepted a new job near San Francisco, she'd gone house hunting in Alameda with him, letting her excitement at finally having a dream house overtake everything else. She'd made it out of her small childhood home, gotten her gorgeous green door, had a successful boyfriend. It was everything she wanted.

But she'd been wrong about him. When she talked about whether they should get a moving truck, he'd laugh. Turned out, he only wanted her designing eye. He was moving on without her. Luna was fun to have around but she wasn't an Alameda girlfriend type. He needed a clean start, one that didn't include her, which felt like history repeating itself.

With distance, she realized she had liked Viggo because he didn't make her feel too much, and he either didn't mind or didn't notice. Feeling too much was risky.

Honesty: There was no way someone like Sam was ever going to get close to a fraction of what Viggo got.

Brutal honesty: The percentage Luna had given Sam was already higher than she had ever intended.

It was time for Luna to turn that brutal honesty on herself because, in spite of who Sam was, he had an ability to make her forget she wasn't supposed to like him.

Most importantly, Sam wasn't supposed to kiss her like that. He wasn't supposed to kiss her in a way that made her feel things, as though somewhere inside was a bare lightbulb flickering in the dark, revealing there was still someone home.

Luna had tricked herself into believing the guy was nothing but the human equivalent of a slight breeze. Then he'd touched her, sending a shockwave of shivers traveling across her skin. Then Sam had said he'd wanted to kiss her, and his surprising boldness sent a thrill to every major pulse point. Luna considered it all harmless fun, and who didn't like a bit of meaningless kissing every now and again?

But when his lips brushed hers, she realized, *Oh, shit! I've been caught in a surprise tornado on a Ferris wheel.* And once one was inside a tornado, no one was coming out cool or arrogant, let alone doing any eyerolls.

His kiss had been gentle and sweet, making her feel both tender and needy. She hadn't felt either of those things in a long time. Luna hadn't wanted it to end. She'd touched him in return, his facial hair scraping the tips of her fingers. Sam had answered her neediness with a deep groan, pulling her closer, his tongue beckoning her to give more. Luna hadn't realized how much she'd missed being wanted. Everything outside the kiss had disappeared. Luna hadn't needed anything else. Wanted anything else. Just this. She had felt something, and it was...perfect.

But it could never be perfect.

Because it was Luna and Sam. The word "and" wasn't something that should ever appear between their names. Not even an "&" or a "+" and especially not preceding a "4ever".

By the time Luna had stopped swirling inside the tornado, she'd realized she'd let things go too far. Tessa had clearly seen what she'd done, and while she hadn't given Mia the hairdresser's information yet, she knew her name. Maybe she was tired of waiting for Luna and would seek Tessa out on her own, make an appointment, and then she'd learn about the Ferris wheel kiss and tell Ross everything. The thought had made Luna's heart panic. She hated herself for having been so reckless just for a bit of meaningless fun.

To reconstruct her barriers, she drew back her arrow, aiming for Sam's center. He didn't even flinch. He took it, his face becoming devoid of every emotion. Obliterating someone never felt as good in reality as it did in theory. When he turned and walked away she felt nothing but emptiness.

The jewelry shop bell jingled.

Luna raised her head from wiping one of the glass jewelry cabinets. Aanya walked in, returning from her lunch break.

"Was it busy while I was away?" Aanya asked her.

"No. Pretty dead."

"I thought maybe there were a lot of customers for you to be wiping the cabinet twice."

Luna slid the glass cleaning supplies away without a word. It was better for the subject to be dropped altogether than for her to admit she'd been standing here, wiping the same spot, since Aanya departed.

Luna was about to leave her spot on the shop floor when the phone rang. Her gaze zipped to Aanya's, who answered, "Lanza's Fine Jewelry." There was a long pause before she said, "Just a moment. Let me see if she's here."

There could have been any number of people who would call Luna, like the bank or a customer, but her stomach went into instant knots.

Aanya put the call on hold. "It's Amy again. Do you want me to take a message?" It was a silly question considering Amy had yet to leave any messages the other times she called. Her mother wasn't giving up.

"What do you think she wants?" Luna asked in a low voice, her gut already churning with nerves.

"Sounds like she wants to talk to you."

Luna had no desire to talk to her, but this also couldn't go on forever. "Fine, I'll take it." Her stomach squeezed tighter. She didn't like the unknown. Taking a deep breath, she took the call off hold. "Hello?"

There was a pause. "Luna?"

"Yes."

"This is Amy."

"I know."

"How are you?"

"Fine. Why are you calling?"

"I-I thought we could talk."

Seriously? Luna had been here before with her mother, but back then she'd been young enough to get her hopes up. Not this time. "About what?"

"How's everything going with you? How's Ross doing?"

"I already said, fine. Now can you tell me why you're calling?" Amy had missed all of her angsty teenage years. It served her right to get a double dose now.

"I've...uh, had a few health problems. I have cancer."

Luna experienced no emotion except for bitterness creeping in. Amy didn't even care when her own father was gravely ill, when she and Ross were left alone to figure things out. "What am I supposed to do with this information?" Luna replied, her tone flat.

"Well, your sisters thought—"

"I have sisters?" Her mother had never mentioned anything before, but it'd been at least fifteen years since the last time Amy had reached out and Luna—excited at the prospect of impressing her mother—she'd spent most of the conversation bragging about how well she was doing in school. But it hadn't mattered. Whether she was good or bad, her mother didn't care. And being good was so much work.

"Yes. Sunny and Skylar. Anyway, they thought…"

So, Amy was only contacting her because her kids thought she should? Did this mean if her mother never got cancer, never got the encouragement, she'd continue living her great new life without giving Luna, her first daughter, a second thought? Did she consider Luna a mistake she'd rather forget?

"What do you think?" her mother finished.

Luna had a lot of thoughts and none of them pertained to whatever her mother said because she hadn't heard any of it.

"Do you regret leaving?"

"Luna, it's ancient history. Maybe we can move forward."

"I'm not sure it can ever be ancient history for me. You left me. Forgot about me. Just moved on like I didn't exist at all."

There was a pause before her mother replied. "Luna, we've discussed this. I asked if you wanted to come with me and you told me you loved Grandpa more than you loved me. Do you know how much that stung?"

There was the sharp feeling of hurt with the realization that all it took was one moment of Luna saying the wrong thing, for some of that brutal honesty to escape from her brain, and people would leave her. There was no grace. The emotion was quickly followed by anger though, which took over completely. "Are you fucking kidding me right now? I was four years old! I don't want to talk about this. I'm sorry cancer got infected with you." Luna disconnected the call.

Every cell in her body trembled. She willed herself not to cry, to not release one single goddamn tear because Amy wasn't worth it. She was done crying over her mother. If she held back more of herself, maybe she'd never have to cry over anyone else ever again.

"Luna," Aanya said, staring at her with wide eyes, not pretending she hadn't overheard the one-sided conversation. Luna had told her own mother, *I'm sorry cancer got infected with you.* There was no use pretending it was anything else. Aanya would realize Luna was a bad person, that she was capable of shooting arrows full of poison. Maybe her mother had sensed the same thing with four-year-old Luna.

"Luna," Aanya said again. "Do you—"

The phone started ringing again, capturing both their gazes.

"I have work to do." Luna fled to the office, soundly shutting the door, wishing there was a way to barricade herself inside forever.

A SOFT KNOCK at the door jolted her from her thoughts while she chewed on a nail.

"I'm busy," she yelled, shuffling papers on the desk in order to appear occupied.

The door clicked, and Ross slipped through with Hermes the dog, shutting the door behind them. *Goddammit.* Aanya probably went straight into Ross's workshop to tell him about out-of-control, heartless, cruel Luna. Luckily, there hadn't been any customers in the store to scare away, but this wasn't Aanya's business, and she had no right to tell Ross anything.

He took a seat, slouched forward, leaning his elbows on his knees while rubbing his hands with a rag. Hermes plopped on the office dog bed, settling into a nap position. Ross glanced at her as though waiting for her to say something. When she didn't, he cleared his throat. "Just got a call from someone named Sky who wants to know why you made her mom cry."

Luna crossed her arms. "Oh, didn't you know? That's one of your other cousins, probably a better one. Sorry you got stuck with me. I don't want to talk about it. And I don't want to talk to any of them." They were lucky they knew where she was at all because, at the moment, she had an urge to jump in her car and drive to Alaska where no one would be able to find her.

Ross held his hands in surrender. He should know better than to force her to do anything. "Okay. I just want to know how you're doing."

"Fine," she replied, gritting her teeth. When was everyone going to stop asking how she was doing?

"You wanna come over for dinner tonight?"

"Why?" She was not in the best mood for company. On top of this, she was feeling guilty for being busy and, as a result, Mia's nursery was still unfinished.

"I don't know. Maybe I miss you. Come over for dinner. Hang out with Mia and me."

That was how Luna ended up at her childhood home after work. Mia was surprised to see her. Ross had forgotten to give his wife the heads-up there'd be one more person at the dinner table tonight. Something that was normally a no-big-deal infraction sullied her mood even more because all she could think about was how they'd probably consider her less and less.

With her appearance, Mia became more flustered, and the kitchen was already in a state of disaster.

"I was making burgers," she said, "but I only bought a pound of beef. Should I run to the store?"

Ross kissed her on the forehead. "Just relax. I'll take care of cooking."

Mia sighed in relief while taking one of the dining table chairs. "Oh, Luna, you wanna stay for a movie? I picked one up when I was at the library today. It looks like a fun one."

"Okay," Luna said. Because what else was she going to do?

"Did you guys have a good day at work?"

"Luna got another interesting call," her cousin said from his spot at the stove.

"Ross," she warned him. "Knock it off."

"What's wrong?" Mia asked.

The grumpiness had fully settled in Luna. "Nothing. I don't want to talk about it."

Mia and Ross exchanged a glance with each other, which Luna didn't appreciate one bit. She didn't want them talking about her, even through non-verbal communication. He was probably going to tell his wife everything as soon as she returned to Schnell Ridge and then Mia would be all up in her business too. Alaska was becoming a more appealing destination all the time.

"Here, eat your slop, peasant," Ross said, dropping a

plate of food in front of Luna.

She took one of the sweet potato fries and ate it slowly while leaning her head against the arm propped on the table. Maybe she shouldn't have come. Luna wasn't the best person for company at the moment. She was miserable and depressed and anxious, all of the emotions she despised the most.

"What movie did you get?" Ross asked Mia, ignoring the lump of crabbiness sitting beside him. "You know if Luna doesn't approve, like the last time, she's never going to let it go. She's not exactly the most forgiving person in the world."

She slid a glare at him. *What the hell did that mean?* Was he implying Luna should roll over and forgive her mother? Luna was not a doormat and Amy had never apologized once. He had better leave it alone before she exploded, because this stick of dynamite was ready to go off.

Mia wiped her hands on a napkin. "Oh, let me get it. It's some old zombie movie."

"Ugh, I hate zombie movies," Luna said, pushing her fries around.

"Probably because you don't like someone reanimating after you consider them dead to you."

She made a face at him. "Shut up, Ross."

Mia returned with a DVD case. "*Night of the Comet.* Have you seen it?" She handed it to her husband who studied the cover.

Ross flipped to the backside of the DVD case. "You might like this one, Lu. It's teenagers who seem to find themselves in trouble with the authorities while trying to fight off zombies."

She rolled her eyes. "As the only person at this table with a record, that seems more like your thing. I'm sure Mia appreciates being reminded that her baby daddy is an ex-con."

The silence that descended in the dining room was immediate. Both Ross and Mia stared at her astounded. Luna then realized she was broken. It's possible she'd been broken since the fair. She hadn't been holding anything back, and the ugliness was pouring out of her.

After a minute of awkward eating, Ross stood, putting his dish in the sink before putting a leash on Hermes and taking the dog for a walk. Mia's gaze followed her husband until he departed and then they landed squarely on Luna. The usual humor lighting Mia's eyes was missing.

"You, of all people, should know better than to talk to Ross like that. You know how hard he's worked to move on from that part of his life."

Luna had never seen this side of Mia before. Her stomach became a nervous pit. She pushed around the fries on her plate, losing her appetite completely, but she couldn't seem to help herself. Once a boulder started rolling downhill, there wasn't a graceful way to stop it. "I was just joking because he's obviously far from being a hardened criminal. He just went to juvie for shoplifting, which I believe we can all thank *your* father for. We all can't be a perfect people-pleaser like you."

Mia's expression grew hard. "Oh, so is this what we're doing today? You're just going to strike out at everyone? Because let me tell you, Luna Lanza, I don't care about my people-pleaser reputation as much as you think I do. Striking at me doesn't change the fact that you clearly hurt Ross, who would do anything for you, by treating his past as a joke."

"No, I didn't. That's just how we tease each other. You wouldn't understand. Today's been rough."

"So, you want it to be rough for all of us?"

"No, I—" Luna wasn't sure what point she was trying to make or how she could defend herself. It didn't matter because, deep down, she knew if she lost easygoing Mia, she must have *really* screwed up. Her cheeks grew hot and frustrated tears threatened to make an appearance.

Luna pushed herself away from the table. "I should leave." She was not in control. Everything was getting away from her. Maybe it was too late and she'd already lost the only family she had.

Mia took her arm as she passed, her gaze unwavering. "I'm not perfect. I've said hurtful things myself. It's a mistake when it happens, but it's a bigger mistake if you don't make it up to the people you love and apologize. You owe Ross as much."

When released, Luna grabbed her bag and left. There was no sign of Ross outside of the home. He probably didn't want to see her anyway. She got in her car and drove, but instead of heading to Schnell Ridge, she got on Highway 50 North. It would be better if she took a few days to get herself together and what better place than Lake Tahoe. She could get a cheap hotel near the state line and take a moment to figure everything out.

Luna didn't have much with her, except for the small bag in the back of her SUV with an emergency change of clothes and some personal supplies like an extra toothbrush and deodorant. It was her bug-out bag for when she couldn't deal anymore. It wasn't enough to get her to Alaska. Lake Tahoe would do for now.

She'd send Aanya a text to tell Ross she wouldn't be in the shop for a few days. He had handled everything fine when she was in school. He didn't exactly need her. Plus, he had Mia, who'd stick up for him, so he didn't need Luna in this area either. Ross had everything he needed.

And Luna? She wasn't sure who she had. At the moment, it seemed as though she had no one. She didn't blame anyone for wanting to pull away from her. Not only were Ross and Mia upset at her, but she had no best friend, no boyfriend, no friends of any kind. Luna wasn't going to cry. She wasn't. She'd go to Lake Tahoe for a few days, take some time to rest, and figure out how to fix her life. If Luna could transform a tired old apartment, she could do the same thing for the other parts of her life. She was resourceful and could try harder to be good. If Ross could forgive her, just this once, Mia would like her again. Hopefully. She didn't want anything more than that.

Suddenly, the lights on her car panel shut off and she started losing speed as the car coasted slower and slower. *What the hell?* She had no choice but to muscle her steering wheel toward the shoulder of the road.

Luna turned the key in the ignition, begging her motor to turn over, to do something other than strand her on the side of the highway. Nothing.

"Fuck!"

Her day had gone from bad to worse to wanting to strangle herself with a seatbelt. This wasn't fair. It wasn't.

She pressed her palms into her eye sockets, taking a few deep breaths. Luna could handle this.

She could call a tow truck. Although, she'd feel more comfortable if she wasn't in the middle of nowhere. Ross's parents were killed somewhere on the 50, after they blew a tire and had to pull over. The two-lane highway was full of narrow twists as the elevation climbed higher through the mountains, and with the tall pine trees, drivers drove between shadow and light.

No one knew where she was. She checked the map on her phone to get a satellite location of where she was. Scrolling her phone address book, she had Mia, Ross, Sam, and Tessa all listed one right after the other. It was a collection of the everyone-who-hated-Luna club. Sam and Tessa were definitely out. Out of Mia and Ross, she could probably face Mia. Or maybe she'd call Ross. He would talk to her more than Sam would, which was fine by her because the apartment manager would be the last person she'd purposely reach out to. Luna pushed the call button.

After a few rings, it was picked up. "What do you need, Luna?"

Wait.

It was a grumpy voice on the other end but it wasn't Ross's. She looked at the phone screen. Sam! She'd accidentally hit Sam's name.

"Shit!" Luna hit the disconnect button.

She jumped when the phone rang in her hand.

"What's wrong?" Sam asked when she answered.

"I didn't mean to…" Her voice had a slight shake and she hated it. Luna disconnected again.

Her phone immediately rang. His name lit the screen. *Dammit! It was an accident!* She smashed the answer button to tell him as much.

"I swear to God, Luna, if you don't tell me what's wrong, I'm going upstairs and—"

"I'm not there. I'm…"

"Where are you?"

"M-my car broke down. I was going to call Ross and I hit your name by accident."

"Where are you?"

"I'm j-just past Ice House."

"You broke down on the highway?"

"It's fine. I'm going to call Ross."

"I'm already out the door. Stay inside your car."

"Sam—hello?" He had disconnected.

Perfect. Just perfect. She didn't want Sam to help her. After the horrible things she had said to him, it didn't seem fair he would ever do anything nice for her again. Considering the abrupt way he answered the phone, he was a reluctant hero, doing it because… To be honest, she didn't know why he was doing it. Luna didn't want to be obligated to him in any way, and rescuing her on the highway would definitely obligate her to…treat him nicely? Was that such a bad thing? She hadn't been nice to him much at all and yet he was still helping her. Luna decided to call him and tell him, never mind, but she got voicemail instead.

Sitting in her car, Luna had time to think. Mia had been right. Ross had done a lot for her. He made sure she never had to worry about anything but her education when she went away to college. He kept the jewelry store going after

Victor died and kept their little family together. She had never thanked him for any of it.

She thought about his parents again. Maybe they had died around this same location. Ross would be devastated if she shared the same fate. Luna couldn't do that to him. He'd been hurt enough in his life, and he didn't need more, especially from her. The winding highway was dangerous and the shoulder she had managed to pull onto wasn't big at all. Someone could whip around the corner and hit her.

She scrambled over the passenger seat, got out, and trekked onto the side of the road filled with a dense amount of pine trees, ferns and sweet pea vines. A car would have to careen off the embankment to hit her now. She sat on a stump and listened to the American River rushing nearby and considered her current predicament.

Chapter Nineteen

S AM RACED ON the highway, exceeding the speed limit to get to Luna. He wasn't sure why he had this uncontrollable urge to help her after their last conversation. He wasn't mad at her, more mad at himself for entertaining the possibility she might actually like him. He was also angry because her words were still able to slice through his callous outer shell and injure him. But mostly he was angry because, in spite of everything, he couldn't stop thinking about the kiss. Their moment on the Ferris wheel had been a gift, one that invaded his mind non-stop, and sheer willpower alone didn't seem to be enough to put an end to it. But he would overcome it. He would, as soon as she was safe and at home.

When he took a curve and saw her SUV a short distance ahead, relief hit him. He rolled alongside her vehicle, turning his head as he passed, and his heart stopped. No one was inside. Shutting off his bike, Sam jerked the kickstand down, ripping the helmet from his head. He rushed to the SUV, but she wasn't there. He shouted her name as worst-case scenarios zipped through his mind.

"Luna!" he yelled into the wilderness, panic taking hold of him.

"I'm here."

He whipped around as she emerged from the brush. Relief transitioned into irritation. "I told you to stay in the car!" He marched closer, jabbing a finger in the direction of the abandoned SUV.

One hand went straight to her hip. "You're not the boss of me!"

"It's not safe!"

"I know!" A slight sob burst through her temper as she slapped a hand across her mouth.

Sam stopped. Luna was a string ready to snap—all large, glossy eyes and trembling shoulders. His anger melted away. He strode to her spot in the woods, pulling her into his arms. He was the right height for her to cry on his shoulder, because this was exactly what she did, as if she'd been holding tears for far too long. Sam took her sorrow as she dampened his jacket and tucked her face into his neck.

When she pulled away, he kept one hand to her back, using his other to push her hair away from her face. Concern filled him when her eyes submerged with tears again. Regardless of how strained their relationship was, he hated seeing her broken.

"Are you okay?" he asked.

She nodded in response.

"Can I have your keys so I can check out your car?"

She surrendered them, remaining on the embankment as Sam investigated her mechanical mystery, discovering her problem soon after.

He returned to her spot, putting the keys in her hands. "I'm going to drive over to Fresh Pond. I'll be back."

"What? Why?" Luna worried her bottom lip between her

teeth.

"It won't take me long. You ran out of gas."

"I—No, I don't think so." She took a moment to think before her cheeks flushed. "Are you sure?"

"Did everything shut off? Was the steering wheel hard to turn?"

Her eyes dropped. "Maybe."

"I'll get some gas and come back."

"Can I go with you?"

"How? I just have my bike."

"I don't know. Can't I ride on the back or on the handlebars or something?"

"No. I'll be fast. Just wait here."

"Please don't leave me, Sam." Her tone became more desperate. "Let me come with you. Please."

Sam couldn't do this. He couldn't. But one glance at her pleading face and he broke. "Have you ever ridden on a motorcycle?"

Her large hazel eyes flicked away as she picked at the bark of a tree. Luna shook her head.

"I don't think it's a good idea," he replied. The thought of her riding on the back of his motorcycle was twisting his stomach into knots.

She chewed on the corner of a nail. "I'll be careful. I'll do whatever you say."

He took another moment staring off into the wilderness in silent debate. He hated this but he also hated the idea of leaving her abandoned on the side of the road, especially with the sun setting. He groaned before returning his gaze to her.

"Do you have a jacket?" Sam asked, eyeing her loose tank top and slim-fitting black jeans.

"No."

"Come here." He opened a storage hatch of his bike, handing her the zippered hoodie he stored in there for emergencies. "Put this on."

She took it from him gingerly. It wasn't dirty, but probably hadn't been worn or washed recently. It was too hot these days to wear a hoodie and if Sam was getting on his bike, he usually slipped on the army-style jacket that used to be Nate's. At the moment, all he cared about was offering her some protection. Without argument, Luna slipped her arms through the hoodie sleeves. She eyed him expectantly, appearing small and vulnerable in the oversized garment.

He approached closer, zipping it as she watched him. His own gaze avoided her face because he'd only think about the kiss and he was doing his best to forget. Sam was here to make sure she got home. Not to contemplate how her hazel eyes captured all the colors of the surrounding forest. Or remember how easily she melted into his arms. Those were all traps for him to avoid.

"Here," Sam said, fitting his helmet on her head.

"What about you?"

"You said you'd do whatever I wanted. I want you to wear the helmet."

She kept her mouth shut. Sam then explained in detail where to sit and where to keep her legs before climbing onto the motorcycle and offering her a hand. "All right, get on."

She mounted the bike behind him, but he couldn't feel her. Maybe she didn't want to touch him, but this was no longer about comfort.

His head turned slightly toward her. "Put your arms around me and you don't let go. Got it?"

Sam didn't have to tell her twice. She pushed forward until her legs bracketed his thighs and wrapped her arms tight around his middle, pressing against his back as much as the helmet allowed.

He'd started the engine, turned them around, and they were cruising on the highway. This time he drove slower than the speed limit. She squeezed his stomach tight as though nervous. Sam was also terrified, but after a few minutes her grip relaxed. When the road straightened, he laid one hand over her locked arms, reassuring himself she was there with him, safe and sound. He could almost forget she despised him.

Sam pulled off the exit ten minutes later, deciding to go to Pollock Pines for gas. He rolled past the station, sliding into a parking spot at Pollock Pines Diner.

"What about the gas?" she asked after he shut off the bike.

He helped her disembark and removed the helmet. "Come on. We need to talk." It might not change anything, but he wasn't going to lose this opportunity to clear the air.

Chapter Twenty

"**B**UT WHY?**" A sinking feeling hit her gut. She never liked the phrase *We need to talk* because, number one, she didn't know what to expect from it, and, number two, it usually meant she was in trouble.

He ignored her, strolling into the diner, and she had no choice but to follow.

"Cup of decaf," Sam ordered from the waitress after taking a seat in a booth.

"Um." Luna scanned the menu. "Can I have a chocolate milkshake?"

Sam shook his head as though he couldn't deal with her ridiculousness.

"What? My grandpa would always take me to get a milkshake when I'd had a rough day and that's exactly what today has been."

When their drinks arrived, Sam poured sugar into his coffee while Luna plucked the Maraschino cherry from the whipped cream and set it aside on a napkin.

"You don't eat the cherry?" He winced after sipping his coffee and added more sugar.

"I don't like them, but I do love extra whipped cream." She slipped a generous spoonful of the dessert into her mouth. "Milkshakes are the Red Cross of food. They always make you feel better in a bad situation."

"Unless you're lactose intolerant," Sam said. "Then it would be the opposite."

She smiled. "Yeah, except that part. I'll have to rethink that one. Did your dad used to take you guys to get milkshakes when you were kids?"

"I'm sure he did but I can't remember anything specifically." His eyes lifted to her. "Do you have siblings?"

For the first time, she wasn't sure how to answer the question. Sunny and Skylar might technically be her sisters, but they were also strangers. Real sisterly relationships were one more thing her mother kept from her.

She shrugged, deciding to keep things simple. "Ross is the closest thing I have to a sibling."

"Nate and I were a couple years apart. He was younger than me, but we were really close." Sam stared into the depths of his cup as though it was the only thing existing in his world. "We would sometimes get ourselves into trouble but we always managed to talk our way out. My birthday is at the end of May and his was the beginning of June so we'd even celebrate our birthdays together.

"He was a great storyteller. We could go to any party, not know a soul, and it would take Nate five minutes to have a new group of friends. There was always a story to weave or exaggerate...mostly exaggerate." A smile slipped across his face as though he was remembering a story in particular.

"On his twenty-first birthday, of course, a big group of us were going to take him out drinking. It wasn't like he hadn't already been drinking before then, and I was quite proficient at the activity myself, but it was his first year being legal and it was his God-given right to get wasted. As the older brother, who had already had his twenty-first birthday celebration, I reluctantly promised my parents I would be the responsible one, watch out for my brother, and be the designated driver. I didn't keep my promise."

Sam swallowed hard. It took several moments before he continued, his voice flat and choking on misery. "In fact, I kept sneaking drinks all night. I had a great fucking time. So much so I ended up passing out. But when one of us failed, the other stepped right in to cover, and while my brother was doing better than me…it wasn't enough."

The muscles worked over his jawline. "I was stuffed into the back seat and my brother had taken the wheel. They found us on the 50, hanging off the embankment. My brother had hit a deer and lost control. I woke up three days later in the hospital. Nate wasn't so lucky. Maybe if I had been conscious—if I could have gotten us help sooner, he would have had a chance.

"And this isn't to shift blame to Nate, to make him the villain of this story. I won't make any excuses. He made a mistake. He shouldn't have done it. He should have called our parents, gotten a ride from somewhere else, left me facedown in that bar and taken care of himself. It doesn't matter. I'm still the villain here, because he was just looking out for me, and I couldn't do the same for him. I'm the one who failed, who made the bad decision. I failed my brother, my family, everyone. But the problem with *too late* is that you usually don't get any warning when it's going to happen. It just happens."

Luna hadn't moved a muscle while he talked. Enjoying her chocolate milkshake while hearing the tragic tale of the Sunderland brothers now seemed inappropriate. She let it melt in its glass. She didn't know what to think, because it all sucked, all of it. She'd have to face the fact that she'd never been so wrong about a person, and she had treated him horribly because of it.

"If you think it doesn't change anything, why are you telling me?" she asked.

Sam kept his eyes glued to his coffee mug. "I don't know. I guess, if you're going to hate me, you might as well know the real truth behind it."

"I don't hate you."

Maybe it was the obligation she owed him for rescuing her. Or maybe it was because he'd been willing to crack himself open to her. He hadn't tried to lie or pass the blame. Sam gave it to her straight, brutal truth and all.

"I don't hate you," she repeated in the hopes he'd believe her words. "I'm...I'm sorry I hurt you. I seem to be doing that a lot lately. At the fair, I—My friend, Tessa... Well, we're not really friends anymore. We used to be best friends."

Luna took a breath. If he could be brave, so could she. "The reason we aren't friends anymore is my fault. We'd always talked about leaving Placerville together and doing big things. But neither one of our situations really allowed for it and after high school, it seemed like maybe we were just going to stay here, which wasn't too bad because we still had each other.

"But, then, I got into college. I was going to Chico, and

while it wasn't a glamorous way to experience the world at large because…well, it's still in California, it's like our plan was back on. And Tessa was a hair stylist, which she could do anywhere, so it made this venture outside of Placerville a little less scary because I'd be doing it with her. Except she had changed her mind and wanted to stay. She abandoned our plan, and it felt like she was abandoning me. And I knew this wasn't fair because she had every right to live her life like she wanted, but I was so mad, I said a lot of mean things, including that she wasn't a good friend and I hoped I'd make better ones at college.

"And it all came to bite me in the ass because here I am back in Placerville, and I could really use a good friend like Tessa but my big mouth ruined it, just like what always happens. I'm the one causing people to leave."

Luna had been picking at her napkin when Sam slid his hand across the table, palm side up. She tentatively laid her hand in his. They were rough but warm. He swept his thumb across her knuckles, and the sweet gesture almost brought tears to her eyes again.

"You won't know if it's too late until you try. If you apologize to Tessa, then you can't be too bad of a person. There's still hope for you," he said.

"Do you think there's hope for you?" Was the question rude? She never knew when she'd pushed things too far. Luna wanted hope for Sam, and to also hold him as he had done for her earlier in the day, so he could feel that things might be okay. It was clear they both needed this reassurance. If they could give it to each other, what was wrong with that?

He frowned. "I don't know. Is there hope for me, Luna?"

She wasn't sure how to answer him, deciding to shift directions instead. "What color door do you want someday?"

He released a small laugh, his face softening. "I'm not familiar enough with this secret code of door colors to know."

"Let me pick one for you. I hope you get a blue door. It means peace and tranquility."

He studied her for what felt like forever, his gaze taking a deep dive into her. Then a small grin cracked his expression. "Which color would mean, 'I wish I had ordered a chocolate milkshake instead?'"

Luna smiled before sliding to his side of the booth. "You can share with me."

"You'd share your milkshake with me?"

"Maybe I'm not the nicest person in the world but I'm not a monster. You are my rescuer after all." She pushed the glass toward him. He did have a nice face, and—good God, those lashes! How'd she missed that before? It wasn't fair he kept surprising her.

"You know what would convince me?" he asked.

"That I'm not a monster? There's more that I have to do besides sharing a milkshake? Now it feels like work." She sucked some wayward whipped cream from her thumb, stretching the moment when she noticed his eyes flicking to her mouth. She released a coy smile. Perhaps he'd been upset at her earlier, but he wasn't immune to her. Teasing him was easy, and she liked it.

Sam blinked. His voice emerged low and rough. "You can let me eat your cherry."

She was shocked at first, but soon threw back her head as laughter bubbled out. Luna slid the napkin with the discarded Maraschino cherry across the table. "My cherry is yours. Knock yourself out."

His wry grin had a touch of danger, increasing his good looks. Her pulse beat harder as he kept those deep brown eyes locked on to her. Luna could develop a penchant for bad boys, even while knowing Sam was more of a reformed one. There might be a little trouble still running through those veins and that excited her as much as riding on the back of his motorcycle.

He took the cherry, popping the whole thing in his mouth, stem and all.

Her expression shifted to confusion. "What the…"

Sam's jaw shifted as though chewing, although it appeared to take more effort. Moments later, he pushed the stem through his lips, before holding it like a trophy. The stem had been tied into a knot.

Luna's jaw dropped. Forget the eyelashes. A whole new side of Sam appeared. "Did you just tie a knot with your tongue?" This certainly explained a few things about how he had kissed her. Luna's body responded by flushing with heat. Perhaps teasing her in return was easy for him as well.

He shrugged, flicking the stem to the napkin. "You ready to get out of here?"

All she could manage was a nod in response.

They swung by the nearest station, purchasing a one-gallon plastic gas can before getting on Highway 50 again. Luna was less nervous about the motorcycle ride this time, enjoying the crisp late summer wind pulling at her clothes.

She reveled in how firm and strong Sam was, encircled tightly in her arms. For as horrible as the day had been, this had been the best part. Maybe the world was resetting itself. She'd make things up to Ross and try harder to be a better person.

After they put gas in her car, it started no problem and she drove home to Schnell Ridge with Sam's motorcycle following behind in the same way a dolphin swam alongside a ship. If dolphins were around, a person knew they were safe.

Once they arrived, Sam followed her as far as the stairs, but she chose to stay at the bottom with him, enjoying the chirp of night crickets. Reaching out, Luna lightly stroked his arm. "Thank you for coming for me, Sam."

She leaned to press a gentle kiss on his cheek. When she pulled away his eyes were closed before slowly opening.

"I remember someone telling me that kissing was never going to happen."

She released a soft chuckle. "And I remember someone saying I should get used to being wrong. But if it makes you feel any better, I still don't think you're very nice."

There was that dangerous grin again. "I don't think you're very nice either."

"Great, then you won't be surprised when I tell you that I'm going to hang on to your hoodie for a little bit longer. Goodnight." She took the stairs two at a time, leaving him at the bottom, letting her laugh trail behind her.

Chapter Twenty-One

SOME OF SAM'S heaviness lifted after his and Luna's conversation. Sure, he was waiting for the return of his hoodie, but he liked that they were somehow connected through his wardrobe now. Luna couldn't hate him if she was borrowing his clothes, right? Why she wanted temporary hoodie ownership was a mystery though.

As promised, Nicholas bought a small grill and some of the residents got together for an impromptu potluck barbecue a few days later. Perhaps he could get his dad to spring for a bigger patio set. The only disappointment was Luna didn't make an appearance. Zabe had excitedly run upstairs to knock on apartment seven's door but there was no answer. He hoped she hadn't become stranded again.

But later, while walking out of his apartment, Sam found Luna setting a tall pot overflowing with plants beside his doormat.

She jumped at his sudden appearance. "Oh, hi! I was trying to be sneaky, but you ruined it."

"What? Why?" He wasn't sure he liked a sneaky Luna. This could mean trouble.

"I wanted to thank you for helping me out last week. I picked up this clay planter at a garage sale for five bucks and filled it with strawberry plants for your patio garden. I thought you might like fresh berries for breakfast or something. You may have to fight the jays or squirrels for them, but you could get one here and there."

Sam was speechless. "You bought me a plant?" Was this how women felt when they got flowers? He was starting to get the appeal.

Her forehead wrinkled. "You don't like it?"

"It's just…" Unexpected. Nice. Warming his heart in a way it hadn't been warmed before.

Luna grew flustered. "It's fine. I can take it to Ross's place. I have to go there anyway for an encore apology tour today, because you weren't the only one I was an asshole to. I'm making finishing Mia's nursery a priority in order to make up for it."

She bent to lug the heavy pot away, but he grabbed her arm. "No, I like it. Thank you." He didn't let go. Her skin was feather-soft. Everything about her made him want to stop and savor. "You could have just returned my hoodie."

"What's the fun in that? Speaking of fun, there was something else I picked up at this garage sale and I was hoping you could put it in for me."

"What's that?"

"A new sink faucet for my bathroom. This one is much nicer than the current one—stainless steel instead of a plastic handle that's all chipped up. See? Fun!"

"Is this supposed to be fun for me or for you?"

"Me, of course."

"I'm not sure if these are thank-you strawberries or bribery ones."

Luna laughed. "Do they taste any different?"

"I believe thank-you strawberries are a sweeter variety."

A smile slipped across her lips, and he developed a craving for watermelon again. "Touché. In that case, consider them thank-you strawberries. Besides, I don't really need you. I'll watch a YouTube video and figure out how to swap the faucet myself. How hard could it be?" she said, flicking her hair.

SAM KNOCKED AT Luna's door the following day, ready to replace her faucet with the yard sale one. Zabe stood beside him, holding his metal toolbox.

"You're going to let me help you this time—right, Sam? How am I going to learn anything if you don't let me help? Please. Pleeeease."

"You're carrying my toolbox. That's already very helpful."

"But I want to do more. I'm going to have to go back to school soon and then I won't be around as much to help you. So, can I?"

"We'll see," Sam replied.

Luna opened the door, taking his breath away. She was wearing tight athletic wear with her hair messily piled on her head and a healthy glow on her skin, appearing as though she'd finished doing yoga or Pilates or whatever pretty people did for exercise. She appealed to him more than a chocolate milkshake on the hottest of days. He made every effort to keep his bottom jaw from dropping on her doorstep with an embarrassing clang.

Zabe was also breathless, but for an entirely different reason. Luna's fuzzy gray and white cat was snuggled to her chest. The kid gasped before squealing, "Oh, kitty! Can I hold it? Pleeeeease, Luna. Sorry, Sam, I can't help you anymore." She whipped the toolbox toward him to relieve herself of helper duties but, in her excitement, slammed the end directly into his junk.

There was a moment of absolute shock as his hips rocked backwards in reflex, his breath whooshing from his lungs. He released an agonizing groan, tears springing to his eyes as shock gave way to shooting pain. His balls felt as though they were trapped in a vicious vise, the kind found in medieval torture chambers. The toolbox clattered to the ground, his body following as his legs lost all their strength. He couldn't move, couldn't think, couldn't care about falling to all fours in front of Luna.

"Oh God," Luna said. "Here, Zabe, take the cat and play inside." She dropped to her knees beside him, gingerly touching his back. "Are you okay?"

He glanced through his arms to make sure the girl was inside, distracted with the animal, before releasing a long "Fuuuuuuck" on a breath. Luna continued to rub along his shoulder. "Just give me a minute," he said, his words strained.

After a while, he began putting himself together, reaching for the tools that had escaped the toolbox since he was on the ground anyway.

"I can do that," Luna said. "Can you get up?"

He inched himself to standing with her taking his arm,

pulling him inside. He delicately made his way to the couch, breathing through a dull throbbing between his legs, before taking a seat. Luna sat close beside him.

The kid, with the cat in her arms, watched him with wide, glossy eyes. "I'm sorry, Sam." Her voice had a slight tremor in it.

"It's okay. You just have to be careful where you fling toolboxes. Not all of us are as tough as you."

"That's what my dad says too. I'm glad I'm a girl."

The small cat released a tiny meow from within the kid's arms.

"She's so cute! I want a kitten. I'm going to ask my dad for one," Zabe said, taking a seat on the rug. "What's her name?"

"Duchess, because I can tell she's going to be an elegant lady cat. I thought about naming the cat Nicholas just to get back at him for Luna, but she's much too sophisticated for that name."

Zabe giggled. "She's too pretty for a name like Nicholas. Do you like kitties, Sam?"

Besides a fish or two he and Nate shared during their childhood, he'd never had a pet before. When the Sunderland brothers made an argument for a dog—they'd decided on a golden retriever—their father shut them down. "It costs too much money to have a dog. What about one of those betta fish?"

After Sam moved out, he was too busy with school, and trying to pick up girls. It wasn't a good lifestyle for pet owning, and he had stopped caring. There was no reason he couldn't have one now. Maybe he'd follow Nicholas's steps and get a little dog, as was his destiny.

"I don't know anything about cats. Don't they prefer to be left alone?" He based his assumption on standard cat stereotypes.

"No," replied Luna. "They just prefer attention on their terms."

Zabe lifted the cat gingerly and approached.

"Oh, no, that's okay. I don't need…" Duchess was placed in his lap, and they stared at each other as if sizing the other up. Should he put a protective hand over his still-sensitive crotch?

"Just pet her like this." Zabe demonstrated this with gentle pets along the tiny animal's spine.

Duchess meowed and he nearly jumped out of his skin. Was it angry? It began climbing his chest, probably to get within biting distance of his face. Sam couldn't move. "Okay, someone take it. I don't want to get scratched."

"Stop being a weenie, which we learned today is very fragile—right, Zabe?"

The kid giggled.

Duchess's destination appeared to be his shoulder, where the feline decided it was a good place for a nap and started purring after settling. He stiffly rotated his head to make eye contact with Luna, surprised to see her expression soft with a wistful smile. "See, it's fine."

"She likes you," Zabe agreed.

Since they'd been on the couch, Luna kept a hand placed on the inside crook of his elbow. If he had been asked, when he was younger, where he wanted a girl to touch him, the elbow was probably not in the top ten. But there was something warm and caring about it. Here he was with a small cat on his shoulder, Luna on his elbow, and Zabe watching him near his knees. Sam wondered if this was what it would be like to have his own little family someday.

And, the same as receiving a plant, he was starting to get the appeal.

Chapter Twenty-Two

L UNA WAS AT Mia's aunt's house in Sacramento for the baby shower. They'd finished playing all the cheesy games, such as guessing how many inches Mia's ballooning waistline was or guessing baby food flavors smeared inside a diaper.

After games and food, everyone chatted, mostly surrounding Mia as she showed off nursery pictures on her phone. While the nursery had turned out fantastic, now that it was done Luna was ready for a new project to capture her attention. Her focus drifted toward the living room fireplace. It wasn't stylized but, rather, the mantel held a variety of framed family photos. She really wanted one, functional or not. Luna did a quick search for DIY faux fireplace ideas, discovering she could reuse an old cabinet or bookshelf with a floating shelf above it to create a similar appearance. That was definitely doable.

In her newfound excitement, she sent Sam a text. *"What are you doing?"*

"Doing work at my mom's place," he responded soon after.

Luna sent a screenshot image to Sam in a text. *"I want to make this since you insist I can't have a real fireplace."*

He responded, *"I give tenants my number in case there's an apartment emergency—not to act as a sounding board to your wild home decorating ideas."*

"This IS an apartment emergency. What if I forget to tell you?"

He replied with an image of his plant with tiny tomatoes growing. *"Did you notice? It's starting to produce!"*

"I give my building managers my number in case there's an apartment emergency. Not to get pictures of your baby balls."

"Please don't mention balls. Mine are still traumatized."

Luna snorted a laugh, which drew Mia's attention. "Who are you talking to?"

"No one. Ross." She couldn't tell her cousin-in-law she was flirting with her landlord—Wait. *Was* she flirting?

She scanned the conversation. There wasn't anything particularly flirty, except for mentioning balls, but talking to Sam gave her the same light flutters she normally got while romantically sparring with a guy. Oh, boy. With full knowledge of Sam's real story, she no longer had a reason for maintaining a flirt embargo. This could be trouble.

"Oh, can you ask Ross if he could pick up some buffalo chicken waffle wraps for dinner? I really need some," Mia said while polishing off a taquito.

"Sure." After messaging Ross, she returned to her conversation with Sam.

"You're also growing cilantro. When you get a couple ripe tomatoes you almost have the ingredients needed to make yourself salsa."

"Really?"

"I think you also need onion and a jalapeño or something."

"Can I grow those in pots?"

"Peppers definitely, not sure about onions." See, this was a nice, normal conversation about gardening. There wasn't anything flirty here.

"I've never made salsa before. When my balls ripen, maybe

you can come over and help me out."

"I am really good at chopping." She added a winking kissing face, a knife, and a smiling devil emoji. Okay, maybe the conversation wasn't innocent after all.

"I'm not sure I like this analogy anymore."

"In all seriousness…you help me with my faux fireplace and I'll help you with salsa?"

"Deal."

"YOU'VE GOT DRIPS on the corner," Sam said, as he stood beside her, inspecting the paint job. He'd become the perfectionist to her *meh, good enough* but she didn't let it ruin her good mood.

They were both on the patio, having taken different parts of the makeshift faux fireplace. Luna was painting the floating shelf with a mahogany stain and finish.

She bumped him away with her hip. "Didn't the teacher ever tell you to keep your eyes on your own work? I'm still working on it. Besides, this might be a right-handed paintbrush. You didn't exactly set me up for success here." She laughed at the idea of there being right and left-handed paintbrushes, but she had to give some excuse.

"The problem is the paintbrush? Nice try. Maybe we need another painting lesson."

"You have a real right-handed privilege vibe going on, do you know that?"

"So, you've noticed how superior I am." His devilish grin was infuriating and hot as hell, which made sense since everyone knew all devils came from Hell.

"Spoken like a man who's never struggled with a pair of scissors in his life. At least left-handed people are creative, probably because of all the work-arounds we do in a right-handed world."

"Is left-handedness the reason you're so stubborn?"

"It's not stubbornness as much as it's an independent desire to do what I want as opposed to doing what you want me to do. No, that amazing trait is due to being a Sagittarius. I'm a cornucopia of complexity, Sam."

"A cornucopia of complexity?"

"It means you should be *thankful* to have met me."

He laughed, the expression more free than she'd ever heard it before. It was deep, came from his gut, and lit his brown eyes. She wanted more of it, and to be the person who caused it.

"I bought some candles to put in my fireplace. It's going to be really cozy."

"All I care about is that you don't burn down the apartment building. If you're going to be the reason I combust, I don't want to be asleep when it happens."

"I figure it's safe since I have a fireman living next door."

"No one wants to come home after work, just to do the same work at home."

Luna chuckled at this. "That must make it especially difficult for you then."

"No kidding. Why am I doing this?" he asked.

She leaned closer, whispering, "Because I'm a cornucopia of complexity."

As if she was made of gravity, he drew nearer. "More like a cornucopia of pain-in-my-ass."

Luna swiped his baseball hat, placing it on her own head. "I think you're confused. I wasn't the one to hit you with that toolbox."

"It's still partially your fault. Are you going to take all my clothes?"

"You'd like that wouldn't you."

Sam's gaze flicked away, his lips pulling into an endearing grin.

She eyed him. "You're not as tough as you think you are, Samderland." Luna bet she could penetrate his shell as easily as breaking a macaron with her finger.

"That's where you're wrong. I don't think I'm tough at all. I don't even know why anyone would want to be that. When I hear *tough*, I think about steak. And how can being so tough and chewy no one wants you be a good thing?"

She pushed a finger into his bicep. "Oh, yes, this steak is nice and tender."

While painting with one hand, he snapped the same arm into a flex pose. Her eyes popped as a boulder developed on his bicep, stressing the sleeve hemline of his T-shirt. "I got your filet mignon right here, Queenie."

Luna threw back her head and laughed. She couldn't help it. They continued chatting while waiting for paint to dry, spending time with both Nicholas and Zabe. What she noticed about Sam was that he had an easy way of conversing with people. Small talk came easy to him, and he had no problems turning it into something interesting. She could get a glimpse of the storyteller in him.

In the evening, it was time to carry the faux fireplace to her apartment. "Are you looking forward to having a roaring fake fire in your fake fireplace? You can roast fake chestnuts and hang fake stockings at fake Christmas," Sam said, reclaiming his hat from her.

"Haven't you ever heard of *fake it 'til you make it*?"

"I think you flipped it. You did *make fake things*."

"Okay, that was a pretty impressive comeback."

"Now I'm impressive? What have I been doing all day?"

"Is this why you were showing off your meat earlier?" she asked.

"Oh, that was just one. I have filet mignon for two, a full rack of ribs, some tenderloins, rump roast, kielbasa and a couple of a-spicy meatballs."

"Look, buddy, if you're going to promise a woman an all-you-can-eat, grade-A beef buffet, you better deliver."

With a huff, they set the faux fireplace in front of apartment seven. Sam gave her a wicked grin before knocking on the door. "Delivery. Your hot beef buffet has arrived."

She rolled her eyes but smiled. "Are you expecting a tip?"

"I've already taken care of it. This delivery offers more than just the tip." He waggled his eyebrows at her.

"I'm not sure if I should leave a review on Grubhub or Pornhub?"

After they got the faux fireplace inside, Luna went into her bedroom to gather some pillar candles while slipping on Sam's hoodie. She should return it, but it was also more comfortable than any of her other hoodies, like a cozy blanket she could wear when it was chilly in the morning or evening. She would return it to him…eventually.

In the living room, he attached the wall mounts for the floating shelf mantel. She took a seat on the rug, switching her phone to camera mode in order to take a picture. After Sam set the shelf in place he took stock of his work.

"What do you think?" he asked.

"I love it." Luna meant it. The mantel was a dark, natural wood color. The bottom portion was painted white, which was created from a small old bookshelf with the shelving removed. Wood was built onto the sides of the bookshelf in order to create the frame of the fireplace. She added the candles at the base of the bookshelf, lighting them to get the full effect. "It's so beautiful."

She took a picture, adding it to an Instagram post. "I need to come up with some good hashtags for this. Hashtag upcycle. Hashtag mood lighting. Hashtag home is where the hearth is."

Sam took a seat beside her on the shag rug. "Do you hashtag everything in your life?"

"Yup," she replied, enjoying his teasing. "Everything. Hashtag my hoodie. Hashtag sucker."

He petted the cat who enjoyed rolling on her back and grabbing the man's hand with her front paws. "You're pretty weird. Ow!" After chomping a finger, Duchess sprinted into the bedroom.

"Pretty weird is still pretty so I'll take it. Did she hurt you?" She inspected his hand for wounds.

"No, just squeezed a little too hard with teeth. You need to make sure she doesn't knock these candles over and—"

"Start a fire. Yes, I know. This may surprise you, but I've owned candles before. But, you have to admit, it would be pretty cute to see a fireman carry her out around their shoulders."

"And where are you in all of this? Would they rescue the cat first?"

"I don't know. I just came up with this fantasy. Oh, maybe she can wear a little firefighter hat. Sam, it would be so adorable."

"I'm glad you're having fun thinking about our possible demise, especially since I'm right below you, which means the floor would probably collapse on top of me. But you're right, let's think about how cute the cat would look in a little firefighter hat. Hashtag kitty fireman. Hashtag dead Sam. There, I've done the hard part for you. You're welcome."

Luna laughed, pushing him playfully. "Now you're getting it."

Sam was funny. Not like a stand-up comedian, but it was more of the quiet kind, the kind no one expected and was able to sneak up on a person. His good sense of humor improved her opinion of him tenfold. She wasn't sure why it had never been on her list of ideal boyfriend qualities before. Luna was changing this immediately, bumping it to spot number one.

She still held his hand in hers. Luna liked comparing her hand size with his. "Thank you for helping me achieve my fireplace dreams today."

He lifted his gaze to her face, those warm brown eyes glowing in candlelight. "Your fake dreams?"

She smiled. "Fake fireplace. Real dreams. Not everything is fake."

Sam's eyes took in her outfit, including the familiar hoodie. "I kinda like the idea of you inside my clothes."

She stole a glance at him from beneath lashes while biting back a smile. "I kinda like the idea of you laid out on my rug."

His head tipped nearer, close enough it wouldn't take any effort to meet.

She tilted her head closer, her breathing becoming light.

His eyes slowly scanned her face, focusing on her mouth before meeting her gaze again. "I'm not going to kiss you. I've already been burned before."

Neither of them moved. Luna raised a hand, her knuckles tracing the line of his cheekbone as his eyes shuttered closed. "That's fair. I was a rude, selfish brat then. This is me kissing you."

She closed the gap between them, pressing her lips to his.

Chapter Twenty-Three

SAM COULD HAVE resisted. He could have gotten up, walked out the door, and demonstrated his unwillingness to be Luna's plaything.

He first drew nearer because there was something appealing about seeing her in his clothes. Also, the scent of his hoodie had changed. She had washed it, imprinting his garment with her own unique aroma. It was equal parts undistinguished floral mixed with something sweet like cotton candy. He wanted his hoodie if only to wrap himself in the smell of her when she wasn't around.

When she pressed her lips to his, he didn't react, didn't kiss her in return. He let her work his lips with her own. But, like snow on a warm day, his resolve melted. Sam latched his hands to the nape of her neck, angling her closer, his tongue sliding into her parted mouth. The flavor of watermelon soaked into his taste buds. A satisfied moan vibrated from Luna, who removed his baseball hat before trailing fingers through his hair and clutching his T-shirt with one hand.

While the kissing continued on a hot and heavy path, he dragged down the zipper of the hoodie. Without breaking stride, Luna shrugged out of it, tossing the garment aside, before throwing her arms around his neck. That threw his balance off, causing her to pitch backwards to the floor and he caught himself on his forearms.

With the room in an early evening shadow, the candle-light highlighted the features of her face in a golden glow. Her brunette locks fanned in a glossy halo around her head on the plush fibers of the rug. His opinion about the rug shifted in a more favorable direction. Everything she'd done to improve the apartment fit her, and that's why he liked it.

Sam ran his finger along the line of her cheek and jaw-bone. She was absolutely perfect. When that same finger brushed along her lips, she kissed the tip gently before taking it into her mouth and swiping her tongue around it. *God damn.* Like Luna wasn't already driving him wild before.

He dove back to kissing her, her legs wrapping around him, forcing his body against her. It must have been a long time since he got this worked up over a woman because he was reverting to his old teenage habit of rubbing himself against her, seeking relief. He brushed one of her soft, bare legs with his fingers and she tugged his hand higher on her thigh. He couldn't quite believe things could shift this quickly between them, but he wasn't about to complain.

Luna broke away from his mouth to yank off her tank top before grabbing him again. She tasted so good, so delicious, his craving for her deepened. His hands migrated from her thigh to her bare torso, her lace bra tempting him to such a degree it was as though his whole crotch was buzzing. That was a new experience—

No, wait.

That wasn't his crotch. It was his phone, literally buzzing in his front pocket.

Part of him was determined to rip the device from his clothes and punt it out the door but, as property manager, he shouldn't ignore calls.

"Wait a minute," he panted while reluctantly pulling away in order to grab the phone from his pocket. It was his father. Dad could wait. He sent the call to voicemail before settling on Luna again to continue the exploration, his hand sliding to a breast.

His phone began buzzing again. *Goddammit!* The old man hated leaving messages and wouldn't stop calling until Sam answered. "Sorry. I have to find out what this is about." He wasn't happy about being cockblocked by his father.

"Yeah?" he answered with more force than he had intended, but he was hoping the call could be finished fast and he could resume a more interesting interaction.

There was a pause. "Sam?"

"Yeah. Dad, I'm kinda in the middle of something. What do you need?"

"Is everything okay? You sound out of breath."

Sam attempted to get his heart rate and breathing under control. "I'm just…working out." He was definitely busy trying to burn some calories here.

"Oh, well, that doesn't sound too important. There are a few things I need to discuss with you."

Great. This conversation wasn't going to be done anytime soon. He let an internal groan roll through his body. Luna watched him, while propped on her elbows. With mussed hair and swollen lips, she was an intoxicating vision of beautiful chaos.

He dropped his head backwards in depressing defeat.

"Okay, just give me a second." Sam muted his dad. "Sorry, I have to take this. It's work stuff," he said to Luna while jamming his hat on his head and grabbing his toolbox. "I'll see you later." And he did the thing he loathed doing the most: leaving her.

Sam unmuted his father as he took the stairs, returning to his apartment. "What's going on, Dad?"

"You know the property on Ponderosa Way?"

"Sure."

"The tenants cut the lease. They had to move unexpectedly across country."

"Okay." So far, Sam wasn't sure what this had to do with him. In addition to Schnell Ridge, his father owned two other apartment complexes and several other rental properties, including the small bungalow.

"It's been having some electrical problems in the kitchen and Leslie called an electrician but they're booked a couple of weeks out. Do you mind swinging by and taking a look at it? Leslie said she'll be there mid-week. You can coordinate with her."

"Fine. I'll take a look. But what's the hurry? Why not just wait for a real electrician?" Sam had done a little bit of everything when it came to maintenance, but he didn't consider himself a professional in this area. For someone who didn't mind cutting a few corners, using his labor made sense (and cents) to his father.

"I was thinking that because there's still some of the summer season remaining, it might be a good idea to switch the property to an Airbnb. Leslie doesn't agree, but I think it'll be a good idea." Leslie was the main manager for all the

El Dorado properties, except Schnell Ridge, since his father moved away.

"Okay." If he agreed with his dad, maybe the call would end soon and he could bolt his ass upstairs.

"If we can get regular occupancy at a higher rate, it'd bring in more money. Maybe we won't have to go through the whole process of losing money while trying to find a new tenant. What do you think?"

Previously, Sam hadn't been interested in his father's business. He'd spent years since the accident, putting his head down and getting through whatever he needed to get done. But doing the bare minimum was no longer fulfilling. It was as though these projects with Luna had unlocked a side of himself he hadn't known existed. He'd found something he could not only do well, but take pride in. He could add value, if he wanted to. He was starting to want to.

"Sam?" his father said. "Are you still there?"

"Why do you have Leslie if you're not going to listen to her? I think she's right. I mean, maybe people might want to stay here because of the proximity to Tahoe but we're still an hour and a half away. Once the bad weather hits, people aren't going to want to drive over the pass in snow, especially when there are plenty of options at the lake. Plus, it's not the same as having a long-term tenant. If you have a new person staying in the place every week, Leslie's going to have to make sure the place is ready and either clean or hire a cleaning person between stays. On top of that, you'd have to completely furnish the place. It sounds like a hassle for taking a chance that you might make more money."

"Okay," his father replied. "If that's what you think we

should do, then we'd have to find a new tenant."

Sam's mind went to one person. "I might know someone who'd take it."

It had been a while since Sam had visited the property, but he could remember most of the details of the little bungalow with white slatted walls that sat prettily on the Ponderosa Way hill. The best way to describe it would be cute. It had been built in the fifties so it had a lot of details people liked: the small enclosed porch, a tiled fireplace, built-in bookshelves, a benched breakfast nook area. It was everything Luna wanted.

After he disconnected the call with his father, Sam stayed put even though his inside caveman desired nothing more than to sprint upstairs, burst through the door, and claim Luna. Him reappearing a half hour later would make it seem as though he was returning expecting to get sex. While he did want that, God knew he did, he also wanted a deeper connection. Not just sex. Her.

The problem was that while he did want her, he had done so at the expense of helping his mom with her dream. His mom had expected him to help her at the house today. Except the last few times he'd gone there, he'd left discouraged. No promises of painting walls or adding a backsplash had led to the kitchen being cleaned enough. Sam knew his mom was trying, and he was trying to appreciate when she was able to let go of a small handful of items, but he was tired. Instead of showing up, he'd made an excuse to stay behind and help Luna with her fake fireplace.

It wasn't fair to his mom, and he had too much to work through to think about getting in a relationship with anyone.

Maybe being cockblocked by his dad wasn't a bad thing. He needed to get his head straight rather than jumping into things, and prove, at least to his parents, that he could be relied upon.

And Luna?

Well, at least in one way, he could give her exactly what she wanted.

Chapter Twenty-Four

L UNA WASN'T ONE to chase after anyone. If anyone had said to her, *I'm not going to kiss you*, the old Luna would have immediately found ten unforgivable faults in the guy before deciding *Boy, bye. I didn't like you anyway.*

What she did with Sam was as close as she ever got to throwing herself at a guy. The fact he'd resisted her obvious advances, and told her he wasn't going to kiss her, somehow piqued her interest more. *Oh, you think you can resist these lips? I'm going to kiss you so well, Sunderland, you're going to melt like a candle in the desert.*

When he did kiss her, *she* was the one swept away, proving he could tie her in a knot as easily as that cherry stem. After he departed her apartment, she found herself waiting, expecting he'd be beating on her door at any moment. But he never came.

She didn't see him the following day, nor the day after that when leaving for work and there hadn't been any text messages from him. She assumed he was avoiding her for whatever ridiculous reason. That made her more annoyed. If anyone was going to reject anyone, it was going to be her and she was rejecting him because…well, she couldn't think of anything at the moment. It wasn't as if there weren't hundreds of possibilities for her to choose from, definitely enough to warrant a TikTok video and the tag of *#ReasonsWhyIHateSamSunderland*

The biggest reason why she hated him was because he made it hard to concentrate at work. She was in her office when a knock came at the door. Mia and her dimple popped through.

"Hey, Luna. I brought you an afternoon treat." She set a coffee on the desk.

"Can I talk to you?"

Mia didn't attempt to cover how much this question lit her insides, acting as if she'd been invited to an exclusive club. "Of course." The woman and her pregnant belly plopped into an office chair and waited expectantly.

Luna wasn't sure how to start the conversation. Tessa would have been an ideal confidant, but she hadn't gotten the courage to send an apology message yet. If her ex-best friend didn't accept her apology, then their friendship was truly dead and incapable of being revived. She wasn't sure if her heart was strong enough to be crushed again. Mia was the next best thing, and she wouldn't give Luna a hard time like Ross.

"Wait, are you supposed to talk or am I? Just so you know, I used the bathroom at Pony Expresso but the timer countdown for the next time I have to use the facilities has already started."

"I kissed Sam," Luna blurted.

Mia's expression didn't change. "I know. I was there." A split second later her brows lifted as the realization clicked. "Oh. Ooooooh, I get it." She took a sip from her iced tea.

"Okay."

"I thought this would get a bigger reaction."

Mia tilted her head in confusion. "Do you want me to get excited? Are you sleeping together?"

"No!" Although, not for a lack of trying.

The woman shrugged. "I guess I'm not that surprised. I sensed something at the fairgrounds, which is why I pulled Ross away. You know he'd just tease you nonstop. Sam seems like a nice guy. I think this is great, Lu."

"You do?"

"Yeah, why not?"

"What about what Natalie said? About the accident and him being an asshole?" Sure, Natalie hadn't been a hundred percent correct, but Mia didn't know this.

"Is he an asshole? You'd know better than her."

"No."

"Well, then whatever. I trust your judgment. And you do know that your cousin doesn't have the best history either."

"Yeah, but Ross—"

"Is family and someone you love. Plus, you see he's not the same person he used to be. His past actions may have helped shape who he is as an adult but he isn't defined by them. The same could be said about a lot of people. I'm not saying we should pretend things didn't happen, but I think someone accepting responsibility for their actions and wanting to change should count for something."

Luna would never be as good as Mia. She doubted the woman ever had to lock away bad thoughts. She was coming to appreciate her cousin-in-law's perspective. "You're going to make a good mom."

"I feel like I have to be because if I'm not, you'll probably tell me."

"Mia Russo, you take that back. I was actually trying to be nice here and you ruined it." But Luna laughed at Mia's audacity to call her out. Perhaps there was some bite to the woman after all.

Her cousin-in-law grinned. "So, you and Sam, huh?"

She released a groan in response, dropping her head into her palms. "No. Not Sam and me…Sam and I? Whatever. I don't care."

"But I thought—"

"We've been sort of hanging out more, not like dating or anything, but the other night we started kissing and—I don't know. He got a phone call and left, and it seems as if he's avoiding me now. I feel like…" Luna wasn't sure how to express all her conflicting thoughts and emotions, opting to throw her hands in the air instead.

Mia's expression crinkled in confusion. "That doesn't make any sense."

"Right?" She didn't understand it either. Why wouldn't Sam be banging on her door? Luna had never been such a willing participant before, and she'd even been nice.

"What was the call about?"

"I don't know. It was his dad, and he said it had to do with apartment business."

Mia shrugged. "Or maybe you think he's avoiding you, but he really is swamped with work."

"So, he's going to make out with me and then go, *what was I doing? Oh, yes, work.*"

Her cousin laughed. "When you put it like that it does

seem impossible he could just tear his lips away from you and go about his business so easily."

"I don't even know what I'm doing anymore. And, as if my life wasn't weird enough, I had to get something out of my car earlier and this was attached to my windshield." Luna unfolded the printout she'd discovered, sliding it across to Mia.

Her cousin took it, studying the one-page with *For Rent* printed at the top along with a phone number scribbled below. The page included a picture of a small white home with a list of features.

"This was on your car here at the jewelry store?"

"Yup. I found it an hour ago. I called the number, and the place is available and it sounded like the lady was already expecting my call. She even asked if I was Luna."

"Okay, that's weird."

"It is, and also this place sounds too good to be true."

"Aren't you in a lease though?"

"Yeah, but it doesn't hurt to look, right?" Luna paused. "I have an appointment this afternoon. Will you go with me? Please?"

"Yeah, of course," Mia replied. "I just have to use the restroom first."

The two women explained to a confused Ross that they were going to view a new available rental property.

"I'm not going to move all your junk up and down the stairs already. Especially now that you have twice as much stuff as before," Ross responded grumpily.

Luna snapped a hand to her hip. "It must be nice that you don't ever have to move your stuff at all because you have Grandpa's house and don't really have to worry about this kind of thing."

A wise Ross closed his mouth and didn't say anything further.

"THIS PLACE ALREADY looks really cute," Mia said when they pulled alongside the curb. "It must have been a guardian angel who put that flyer on your windshield."

Luna was apt to agree with Mia. It was nestled in between old trees. A stone pathway was hugged by grass on either side, and it had a healthy growth of white Shasta daisies and purple lupin. Luna was halfway in love already. It was better than the duplex from a few months prior. Even so, she tried to temper her excitement.

An older woman with a friendly disposition and wild gray curls approached from the covered patio. "Hello! I'm Leslie and which one of you is Luna?"

Luna raised her hand shyly. She was suddenly nervous and glad Mia had come with her. She removed her shoes before stepping foot in the place because she wasn't taking any chances this time. The house was tiny but it already felt like a home. She wanted this place with all her heart.

"Luna," Mia said, poking her side with an elbow.

"What?"

"Leslie asked what you thought."

"Oh. Yeah, I really like it. Do you have an application so I can start the process for the credit check?"

Leslie removed a long sheet from her black portfolio

folder and handed it to Luna. "We already have the necessary information. If you're willing to pay first month and deposit today, we can go straight to signing the lease."

"Huh?" Even Mia was confused as she shared a glance with Luna. This was all happening too fast.

Luna's gaze dropped to the lease in her hand and the mystery surrounding the place shifted into focus. It was a Sunderland property. She cleared her throat, attempting to appear casual. "Sure. I'm assuming you got my information from Sam."

Mia's eyes were about to pop from their sockets.

"Yes, of course," Leslie replied.

"Sam?" Mia said after Luna had done all the necessary paperwork and they returned to Luna's SUV. "What is going on?"

"That sneak! Now he's trying to get rid of me!"

Mia gave her an incredulous look. "I mean, he's giving you exactly what you wanted. Are you actually mad at him? Aren't we supposed to be celebrating that you're getting a cute little place? It's not like the guy threw your stuff out on the street and changed the lock on your apartment."

"You don't find it weird that he just quietly leaves a flyer on my car like a creeper. Why didn't he come talk to me?"

Mia snorted. "Like you've never done anything weird or sneaky."

Luna released a squeak. Her cousin was getting braver all the time. "Whatever. I can be both happy and mad at the same time. It's not impossible to feel both of those things together, especially in regards to men."

She pulled alongside the curb of Lanza Fine Jewelry to

drop Mia off.

"You're not going back to work?" her cousin asked while easing herself from the vehicle.

"No. I need to have a few words with someone. He can't avoid me forever. Oh, can you let Ross know something came up and I have to run home?"

"Just remember, you got the keys to a really nice place today, so maybe do more kissing than yelling at the poor man."

"Ha! Sam has no idea what he's in for…and neither do I because I haven't decided what that is yet."

As soon as Mia shut the door, Luna drove off. With each block closer, the more aggravated she got. She didn't even know why she was upset. Mia was correct. Sneaky as it was, Sam had done a nice thing for her. But why was he pushing her away? He liked her. Right?

As soon as she parked, she marched to his door, and knocked sternly.

No answer.

His motorcycle was in its normal spot. She knocked harder. Was he really going to ignore her? Because how dare he! She pounded her fist on the door. "I know you're in there, Sam Sunderland! You come out here and talk to me, you big coward!"

She was about to bang some more, when it jerked open, revealing a damp, naked Sam holding a white towel around his waist. "What in the hell is going on?"

Luna's knocking hand held midair, her jaw jarring apart. His bare chest, speckled with water droplets, was absolutely lickable. It was one thing to feel the man's solidness while kissing him. It was another thing to actually witness it with her eyes. When one was as thirsty as her, she'd take every last drop of him.

"Is there an emergency or not?" Sam asked, growing impatient.

"I..."

What was she supposed to talk to him about? She couldn't remember anything.

With his one free hand, (not the one holding the towel in place), Sam grabbed her arm, pulling her inside his apartment before slamming the door shut.

Chapter Twenty-Five

ALL SAM HAD been doing was taking a shower after getting sweaty from working at his mom's house, helping her *organize*. This mainly consisted of moving one pile of stuff to another section of the house. His calming shower shifted into panic when the sound of pounding echoed through his apartment. After he shut off the water, the noise persisted along with yelling. Grabbing his bathroom towel, Sam wrapped it around his waist before rushing to discover which apartment had a burst pipe.

Of course, it wasn't an emergency. It was only Luna, who was the number-one leading cause of his heart palpitations these days. On the patio Nicholas was throwing a quizzical glance in their direction. Sam didn't think, just pulled her inside his apartment to hash out whatever was bothering her. Anything to prevent having to stand in the open doorway with a single towel to protect him from indecent exposure.

"What do you need, Luna?" he asked while tucking the edge of the towel in place at his waist, freeing his hands.

She didn't answer; her gaze instead swept his apartment. Sam shifted uncomfortably as his place was nowhere near her standards. Most of his furniture was brought in by his dad, and he suspected most of it had been abandoned by old tenants. His bed was the single thing he'd purchased because he was tired of waking with a sore back. His body had dealt with enough problems, and he didn't need any more.

Sam was worn out, and not in the mood for any decorating judgments. "Luna."

"What?"

"What do you want? If there's no emergency, I'd like to put some clothes on."

This snapped Luna from her daze, although her eyes shifted to his body with a laser-focused intensity. "I'm mad at you."

"No, you're not."

She huffed a breath, crossing her arms. "You don't get to tell me when I'm mad."

"I've seen you angry. This isn't it."

"You sneakily left that flyer on my car instead of talking to me."

His hands rested on his hips. "I wasn't being sneaky. I just happened to drive by the jewelry store on the way to my mom's house and forgot to text you. So? Did you call Leslie?"

"I just signed the lease."

Sam shrugged. "Good. I can help you find moving boxes if you need them."

"I'll have to break my lease." Her eyes sparked as if daring him to get upset.

"Don't worry. I'll take care of it."

Luna threw her hands up in clear frustration. "I don't get you at all, Sam."

"And I don't get you. Isn't this what you wanted?"

She looked him dead in the eye, her jaw shifting into place. "Are you just trying to get rid of me?"

Sam could detect a hint of vulnerability in the question, and it stopped him. His arms dropped with a sigh. "No. I didn't do it for me. I did it for you."

The stubborn set of her jaw melted. Luna pushed nearer, close enough her light breathing could be detected across his skin. Her eyes dropped away, dark lashes fanning across her cheeks. "I haven't done a whole lot lately to deserve this," she replied in a low voice.

"Luna. You have. Take it." Despite their chaotic ride of a relationship, he'd come to really like Luna. It put a warm glow in his chest at being able to offer her a dream place now instead of her hanging around Schnell Ridge for twenty years.

She didn't move. The atmosphere around them grew heavy and intoxicating. He didn't know this was possible without actual alcohol involved.

One of her small, graceful hands drew down the center of his bare chest, sending sparks along his skin, her mouth tilting closer. "Sam."

He wasn't strong. His resolve was as brittle as a twig during a drought, ready to snap at any moment. Sam steeled himself as much as he could, because if he allowed himself to tumble down with her, he might not have the desire to ever escape. "Have you realized that you're not actually mad?" he asked in a low, calm voice.

She nodded. "I'm not mad."

"Good." He grabbed her arm, rotating her to the door.

"You should probably start packing your stuff."

Sam turned the knob, the door cracking open before her hand raised, slamming it shut. The front of his body collided with her back as Luna became an immovable mountain.

"No," she said. "I'm not done with you. I know you want me."

Yeah, no shit. He couldn't hide this fact any more than he could hide an erection in a bath towel, something he was currently familiar with. "Stop it, Luna. Get out of my apartment."

"No, *you* stop it."

"You're the most stubborn woman—"

"I don't know what switched between the other night and today, but I'm not leaving until whatever is going on between us gets hashed out. So, if you want to put on some clothes and get comfortable, that's fine because I'm still going to be right here. But between you and me, I'd rather you didn't put any clothes on."

Well, those words made everything harder. He swallowed, gathering his strength. "I don't..." She leaned against him. "I shouldn't..." Her head tipped sideways, exposing her slender neck to him and he inhaled the full scent of flowers and cotton candy. Of their own accord, his arms grasped around her waist, his nose pressing against her skin, all his senses experiencing paradise.

She sighed, rotating to face him before kissing his lips at a slow, tender pace, drawing him deeper and deeper into this fog of sensations. He didn't even notice her fingers running along the edge of his towel, until he became *very* aware. Her lovely hazel eyes lifted to his and Sam nodded. A second later his towel lay in a heap at his feet, and she took hold of his dick with her hand, grasping it firmly. He drew in a sharp breath, breaking away from her mouth. "Lu." He rested his head against a fist on the door as she stroked him and kissed the skin along the pulse of his neck, his breathing becoming uneven. It was the most delicious torture.

Her eyes were dark and glittering. She was the type of audacious person who'd wear red while walking past a bullpen before tossing her head back and laughing as the teased animal raged...or begged. He wasn't beyond begging at this point.

Two years ago, Sam was particularly lonely and wasn't sure what to do about it. He had downloaded a dating app, purchased a box of condoms, because *Why the hell not?* Logging on for the first time, he'd been so overwhelmed by the prospect of trying to establish a connection with someone, he never took the first step and soon deleted the app altogether, stuffing the condoms somewhere in his bedroom. At this exact moment, his overstimulated brain was trying to pinpoint where he'd stashed the box, like a horny pirate attempting to locate an old treasure without the use of a map.

He grabbed both of Luna's hands, disconnecting her from him and locking them against the surface of the door on either side of her head, giving them both a moment to think. "What do you want, Luna?"

Her skin was flushed but her voice was confident. "The same as you. Just this."

The condoms. They were under his bed.

Sam eased the grip on her wrists, his eye drawing to the

dip between her collarbone, wishing to circle his tongue there. A breath shuttered from his lungs, the final resolve leaving his body. "Okay." His head dropped to her neck, pressing his mouth to her warm skin, inhaling her sweet scent. Her arms enveloped his neck and head. Luna could have whatever she wanted as long as she continued to show this kind of mercy to him. He wanted to weep.

Sam didn't weep, because the other half of him was so aroused at this point, he would either take her against the door or carry her to the bedroom. Reality told him neither option would be good for his knee, but when had his dick ever been considerate for any other body part?

Instead, Sam decided to go with pulling and kissing Luna on a direct trajectory to his bedroom. After he deposited her on the mattress, he sat on the edge of the bed, his hand sweeping beneath the frame and locating the box of condoms, much to his relief. Finally! Something went right for him. However, his celebration was short-lived when his fumbling fingers had trouble breaking the outside plastic wrapping and had to resort to using his teeth, ending with a mouth full of dirt particles. He coughed.

"Ew. Dusty. There's probably a metaphor here about your sex life," she said while releasing a small laugh.

"Can you at least pretend not to notice? I'd like to have some dignity and not look as desperate as I feel right now."

"Are you sure those are still good? How long do condoms last before they expire?"

Oh, dear God, no. It seemed cruel for something like the passage of time cockblocking him at this moment. With his heart beating in the depths of his stomach, he snatched a condom wrapper and scanned the package for a date. Sam released a sigh of relief. "It's still good for another year." He ripped the squared packaging and rolled one on.

Luna traced a finger along his back "But you were a little scared, right?"

"No, I was perfectly cool. Not worried at all." He glanced at her. "Okay, I was a little nervous. Would you blame me?"

"No, because then you'd have to face my wrath." Luna removed her shoes with her feet.

He stretched alongside her body, any weariness from earlier had melted away. Everything inside him was focused and ready. "Like I could have predicted I would be serving myself up to her majesty today."

She narrowed her eyes as he helped peel her shirt from her body. "Maybe if you hadn't been hiding from me, you would have gotten a hint."

He laughed. "I told you, I wasn't being sneaky. And you're not supposed to be getting mad at me right now."

"You don't get to tell me when or when not I can get— Oh God, Sam." She moaned. He slid a bra cup down and swept the tip of her breast into his mouth, teasing it with his tongue, the sound she made was mesmerizing. Sam returned to her mouth, pulling heated kisses from her as he went to work removing her bra and sliding down the zipper of her shorts. Luna lifted her hips to wiggle out of the garment herself. He broke the kiss to get a good look, but she grabbed his face.

"Don't look. Can't you just keep your eyes closed?" It was the middle of the day. His bedroom wasn't close to being dark.

Yeah, that was not going to happen because it was all he'd been fantasizing about for weeks now. "That's not fair. I've been naked in front of you for a good ten minutes already."

"Yeah, but you look really good and I'm not perfect."

His ego swelled at this but he pulled back. "I'm going to look." He sat on his haunches, getting the full effect and letting his gaze linger across every curve, dip, and freckle. He had no idea what she was concerned about because she was the most beautiful thing he'd ever seen before.

Her skin flushed pink as she covered her face. "Okay, you've stared long enough."

Sam removed her hands. "You have the body of a queen."

"Oh? You've seen a lot of naked queens before? Sicko."

"Stop trying to get me into trouble just because you like being mad at me." Sam crawled on top of her, kissing from her jawline to her ear. "You're breathtaking." She was, in every sense of the word.

Her arms slipped around him, fingers drifting along the hair at the nape of his neck and Sam knew there would be no more talking. Nothing else needed to be said. He took her mouth with his again, sliding his tongue along hers as his hand grazed across her body, taking her thighs and gripping them higher on his waist. The temperature increased between them as each of their demands grew stronger, until he couldn't resist not being inside her any longer.

Sam soon realized his bed frame might have been too close to the wall. Every time he pushed into her there was a bang. They were literally banging. And since he shared a bedroom wall with Nicholas, he was expecting to get a knock on the door at any moment—not that he was going to answer. The whole apartment complex could be on fire and Sam wasn't leaving this bed until both of them were satisfied.

Luna felt so good. He couldn't stop himself from groaning as he began pumping into her harder, grasping her hips as beads of sweat dotted his skin. The pillowcase twisted in her hand as she muttered something unintelligibly, before squirming and arching against him, her sweet pink mouth popping open. When she cried out, it set him off. Every tremor vibrated through him like an aftershock.

God damn!

Sam collapsed, his heart racing a mile a minute as he tried to catch his breath. He had a desire to wrap her in his arms, nuzzle against her body, and take the longest, most restful nap he ever had in his life. Instead, he used all his remaining energy to carefully roll off her and slip into the bathroom.

As he cleaned himself, he glanced at his reflection, noticing a goofy half-smile that he did his best to school away because this could all mean nothing. He was convinced Luna was part human and part mischievous sprite and, therefore, it was hard to tell how much she did for her own amusement. He cracked the door, expecting to see his bed empty as though the whole thing had been a fever dream.

To his surprise, she had slid beneath the sheet, lying on her side, those astute hazel eyes watching him. He slipped into bed, facing her, unsure of what was supposed to happen now.

She pulled her fingers through the ends of her hair. "I forgot to say thank you for helping me get the new place."

"Is that what this was?"

She at least appeared shocked at his question. "What? No. I—What are you saying?"

Relief swept through him. What they did in his bedroom could mean a lot of things, but he didn't want it to be that. "I just want you to know that you don't owe me anything. I don't expect anything from you."

"Okay, then. Just know I would never give you anything even if you did feel like I owed you. I'm beholden to no one."

Sam laughed, slipping a strand of hair behind her ear. "Good. I'm glad to hear it."

"But I do mean it, Sam. Thank you for helping me."

A bubble of warmth stretched the confines of his chest. "You love it?"

"Yes. It's exactly what I wanted."

"Well, not *exactly*."

"What do you mean?"

"It doesn't have a green door."

She smiled. "That's true. Maybe you get the door you need, not what you want. A red door is good too."

"Is it? Does it mean death and vengeance upon your enemies?" He was tempted again to kiss the spot in the center of her collarbone. It seemed to have been made for his lips and she tasted amazing.

"Off with your head, pleb. Nope. Try again."

Sam squinted an eye as he ran through options in his head.

"God, don't hurt yourself," she said, laughing lightly while soothing a finger along his forehead. The action was light and tender, and he considered snuggling with her again.

"Does it have something to do with love?" A brief thought flashed through his mind about how he didn't want her in a love house unless he got to be there as well. He shoved the unsaid commentary into the dark depths where it belonged.

Luna laughed. "That's a good guess but no." She continued trailing a finger on him, drawing a line from his shoulder, across his bicep and ending at his hand. "A red door means safe harbor, a sanctuary. Welcome. *You* would be welcomed."

He wasn't sure if she was referring to him specifically with such an invitation or tossing a general *you* into the conversation. He didn't consider the conversation serious and decided to keep it that way. "It's nice you at least have a door to welcome you home. I'm happy for you."

Luna drew her hand away. "You don't want to go to a place like that?"

He didn't know how to answer this and found himself muttering, "I don't know. I have a lot going on right now. Probably best if you just stick with the door for now. It's more reliable."

She sat up and fumbled through the blankets, searching for her clothes. "Well, good to know." She slipped into her underwear in short jerky motions.

"Where are you going?" Sam wasn't sure what was happening right now, but he wasn't ready to let her go yet, not when she was clearly miffed about something.

"Where do you think? To find moving boxes." She scooped the rest of her clothes, attempting to dress and march from his bedroom at the same time.

Sam scrambled from the bed, grabbing a pair of boxer briefs from his dresser and almost tripping in the process. "Do you need help moving your stuff out?"

"No! I don't need your help ever. I can handle it myself."

He threw his hands in the air. "What the hell is wrong with you?"

She was dressed at this point and flicked her hair from her shoulder. "You just make me so goddamn mad." The door slammed behind her as she departed.

This time, he believed her.

Chapter Twenty-Six

T HE NEXT TIME Sam saw Luna, for more than a minute, was when she and Ross were carrying things from her apartment to the moving truck. Zabe abandoned him to run to her, wrapping her arms around Luna's waist.

"Why are you leaving? Don't you like being neighbors with us? Is it because Sam won't put in a pool?" The kid's questions cracked with obvious sorrow.

"Of course, I like being your neighbor. That's not why I'm leaving."

"But why? You just moved here."

"I'm not moving that far. We'll still be in the same zip code."

"So, you'll come back to visit us?"

Luna patted her. "I don't know."

Zabe ran a hand across her nose. "Can't you at least say, 'we'll see,' like all the other adults who don't want to say no?"

"Tell you what. You keep an eye on the place and, if it's okay with your dad, you can someday come visit my new house and hang out with me and Duchess. We can eat pizza while you tell me all the gossip I've missed."

Zabe's face brightened. "Really? Okay, I'm going to ask

Dad right now." She ran to her apartment.

Luna made brief eye contact with Sam.

"You guys need any help?" he asked.

"Nope," she replied in a hard tone.

Ross, who was crossing the patio, glanced between them before shrugging his shoulders. Luna wasn't against all help as she accepted assistance from Fireman Ryan with a glittering smile when he helped get the couch downstairs. Sam pulled his hat lower on his head so he could block it. The alternative was shooting eye daggers at the guy, which wasn't professional landlord behavior.

Then she was gone.

For a couple nights, Sam lay in his bed, facing an unused pillow. She hadn't occupied the space long, but his bed felt empty all the same. He regretted saying anything to her when he had returned from the bathroom. If he'd been smart, he would have pulled her into his arms so that they could simply be. His ears strained for the familiar sounds of someone moving around in the apartment upstairs, but there was nothing. The box of condoms was pushed beneath his bed to gather more dust.

A few days later, he didn't have the luxury of avoiding apartment seven any longer. Business dictated it was time to move on. When the key clicked in the lock, and he bumped his shoulder to force the door open, he was hit with the warm, welcoming scent of Luna's home, the same cozy, spicy fall smell it always had. The furniture was missing but everything else she had done to transform the place remained. The walls had the added color, the shades were on the window, the kitchen still had its modern facelift. In fact, the place was as pristine as it had ever looked, as though a cleaning crew had already been there. Sam would still hire someone, because the law dictated he had to, but he didn't want to destroy her work. He took apartment pictures as is. What his dad didn't know couldn't hurt him, which in this case meant extra work.

Back in his own place, he added the photos to an apartment listing rental, and published it to all the standard channels before leaving to do work at his mother's place.

"Is everything okay, Sammy?" his mother asked.

His phone had buzzed with a call for the third time, but not recognizing the number he returned the device to his pocket. "Yeah, fine."

"I want to show you this new cute thing I bought—"

"What?" Sam couldn't stop the agitation from infiltrating his voice. "Mom, you need to stop. This is all hard enough. We've been working at this for weeks now and have barely gotten anywhere. I feel like I'm in an uphill battle and my own mother is working against me."

He stopped when her large gray eyes turned watery. "I'm sorry," he said. "I'm really sorry. I-I'm just tired today is all. What did you want to show me?"

Sam felt even worse when his mother showed him a desk organizer in the shape of a raccoon. It sat in a crowded landscape of chaos but she showed him how she'd used it to organize some of her pens because she was tired of never being able to find one.

"I'm really trying," his mother said. "You believe me, right?"

"I know you are." He wasn't sure how either of them

would ever come out on the other side of the hoard, but he did his best to push those thoughts aside, giving her a small smile. "I like it. It's really cute."

After a few hours of negotiation over things his mother couldn't let go of, Sam had had enough. He left to return home, realizing his phone had several voicemails and even more emails, all in regards to the new apartment listing. Schnell Ridge had never been overwhelmed with interest like this before. Obviously, whatever Luna had done to the place made it in high demand.

He set up appointments over the next several days but he had to do one thing first and purchased new paint. Out of all the potential tenants who came by, only one asked him why the outside door was red when all the other doors were white. It was a single mom who'd recently gone through a bad divorce, and Charlene eyed him warily. He realized it did appear odd but maybe he'd eventually paint everyone's door a different color. When Sam explained the meaning behind the red door, her eyes glittered with unspent tears, with one spilling over as she looked at Luna's decorating vision. A feeling of pride went through him.

More surprising was finding his dad's car in the parking lot a few days later when he pulled in with his motorcycle after getting groceries. He hadn't seen his dad for a good year and a half, although they talked about business fairly regularly. The overly tanned man sat in a patio chair, sporting a trimmed beard with his hair swept back and wearing a Hawaiian shirt and sunglasses.

"Dad?" Sam said as he approached.

"You're still riding that thing? I bet that makes your

mother unhappy." His father jerked a chin in the direction of the motorcycle.

"Yeah. I…I didn't know you were coming."

"I see you've made a few changes. You decided to go ahead with the plants."

"I used my own money." Sam adjusted his baseball hat. "The tenants like it."

"Yeah, I bet. It's like free food included with the rent."

While the little garden was producing some stuff, it wasn't as though the tenants, or Sam, could forgo going to the grocery store, made clear by the bag he held in his hand. "Well, you always hated wasted space. And now it's no longer wasted."

His father eyed him. "So, you rented out that new vacancy pretty quickly I see."

Sam's stomach dropped. There was no way to hide the red door, and it only hinted at what was hidden inside the apartment. He tried to play it cool because what was done was done. "Yeah, pretty fast."

"I got curious because we received some emails on the Sunderland Properties website, people asking to be put on a waiting list for Schnell Ridge."

"Oh, yeah?" Sam feigned surprise despite experiencing the same thing on his end. "Sorry about that. It's been a little busy. Is that why you're here?"

His dad sighed. "I saw the pictures. After several emails, I had to look up your listing to see what all the buzz was about."

"Okay." Sam didn't have anything else to say.

"Can I take a look inside?" the older man asked, as if

Sam had any choice in the matter.

"Let me just drop off my groceries and grab the key."

Inside the improved apartment, his father didn't say anything, just wandered through the place. In spite of how Sam tried to justify everything that had taken place at the apartment complex in the last few months, deep down he was at least guilty of going against policy. He waited for the disappointment to roll in.

"She must be pretty." His father threw a stern eye in his direction.

He didn't try to pretend not to understand the implication. Sam slipped his hat off, running a hand through his hair before returning the cap to his head. "The situation was a little more complex than that."

"Right," the man replied with a shake of his head. "Look, I don't know if you're just lonely or horny or what, but you understand why we can't allow stuff like this to happen, right?"

The logical argument was because most people could do serious damage, costing the property company more money to fix. "I know, Dad. I—Like I said, the situation was more complex. Most of everything in here was done with my supervision."

"Your supervision?"

He sighed. "My help."

"And the person you approved to take over the place. What was that? Because with all the interest in the place, I find it hard to believe this was the most financially sound tenant you could have chosen."

"Her name is Charlene. She's going through a tough

time and it seemed like she really needed a break. I gave it to her." He was prepared for his father to be angry but, amazingly, he didn't care. Sam didn't regret anything.

His father shook his head. "It must be nice that you can be so generous with a property on my dime."

"I'm sorry...but I'm actually not sorry, because all this stuff that I've been doing, I like it, and maybe I want to do more than save a dime here and there. Because I, of all people, know that second chances don't come along very often, and it's the people who don't expect to get one that appreciate it the most.

"Go ahead and fire me. Find someone else to do the bare minimum to make you a buck. But if you keep me on, I'm going to manage the way that I think is best and sometimes that means going a little outside the box. If you don't want to take ownership of Schnell Ridge, I will because I live here."

Sam's dad pulled him into a weird half-hug. "Okay, okay, I get it." His father removed a phone from his pocket, retrieving a photo. "Have I ever shown you my garden? Maybe next season, I'll send you some of my heirloom seeds."

"Okay," Sam replied, thrown off by the turn of conversation.

"And, yes, I'm disappointed you basically went behind my back to do all this. I thought you were smarter than to allow yourself to be persuaded by a smile from a pretty girl. But you clearly feel passionate about whatever all this is, and I miss seeing that side of you. If you got ideas, let's hear them, but I'd rather we be a team. You're still my son and I love you."

His father continued. "The place looks good. Clearly, other people agree. If you want to do more in the company, then let's talk and figure something out."

"Okay," Sam said again. For once, he didn't feel as though he was fighting against something, and maybe he could do this. With his experiences with Luna and Charlene and the rest of the residents at Schnell Ridge, he was starting to have ideas, different ideas his dad probably wasn't going to like. But they were motivating him in a way that he hadn't felt in a while.

Instead of seeing the apartment complex as a trap, he was starting to realize he had access to a resource that could help people. It wasn't sports medicine but watching Charlene sign the lease paperwork with a quiet excitement, the pages slightly shaking in her hands, he had the epiphany that Luna had been right the whole time. Coming home to someplace special meant something. Why did a person need to wait decades for something they wanted?

At the moment, he wanted Luna. And he had thought he had to wait until his mom's house was sold or work was better or for a moment when life stopped throwing curve-balls and everything was easy. But that magical period of time may never happen.

He kept waiting for his luck to strike. Maybe it was time for him to do some striking of his own.

Chapter Twenty-Seven

PERFECT.

Everything was perfect in Luna's new place. It took her about a week to set everything exactly how she had envisioned it. Rental or not, it was hers for the foreseeable future.

That evening, she brushed her hair into soft waves, slipped on a luxurious, floor-length royal blue velour robe, and grabbed a glass of red wine. From her bookshelf, Luna retrieved a literary novel to read on the couch. Duchess the cat cleaned herself on the shag rug before curling into a tight circle. This was how her evening should be. #PonderosaDream #AdultingRight #Blessed

Her place was quiet, almost too quiet. Luna streamed some music on her phone. Classical, right? The music made it hard to concentrate on her book or it could have been paragraphs upon paragraphs of reading about a middle-aged man who may or may not be in a tent in the woods while also recounting the time he was an astronaut with Werner Herzog or something. She sighed while flipping through the pages. God, her hair was annoying, and she couldn't get comfortable at all.

Ten minutes later, she'd thrown her hair into a sloppy

bun, put on an old pair of flannel pajama bottoms with her lion tank top that still contained a few paint splatters. She turned on an episode of some garbage TV show and sprinkled chocolate chips into a jar of peanut butter to snack on with a spoon.

This was better—or at least she was more comfortable. The problem was, she was still lonely. At least at Schnell Ridge there was activity always happening on the property. Here there was nothing.

Luna retrieved her phone and scrolled through her contact list. She missed Tessa. After debating with herself, she composed a message. *"I miss talking with you."* She sat with it for a few moments. Was it enough of a start? She grew impatient and hit send, taking the risk.

Luna had anxiety over how Tessa might reply. She no longer cared which woman on *More Than Skin Deep* got picked by the bachelor surgeon searching for love but also performing plastic surgery on the winner to create his ideal woman. A happy ending wasn't guaranteed, not for the contestants of the show and certainly not for her.

Her phone buzzed.

"How's the new place working?"

Sam.

She should ignore him, teach him a lesson for making her angry. Truth be told, she was more aggravated than mad. That day in his apartment had proven one thing. She could wear him down and have him physically but, other than that, he could take her or leave her without being affected too much. In the end, she'd been the one to foolishly entertain the possibility of her and Sam being something more, only for him to inform her she shouldn't rely on him for anything substantial. She'd gotten the hint clear enough, and her heart had bolted.

But staying angry for the long term took a lot of energy. Her temper came in a burst before fizzling out quickly. She'd rather spite him instead. *"Why do you care? Isn't that Leslie's problem now?"*

"I'm not asking as a property manager."

He had her interest. *"What are you asking as then?"*

He didn't respond straight away. Perhaps she'd already pushed him too far. So much for a distraction.

Her phone buzzed and she snatched it from the couch. *"Just regular old Sam."*

"Have I interacted much with regular old Sam? How would I know the difference? Does he have less of a stick up his ass?"

"You've interacted with him lots of times. At the fair. The nursery. In my apartment. As far as my ass is concerned, you should know."

Her mouth sprung ajar in shock. But she wasn't going to make it too easy for him. *"I thought your ass had too much going on."*

"My ass was being an ass." He soon followed with: *"Regular old Sam wants however much of you he can get. But we'll keep the ball in your court. If you ever need me, you know the code."*

Luna stared at the message, rereading it several times. Did he actually mean it? Would he come if she asked? Part of her had a desire to test him, the other part only had a burning desire.

The heart inside her chest beat hard and her fingers typed, *"S.O.S."* She paused briefly, hitting send before her mind could be changed. No one would ever accuse her of not being gutsy but mainly because she was curious about what would happen.

She waited a moment to see if he'd replied but there wasn't anything. Luna wasn't even sure what it meant or what he was offering. Was he on his way? Just in case, she should probably change her clothes into something more—

There was a knock at the door.

She jumped.

"Who is it?" she yelled with suspicion, willing her voice to sound tough.

"Sam," came the muffled response from the porch.

Luna glanced at her phone. She'd sent the text a minute prior. Even with Schnell Ridge close by, he wouldn't have been able to arrive any faster than if he had flown. Luna stood, touching a hand to her hair. She was the unsexiest version of herself. God, she wasn't even wearing a bra. How was she supposed to know an *S.O.S.* message would be so powerful?

She peered through the peephole. It was Sam all right, right down to the old River Cats baseball hat.

"How'd you get here so fast?" Luna asked after cracking the door.

He rubbed his neck. "I was already in the neighborhood." His motorcycle was parked across the street. She wondered if he'd been texting her from that exact spot the whole time. Despite her unsexy wardrobe situation, she welcomed him inside.

After his gaze swept the room, they locked on to the jar of peanut butter in her hand. "Am I interrupting something?"

"Yeah, you just missed the party."

"Did I?" He helped himself to the spoon in the peanut butter jar, smearing a big glob on his middle finger before returning the spoon to the container. Keeping his eyes locked on her, he achingly, slowly, licked the peanut butter from it. Luna almost dropped the jar. Clearly, there was nothing "regular" nor "old" about Sam. Her mouth grew dry as she became more conscious about her lack of bra. Maybe he did too because his attention dropped to her bedtime-casual outfit. Those eyes had enough intensity to burn holes in the fabric.

She cleared her throat, attempting to harness some control. It didn't seem fair the man had the ability to keep sneaking up on her. "What exactly is supposed to happen now?" she asked in a low voice.

"Whatever you need, Queenie." He licked his lips.

Luna may have stopped breathing at this point. His eye contact was unwavering.

"You really think you can put up with me?"

"Yes."

"You won't...leave?"

"No," he replied, shaking his head. "I won't leave until you want me to."

Luna lifted her chin, meeting his gaze with a blazing look of her own. "Show me."

In a single graceful motion, Sam's hand shot out, he grabbed a handful of her shirt and yanked her to him. He absorbed her gasp when his mouth covered hers. Shock turned into longing as she melted into him, kissing him in return. He tasted of peanut butter; his tongue smooth as it glided into her mouth. Luna wrapped her arms around his neck, her free hand grazing his skin and sliding to his jawline. His grip went around her back before landing on its final destination of her ass and he squeezed.

Luna pushed the man to the couch, setting the peanut butter container on an end table before straddling Sam's lap. She tossed away his hat before returning to his mouth. It was as though she didn't realize how hungry she was until a feast was placed within reach or how much she craved someone equally starving.

Without any ceremony, he peeled the shirt from her body, his lips going to the heart of her collarbone, leaving wet hot kisses there before dragging them to her breasts. Her head tipped backwards as she allowed his tongue to titillate, her breathing transitioning to whimpers.

"You have no idea how much I've been aching to feel you again," he said.

"Please tell me you came prepared tonight."

He nibbled her neck with lips and tongue and teeth before smiling against her skin. "You need it bad, huh?"

"I don't need anything," she said between breaths. "I'm like a camel storing water in my hump. I can manage a long time without sex." Needing led to expectations and disappointment. Luna didn't want any of it.

"Mm-hmm. I really like your humps." His hand slid under the elastic waistband of her pajamas. All his rough, calloused touches were going to be the death of her. She moaned.

"But if I *did* want something, you came prepared, right?"

"You can relax. I came prepared."

"Relaxing is the last thing I want to do right now."

He stared into her eyes. "You can have as much of me as you can take, Queenie."

Luna's breath hitched. She looked past his dark, intense eyes, and suddenly she could see him. Really see him. Her finger brushed the scar on his eyebrow, down a sharp cheekbone to his soft lips. He was beautiful.

"Sam," she whispered before pressing a gentle kiss to his lips. "Just be with me."

"Okay."

She pulled his shirt off, her fingers eager to trace the solid lines of his chest, the smattering of chest hair, as her mouth returned to his again and again. She needed more of him even while feeling there was an abundance of everything, more than her heart knew what to do with.

"More," was all she could say between kisses. Her possessive hands were already making work with the fasteners on his pants. They discarded the rest of the clothes and Sam made use of the condom he'd brought with him.

"God," he groaned when Luna sank down on him.

She liked that Sam wasn't quiet. He pressed moans into her skin or dropped her name in between swear words. As she rocked against him, she found herself whimpering his name in return. Luna pushed them until she couldn't hold back the overwhelming pleasure any longer, her body breaking apart around him. Sam dropped her onto the couch as he pumped into her hard until he also slumped, completely spent.

"You'll come back, right?" she said, wrapping them in a big, fuzzy blanket after cleanup. Luna had never been much of a cuddler but she was beyond relaxed, curling into the space between his arm and body.

He held her while brushing soft kisses to her temple. "I'll come back. Whenever you need me. You know the code."

Chapter Twenty-Eight

F OR THE LAST month, Sam would visit the Ponderosa bungalow once or twice a week, whenever he got an *S.O.S.* message. They never went out or did anything other than try to get under each other's skin in the best possible way. But he could sense she was holding some part of herself back, keeping their interactions on the surface, a sex-only type of affair.

"Guess what?" he said one time while they relaxed on her couch. "Nicholas and Little Luna are moving out at the end of the month."

"This better not be the way I discover people refer to me as Big Tuna Luna."

He laughed, tracing the different parts of her hand. He liked how hers were smaller and more delicate than his. "What? No, you're just regular Luna."

Luna snatched a throw pillow, smacking him in the shoulder with it.

"What the hell was that for?" he asked.

"I don't want to be just regular Luna."

"You're right. There's nothing regular about you."

"You're damn right there's not."

He kissed along her neck. "Anyway, Nicholas met a lady

friend at some dog club and he's moving in with her."

"Aw, good for him. I'm happy he found love."

"Yeah, me too. Can I talk to you about something?"

"It's not something serious, is it?" Her shoulders stiffened, clearly betraying her dislike of the idea of a serious conversation.

He pushed away the unease of what this meant, especially if he wanted to have a serious conversation about their relationship at some point. "Well, it's serious about the apartment complex. I just want your opinion."

She relaxed into him. "Oh, in that case, talk to me. I do love giving my opinion."

"I'm trying to convince my dad to turn Schnell Ridge into a low-income apartment complex, one that accepts housing vouchers for rental assistance. I've looked into it and it provides some tax credit and benefits from the city, but my dad is pretty conservative about that kind of thing, like it's somehow going to ruin our reputation." He rolled his eyes at this.

"I want to make Schnell Ridge into something more unique than other low-income options, something that truly offers people a second chance and part of it is making the individual units something special. I don't have a very big budget, but Nicholas has been in the place a long time so I pretty much will have to replace everything. Anyway, as far as the design is concerned, you have more of an eye than me." He brushed a strand of hair from her neck, placing a kiss there. "Maybe you wouldn't mind helping me, give the apartment the Luna touch."

She turned to him, her gaze soft. "Really?"

"Yeah. It can be like old times. Hashtag new Schnell Ridge apartments."

"Wow. You're really terrible at coming up with hashtags." She smiled, weaving an arm around his middle. "But, yes, I'll do it. I've really missed doing apartment improvements." His heart did a kick knowing he had made her happy again.

"IS EVERYTHING OKAY?" Zabe asked a few weeks later.

"Hmm?" Sam glanced away from his phone, returning to the small box planter he was putting together for the girl. "Yeah, fine."

It was fine, except he *really* wanted to see Luna and his phone remained frustratingly silent. The problem with having a one-sided code word was he didn't have one for himself. This was a definite flaw in the system.

She studied him. "You leave a lot lately. My dad said you might have a girlfriend. Do you? What about Luna?"

Sam fiddled with the tool in his hand because there wasn't a good answer. He wasn't sure if what they had was as solid as a boyfriend/girlfriend relationship. The words had yet to be uttered. He wanted to do something normal such as bring her a plant or go for a walk and hold her hand, but he wasn't sure about anything. It was tricky trying to balance his normal management work, helping his mother on the weekends, and then trying to see Luna in the evenings. How strange it was to experience having a full life again. "I've been hanging out with a friend," he replied to the kid.

When she wasn't paying attention, he slipped the phone from his pocket and took a chance. *"Miss you,"* he sent in a text.

Five minutes later Luna replied, *"Funny. Just got the same message from my dentist. I'm due for a cleaning."*

Sam shook his head. Anything resembling a relationship-type sentiment always got sidestepped. *"You're due for more than that. You free tonight?"*

"Going to Ross and Mia's to see the baby and have pizza."

Well, so much for his plan.

He was shocked when her message was soon followed with, *"Want to come with me?"*

Since the baby had been born, he'd known Luna had visited the family several times, but he had yet to see the baby himself. *"I don't want to crash a family thing."*

Luna replied with a rolling-eyes emoji. *"It's a casual last-minute thing. Their besties will be there. And Mia's dad. Ugh. I don't like him. It's only fair I get to bring along a buddy."*

There were some things to unpack there but, at the moment, Sam didn't care. *"Okay, as long as your family doesn't mind."*

"Ross already said okay. Do you want to come to my place and we'll drive together after work?"

"Can I just meet you there?"

She texted him the address.

A little after six, Sam's motorcycle parked outside the older ranch-style home. Her white SUV was already in the driveway. He pushed away a bout of butterflies in his stomach. He wasn't sure what the nerves were about. Why should he care about impressing Mia's dad? Perhaps it was a case of being invited by Luna to be a part of this get-together, as though they were a real couple. He wanted to be accepted by the group, to feel as though he belonged with her.

Ross answered his knock. He remembered the guy as being sullen in school, but the adult version was more at ease and, clearly, happy with his current life. A small sting of jealousy invaded Sam's body.

"Oh, hey, man." Ross welcomed him into the house. "Want a beer or something?"

"I'm good, thanks."

"We're all eating in the family room."

The inside of the home was quite lived in. Luna's elegant, sophisticated style wasn't on display here. It was a warm, standard home of mismatched furniture and lots of photos on the wall. In the living room, Mia sat on a dining room chair and a stern-looking older man with arctic blue eyes relaxed on a recliner. Sam was introduced to a couple named Natalie and Mason, who sat on the floor with their toddler, Alex, who was doing his best to put everything in his mouth, while Mason discussed why honey should be a standard topping on pizza. The only thing Sam cared about was Luna. Refreshed and gorgeous as ever, she took his breath away from her spot on a worn floral sofa, a baby bundle in her arms.

She glanced in his direction before returning her attention to the baby, a bright smile on her lips. "Who's that? Huh? Is that Sam?" Luna said this in a light, baby-friendly voice. "Yeah, it's Sam. Hi, Sam." She delicately grasped a baby wrist and waved it in his direction.

He swallowed down the emotions, unsure what to do

with himself, taking a seat beside her. Being included at a family-type function hadn't happened for him in a long time. The realization hit him in the gut.

"Oh, this is Mia's dad, Judge Russo," Ross said, sitting beside his wife and slipping an arm around her shoulders. "Help yourself to some pizza."

"Do you want some more, Judge?" Mia asked her father. Sam was confused. Was the guy's name Judge or was he a judge?

"I'm just waiting for my turn to hold my own grandchild," the older man said gruffly.

"Oh, stop," Mia replied. "You've had way more opportunities to hold Victoria than Luna."

"Yeah, I've hardly got to hold you at all," Luna said in the same soft sing-song voice to baby Victoria. The infant stared at her with big, dark eyes full of infinite curiosity.

"Let me have your hand." Luna took hold of Sam, bringing his hand closer to the baby. Victoria's small one clasped a finger. His own were rough and tanned in comparison. "She's got a good grip, right?"

"Yeah." The kid's hold was surprisingly strong. How lucky Ross was. The man had found a way to build a new family.

"This kid is going to be a firecracker just like the rest of the women in this family," Luna said. "I can tell."

"Please. Not too much of a firecracker. I don't know if my heart can take it," Ross replied.

"And we thought the dog was spoiled," Mia said while patting her husband's knee. "The kid coughs and Ross practically has a panic attack."

Mason laughed at this as he turned his own kid upside down to his squealing delight.

"Men are so fragile, Victoria. That's why you gotta be a little firecracker to keep them on their toes," Luna responded.

"Okay, I think it's time for the judge to hold her," Ross said. "You don't need to influence the kid anymore." He stood, removing the baby from her arms as she protested.

Luna pouted. "You're so mean. You're going to be the meanest dad ever."

Ross ignored her. "Hey, baby," he said, kissing the infant on one chubby cheek before relinquishing her to the older man's arms.

Judge Russo's face transformed into something softer as he took Victoria into his arms.

"When I have a kid, mine is going to be even cuter," Luna said, pulling her legs to her body and relaxing into Sam as though it was the most natural thing in the world.

"How dare you not agree that this is the cutest baby that has or will ever exist," Ross replied.

"She's cute, which I find to be a miracle considering she has half your DNA. I'm sure Mia's side had to work extra hard to overcome such obstacles."

Ross looked pointedly at Sam. "You really want to put up with this brat?"

Luna's body stiffened beside him.

"Luna keeps you grounded." Sam's eyes were drawn to her, and he saw she was watching him. "When you do get something nice, it makes you feel like you really earned it."

Mia and Natalie exchanged an amused glance between

them, but Ross snorted, taking a sip from his beer bottle. "She'll keep you grounded all right, right into the ground." Mia elbowed her husband, causing him to dribble his drink. All Sam cared about was the small smile Luna gave him before interlacing their fingers together. Yeah, there was nothing regular about Luna.

"Wanna come over?" she asked as she walked him to his motorcycle later.

"Yeah."

"Okay. See you there."

Sam's motorcycle followed her SUV while he pondered all the things he'd say if he had the courage. He removed his work boots on the enclosed porch before following her inside.

"You don't have to defend me when I'm being a brat—which I was, obviously. Ross and I have always given each other a hard time," she said while slipping off her shoes.

"Yeah, same with my brother and me. Can I stay overnight?"

Her eyes reflected surprise. "You want to stay?"

"I want to stay every night." Fooling around and leaving afterwards wasn't enough anymore.

They stood there at what appeared to be an impasse. Sam may want her, but he wasn't going to push or beg. He wasn't going to accept anything she wasn't a hundred percent willing to give. Maybe an invitation to a family get-together and hand-holding didn't mean anything after all.

"It's okay. I think I better get home." He pushed his feet into his boots and was halfway across the yard when she called his name.

"Sam," she called again. "You can stay."

They spent an hour watching some show. Sam couldn't even describe what it was about. There was too much nervous energy, either from him or her or both of them. He then watched her go through her ritual of getting ready for bed: changing into pajama shorts and a tank top before slipping on his hoodie to wash her face and brush her teeth. She handed him an extra new toothbrush that had been stored in the cabinet. Luna removed the hoodie, put on the fuzziest socks he'd ever seen, before sliding beneath a big, fluffy white comforter.

She watched him as he peeled off his clothes, except his boxer briefs, before climbing into bed. It was hard to explain why all of this was nerve-racking, and more intimate than sex, but it was. Luna had become withdrawn. There was none of the usual banter to ease the tension.

As soon as the lights flicked off, she captured his mouth in an aggressive kiss, but he pulled away. "Wait. Let's just stop for a minute."

Luna shrank to her side of the bed.

Sam brushed the hair from her cheek. "What exactly do you want, Lu?"

"I don't want to want anything."

He wasn't sure why she would say that but he understood the sentiment itself. "Okay." His thumb traced along her cheekbone. "After the accident, I didn't want to want anything either. It's tricky, right? You can't stop yourself from wanting things but knowing it can all be taken away can be pretty scary."

"Yeah." Even in the darkness of the room her eyes stayed

with him. "What do you want, Sam?"

"Can we start with something simple?"

"Sure."

"Turn over to your other side."

Luna turned away from him, and he molded his body to hers, pressing his face into the soft skin at her neck. The scent of flowers and cotton candy enveloped his head, and he took a long, deep breath, soaking the smell into his lungs. He lived for this scent now.

"You want to spoon me in bed?" she asked, sounding incredulous.

"Yeah, for a whole month now. There's this feisty, stubborn woman who doesn't seem to be afraid of anything, so this is probably the safest position for me. If something leaps through the door, you can protect me, or, if you get mad at me, you're at least faced in the wrong direction. Ripping out my throat might still be possible but at least it gives me a fighting chance. Yes, this feels very secure, like I can finally get a decent night's sleep."

Her body relaxed into his. "What else do you want?"

"I would like to take this same feisty, stubborn woman out sometimes."

That was met with silence. It was as though he'd pushed his heart to the outside of his chest, but Luna hadn't taken it yet and the dejected organ was shriveling in the cold. His inability to figure her out was becoming a sticking point of frustration. Sam pulled away, sitting on the edge of the bed and leaning his elbows against his knees.

Luna turned around. "You're not leaving, are you?"

"You know what I want? Really want? I want a girlfriend.

Something real. Not a fling or a thing with benefits. I want you. So, yes, I want to take you out and sleep next to you at night. I want to know that I'm not going to be alone here, that you're going to claim me."

Before he could act, a pair of warm arms slipped around his chest as Luna pressed against his back, her mouth at his ear. "Some guy asked me out the other day, and I told him I had a boyfriend." She kissed his neck.

Sam closed his eyes, all his muscles relaxing. "You have a boyfriend?"

"Mm-hmm. Could we go on your motorcycle and get milkshakes when you take me out?"

He bit his lip to keep a giant grin from spreading across his face. "Well, the weather is going to get bad soon, so maybe the bike isn't a good idea, but, yes, if you want to be a cheap date and get a milkshake, that's fine with me."

She released a contented sigh, pressing more kisses to his back. "What else do you want?"

He couldn't remember ever feeling so free and full of joy before. He put his hands over her arms, keeping her pressed to his back. "I want to make you feel as warm and safe inside as I feel when I'm with you. I want to make you laugh so hard you throw your head back. I want to give you all my hoodies so you're never cold. And I want to make sure that when you're out exploring, you never end up stranded anywhere. You can call me if you need to."

"Those are a lot of wants and they aren't even remotely selfish. You lied to me, and you're actually a nice guy after all. This is a horrible thing to find out now."

That opinion could not stand. Sam whipped around,

tackling her to the mattress, a burst of giggles escaping as he nipped her skin with his teeth. "Ross is right. You're the worst kind of brat. Take it back."

She laughed until breathless. His heart stretched from being absolutely full of her. Cracks of lightning were breaking apart what remained of his pessimism, replacing it with something else.

"What do you want, Luna?"

She turned serious again. "I want...to let my guard down, to let myself feel something with abandon but, mostly, I want to be in a relationship where I don't feel I'm constantly letting someone down because I can't stop myself from being who I am."

He raked his fingers through her hair and gently kissed her.

"I like you," she whispered.

Sam, finally, had all the time in the world: a whole night. He kissed her, pressing himself into her. His hand slipped beneath the tank top to stroke her breasts. When she gasped, his whole body responded to it. Having her became all that mattered.

With clumsy fingers he drew her pajama shorts and underwear down. Sam dragged slow kisses along the inside of her thigh, before using his tongue to feast on her, sucking and licking until she was a whimpering, trembling mess. He smiled, loving nothing better than reducing her to that state.

Sam pulled himself over her again, kissing across her collarbone. Luna's nails dug into him. He wanted to tattoo the crescent-shaped marks all over his body, to feel her over every inch of his skin. She breathed out his name and arched against him. His brain was already a hazy mess and getting worse. "I need to get a—"

"No," she responded.

"No?"

"I'm on birth control. It's okay."

His brain stuttered for a moment. "Are you sure?"

She nodded. Sam took a second to enjoy the sweet taste of her mouth before sliding his boxers down. He was sure he saw starbursts when he pushed into her, forcing a breath through his nose. It was the feel and heat of her at a hundred percent.

"Fuck, Luna," he said, pressing his face into her neck. He wasn't going to be able to control it because, this time, he knew she was his.

SAM WOKE EARLY the following morning on his back with Luna's arm slung across his stomach and Duchess the cat on his chest in full loaf position. While his mattress was probably better than hers, he couldn't remember when he'd slept so well.

Too bad he had to go to work. Lifting the sleeping cat from his chest, he resettled her on the pillow before slipping from the bed to get dressed. Sam kneeled on the bed beside Luna, brushing a mahogany strand away and planting a tender kiss on her cheek. "Hey, Queenie, I have to go to work. Gotta rip out some old carpeting in Nicholas's place."

"Hmm?" she replied half asleep. "Okay, I'm going to visit some thrift stores today to see if I can find anything for the place. You'll take me out later?"

Sam smiled as he nuzzled her jawline. "Yeah, you check your calendar and let me know when you're free. I'll text you later, okay?"

"Okay." She curled deeper within the comforter.

While Sam hated leaving, he also felt pretty good. And if Zabe asked about his whereabouts, he could say he'd definitely been visiting his girlfriend.

Chapter Twenty-Nine

FOR LUNA, BEING in a relationship had always been a balancing act. There were guys who immediately demanded more of her than she had been willing to give, which caused her to release the guy immediately. And there was someone like Viggo, who didn't care about having more of her, as though having less than a hundred percent was fine.

Sam was different. Here was a man who was aware of all the undesirable bits of her personality, someone she'd already tested and pushed away, and yet he remained. Luna could try to get away with her usual tactics to prevent him from getting too close, but she didn't have the desire for it, especially when he treated her as though she was something special. Finding someone she didn't have to pretend with, who gave it to her straight, with no games, was a rare find in her world. Perhaps if she gave a little more of herself, he wouldn't leave. Luna had agreed to give their relationship a chance but, in a sense, she was also agreeing to give herself one as well. It was a challenge to keep herself grounded and fight the desire to flee.

Surprisingly, Luna discovered she could be with someone and not be suffocated or bored. Sam did his own things but would check to see if she wanted to meet him somewhere, never being pushy about it. She actually wanted to be with him. On the physical side, he excited her. His touch and kisses could be electric, lighting every cell in her body. No matter how many nights he slept in her bed, he still had the ability to sneak up and surprise her.

"The place is looking really nice," Luna said while touring Nicholas's old apartment. "You did a good job, pleb." The transformation from old and rundown to modern was as exciting as it had ever been.

When he'd told her about his vision for Schnell Ridge, she'd loved the idea straight away. She liked shopping for a purpose, and she wanted to make him happy. Plus, helping to show up Sam's father, proving he was wrong about this, was icing on the cake for Luna. On top of that, she was hoping this was the beginning of something new for her too, perhaps she'd do more than the accounting at the jewelry store.

"The new flooring should be arriving tomorrow. Thanks for getting that extra discount so I could make the budget."

"Hashtag dimpled secret weapon."

He laughed. "You see that edging?" Sam wrapped his arms around her from behind while keeping his paint-speckled hands off her body. He sunk his face into the nook where her neck met her shoulder.

"Mm-hmm. Looks like you've been edging all day, you poor thing."

He snorted a laugh into her skin. "That could be why I'm so happy to see you. I'd grab you right now, but I don't want to get you dirty."

"I don't mind getting a little dirty."

Sam groaned in frustration. "You look at the rest of the place. I'm going to wash my hands at least."

He later found her perusing the bathroom. The walls were a warm gray and the cabinet had been replaced with an ebony one with a bright white countertop. The mirror was large and circular with a gold frame Luna found at a thrift store for fifteen dollars. It was fun to add her own unique touches, which had hardly cost anything for Schnell Ridge.

"Nice," she said.

"You like it?"

"I like it a lot, Sunderland."

His smile grew dangerous. "I like you a lot."

"Is that so?"

Sam shut the bathroom door before grabbing and yanking her close, pressing her back to his front. She gasped a laugh as he nibbled an earlobe, his hands sliding along the curves of her body.

"These leggings are really doing it for me." One of Sam's hands dipped past the waistline, his fingers slipping between her legs.

Luna sighed softly, her whole body heating. Her reflection confirmed a deep flush spreading across her skin. His gaze met hers with a devilish glint. Oh God, she was going to get caught in the tornado again, wasn't she?

She couldn't keep her eyes from the mirror, watching as he closed his eyes while slowly kissing along her neck, his other hand continuing to stroke her. He seemed to sense when her body weakened, his eyes opening and lighting with hunger when she let out a breathy moan.

"What do you want, Luna?"

"You." The word barely got out.

He peeled her leggings and underwear down, pushing her forward into the counter as he ungracefully undid his pants. Sam's dick slid into her from behind, his torso draping over her, holding her to him. "I want all of you," he said.

Her gaze lifted to the mirror again, his expression as fevered as her own, but his eyes were steady as if trying to give his comment more weight. It kind of thrilled her, kind of scared her.

Luna let the tornado overtake her.

"CAN I STAY tonight?" Sam asked a few days later.

"You can if you want, but I just started my period so I might not be the best company in bed." Luna was used to guys making themselves scarce whenever she mentioned the P-word as though she was somehow diseased.

"I'll keep you and Duchess company."

"Okay." Her heart may have expanded a smidge.

That's exactly what happened. They lay in bed, facing each other and Sam stroked her arm, his presence and touch soothing.

"If I say anything mean to you while on my period, I'm apologizing now," Luna said.

"Are you going to say my nose is too big or something?"

"No, I wouldn't say that because it's not true. You have a great nose. I don't like to say anything I don't truly feel. It's a curse. If I were to say something, it'll probably be about your facial hair. Are you really bad at growing a beard? Do you have a shitty razor? What's going on here?"

"Wow, you weren't kidding. You just jumped right in there."

Luna laughed, covering her face with her hands. "Oh my God. I'm so sorry. See, it's a curse. But you know I'm right. Please don't leave."

She kissed his fingertips, and he continued trailing them on her skin. "Sam?"

"Hmm?"

"I really do want to be better. I sent a message to my friend, Tessa, a couple months ago, but she never responded."

"You can always send another one."

"I don't know. Maybe she's truly gone. It's not like it wasn't my fault. I should be able to control my mouth."

"Have you always been so brutally honest? Were you one of those kids that your mom had to apologize to strangers for because you hurt their feelings?"

"My mom left me when I was four."

"Oh, shit. Sorry. Now I feel like my big mouth is cursed."

Luna wasn't mad. It was as though the door had been cracked into this sensitive subject, freeing her to tell him. "She called a few months ago. All these years of nothing and suddenly she started calling."

"She wants to reconnect?"

Luna nodded. "She said she has cancer and her new family, apparently I have sisters, thought she should reach

out. I said something really mean and then hung up on her."
She couldn't reveal what she had actually said. It was too
horrible. What if it changed his opinion of her?

"Do you regret it?"

"I always regret saying something mean, but it's not because I don't think she deserves it. It's more that I don't
want to be like that."

"Have you heard from her since?" he asked.

"No. I'm sure they all hate me now."

"Have you talked to your cousin about it?"

"Yeah, but it's not easy to talk to him about this."

"Why?"

"He has his own life going on with Mia and the baby,
but mostly because he lost his parents in an accident and, of
course, he'd do anything to have them back, especially now.
Ross thinks I'm wasting a chance to make amends, and
maybe have a parent again, that I should forgive and forget."

She swallowed to keep her voice from cracking. "But I
will never forget. It's not the same thing as losing someone
you loved, who loved you back. I've had to go my whole life
knowing my mother didn't think I was important enough to
check in, to make sure I was okay. And it's so hard because
I'd really love to have a mom, but not that one. She's already
broken me." There were tears burning on the brims of her
eyes, but she wouldn't let them go. Luna was done crying
over her mother, over herself, over the unending sense of
what she'd never have.

"Come here." He encouraged her closer and she turned,
assuming the small spoon position as Sam held her. She
wasn't a cuddler, she wasn't, but Luna could also close her

eyes and breathe, absorbing the comfort his presence offered.

"You're resourceful and smart and resilient, not to mention beautiful," he said into her ear. "If there's anyone walking around with regrets, it's probably your mom because she missed out on all of this."

She sniffed and took his arm draped across her, hugging it to her chest. "I was definitely kissing you when we were on the Ferris wheel."

Sam gave a small chuckle. "Oh, it was pretty obvious you wanted this body ever since the park."

"Wow. You're a real arrogant ass."

"But I'm *your* arrogant ass."

Luna rolled her eyes while pushing him away. "All right, you big goof, I love you but it's time to go to sleep."

He kissed her forehead. "Night, Queenie."

She didn't react, didn't reply, didn't move because she couldn't. The words, which had popped from her mouth, echoed in her head. Maybe he hadn't heard her, or he realized it was a joke. Clearly, it was a joke, right? What else could it be? People said "I love you" all the time about all kinds of things but it wasn't a real declaration.

And yet…

And yet, earlier Luna had stated she didn't like to say anything she didn't truly feel.

Sam had fallen asleep on his back, his breathing slow and deep. Duchess settled on the pillow beside his head. One of Luna's hands rested on his chest and, even in his sleep, he held it there. As she studied the outline of his profile, something stirred within her chest.

Maybe there was something here, something deep between them. Maybe he'd stay and maybe she didn't need a bug-out bag anymore. Maybe when Spring arrived, she'd let him take over the yard and plant whatever type of garden he wanted, regardless of whether it was aesthetically pleasing or not. A whole world of maybes opened to her.

What would happen if she made a real declaration?

Sam knew almost everything there was to know about Luna, even more than Viggo, and he was still here. Did he love her? She resisted waking him to ask. It was probably hard to love someone who woke you in the middle of the night in order to ask pressing relationship questions.

Instead, Luna rested her head against his bare shoulder and listened to him breathe. She wondered what his parents were like. Sam didn't talk about them often, unless he was recounting a story from when he was a kid. She remembered they were divorced, and his dad lived somewhere else, but his mom was in town. How long until Sam introduced them? Would his mom like her? Would his mother fold her in as if she was part of the family?

Viggo's mom had always been sweet to Luna's face, but it had all been a thin veneer. Luna had overheard her tell Viggo's sister that she found Luna to be 'a little too brazen' and hopefully her son would get over the phase soon.

Surely Sam's mom would be different. Luna could also be different from who she used to be. She could be someone who was lovable.

And this feeling of hope inside her? That was also different.

Chapter Thirty

THE DISCUSSION HAD started innocently enough.

Sam and Luna had been relaxing on her couch, watching some movie on Netflix while sharing a bowl of popcorn. She had insisted on making them some gourmet flavor, rosemary parmesan.

"Really?" He made a face.

"It's fun to try something new. Don't be boring," she replied.

He did try it. While it wasn't horrible, why couldn't he have regular butter popcorn? At least butter didn't overpower his taste buds like rosemary did. Sam had a sneaking suspicion Luna held a similar opinion because she lost interest after a few handfuls, preferring to trail her fingers across his forearms.

"My birthday is at the end of the month, just after Thanksgiving," she said.

"Do you want to do something special?"

Her hazel eyes lit. "Can you take me somewhere on your motorcycle? Maybe we can go to Tahoe."

She'd made it clear a few times how eager she was to go for a ride. Every time she mentioned the subject, Sam treated the request the same as Zabe asking for a pool. He pushed the conversation aside, hoping she'd forget.

"I don't know if that'll be a good idea. It's probably going to be all snowy and cold. Let's do something indoors where I can keep you nice and toasty." He dropped some kisses on her jaw.

"Yeah, but you're still riding your bike."

"Sure, because it's my only mode of transportation and I'm making short trips to get food or see my mom or see you. I'd brave any type of bad weather to be with you."

Luna slouched into the couch cushions, crossing her arms, not at all impressed with his attempt to be romantic. "Okay, but what if I promise to bundle up well? Or we can head south where it'll be warmer."

He sighed. "Come on, Lu. You're going to be able to hold on to me in a really thick coat? Your birthday is going to suck if you fall off. Why can't you just pick something else you want to do?"

"We're in Placerville. It's not like there are a lot of options. You asked me what I wanted to do, and this is it."

"I just think you should pick something more practical."

Luna glared, but Sam didn't care at the moment. He wasn't risking safety to give in to her careless whims.

"Here. Have more of this amazing popcorn you're making us eat," he said.

She didn't respond for several minutes. "Fine. I've come up with something else."

"Great."

"We can take my car for the trip. Maybe we can go to the coast for a few days. But I still want my own motorcycle helmet for when the weather gets nicer. Do they come in different colors? I don't want something boring."

"You do realize that a helmet, even a boring black one, is going to cost over a hundred dollars for a good one."

"Did I say you have to buy it for me? I have my own money."

"I just don't want you to waste it."

"And why would I be wasting my money? As long as you help me pick out a good one, what exactly is the problem?"

The last thing Sam wanted was to get into a fight. "Let's watch the movie and talk about this later."

They watched the movie for a few minutes but Luna sat apart from him, her arms remaining crossed. Sam stuffed more popcorn into his mouth.

"But if I did buy a helmet, you'll take me somewhere during the summer, right?"

He resisted the urge to groan. "I don't know. We'll see."

"What is there to see?" she asked, her tone rising. "Do you think we're not going to be together then? Are you planning to sell your bike? If you don't want to take me for a ride, just say so instead of coming up with all these excuses."

"I don't want to take you for a ride," he said, his frustration coming out. "Can we just watch the movie? I don't even know what's going on anymore."

"But why? I've already been on the bike. How is this any different—"

"I was scared as shit the whole time! And that was before we were even together. There's no way I'm doing it now."

Her brow furrowed as she studied him. He prayed she'd understand and stop pushing. All of this was too hard.

"Okay," she replied.

Sam reached across the gap between them and stroked her arm. "We'll still do something nice for your birthday. Maybe I'll hire a clown or something."

She rolled her eyes, not amused in the least. "What about my other idea?"

"What other idea?"

"We can take my car and go to the coast."

"Why do you want to go so far? What if we just do a day trip to Sacramento or something?"

"Because I don't want to go to Sacramento. What am I going to do in Sacramento?"

"It's a major city. They have lots of things to do there."

"I'm sorry, is this my birthday or your birthday?"

"It's just a long way to go on my motorcycle and if there's an apartment issue—"

"So, you're never allowed to ever take a vacation? I find it hard to believe that Leslie couldn't handle emergencies while you're away for a few days. And you wouldn't be taking your motorcycle because we'd take the SUV."

Sam didn't reply, working the muscles over his jaw.

"Now what's the problem?" she asked. "I'll have you know I'm a careful driver. I've never even gotten a speeding ticket."

"No, you just ran out of gas."

"Are you kidding me? That was one time. And all you're doing is playing games with me, which I hate. If you don't just tell me straight what the issue is than I'm going to—"

"I don't like riding with other people."

She stopped again. "You haven't ridden with anyone since the accident?"

"Not if I can help it."

"So, are we just never going to share a car together? What if we go on a trip somewhere? Or what if we have kids someday? Is Daddy just always going to ride separately?"

Sam removed his hat to run his hands through his hair before replacing it. He honestly hadn't allowed himself to entertain any of these imagined scenarios. He was surprised she had. Had she meant it when she said she loved him? Was she considering a real future with him? "I don't know. I don't think this is something I'll have to deal with anytime soon."

The expression on her face was dangerous, as though she was trying to decide whether or not to dump the entire bowl of popcorn on his head. Sam wasn't sure how to get things back on a non-aggressive track when the whole conversation hadn't put him in the best mood either.

"How about we worry about this later. Your birthday isn't until after Thanksgiving, so we have a few weeks to figure things out and come up with ideas."

Her expression softened and Luna scooted closer. "What are you doing for Thanksgiving?"

"Nothing much. I just go to my mom's house and eat whatever she makes." 'Nothing much' was right. These days, Sam wasn't sure if his mom could cook a full meal considering she didn't leave herself any countertop space. He should text his mom and see if he could bring burgers or something easy.

"Ross and Mia are having Thanksgiving at the judge's house because he bought all the stuff to deep-fry a turkey. They invited me along but, you know, I can't stand the man so…" Luna shrugged.

"Is he an actual judge or is that his name? I'm so confused."

"He's a real judge. Or was. He's mostly retired now."

"You don't think it's weird that he makes his own family call him by his title?"

"Whatever. All I know is I'd rather avoid him and that includes holidays."

"You get to eat fried turkey and see the baby. It doesn't sound too horrible."

Luna's forehead pinched together, but her face switched to a hopeful expression. "Okay, but what if I go with you? I'd like to meet your mom."

Sam's blood ran cold, and he wasn't sure if he started sweating but he was close. He couldn't make eye contact, preferring to stare into the bowl of popcorn as though the kernels had the ability to rescue him from this situation. "I'm not sure that option is any better than going to the judge's house. I don't even know what we're eating since my mom isn't much of a cook."

"I can help. I know how to make a really good sausage and walnut stuffing. Oh, and I can do a goat cheese beet salad. It'll be really elegant."

"I—" Sam was speechless. He wasn't prepared for this at all.

Her face fell. "Do you not want your mom to meet me?"

How did this happen? What Sam wanted was Luna. He wanted her to infiltrate every aspect of his life. Yet, he realized how compartmentalized everything had become and maybe it was because he liked it that way. It was easier.

Her hazel eyes grew large. "Do you think your mom won't...like me?"

"No, it's just—my mom has been really fragile. I-I'm just trying to protect her."

Luna blinked, her intake of breath stuttering, and her body stiffened as though Sam had verbally slapped her. "You're trying to protect your mom from me?"

"N-no." Yes. Or rather he was attempting to protect himself. Because however his mom was, it was his fault. He wouldn't throw his mom under the bus for something he caused. The situation wasn't so simple. "I mean—it's not easy to explain."

But it was too late. He could see it was too late by the way she blankly stared at the wall on the opposite end of the room. Sam was losing. "Lu, I'm sorry. It's not what you th—"

"I want you to leave." Her jaw tightened, chin lifting.

If only she'd yell at him, say something biting, punch him. He preferred any of these. Sam knew how to react to her normal level of anger. This was a level of upset past that and he wasn't sure he could fix it.

He set the popcorn aside, slid closer, his hand covering the cold fist on her lap. Sam pressed his forehead to her temple. "Luna, listen, everything came out wrong. I fucked up."

Sam stroked a hand along her spine, but she'd become marble, unreachable.

"Get out," she repeated. "You said you would stay until I wanted you to leave. I want you to leave."

He grabbed his jacket and stumbled trying to put his boots on his feet as he left her place. Sam couldn't believe how much he'd fucked that up. He'd spend wakeless hours debating how he could have done everything differently. He could have answered her in a way that made it clear he wanted a future with her as well.

The problem was him. Because considering this future, one where everything was laid out on the table, put his mind right back on that motorcycle with her arms clinging to his midsection as they flew down the highway. And he was still scared as shit.

Chapter Thirty-One

LUNA WAS SAD-NAPPING on her couch, buried beneath a comforter, when a knock woke her. Besides going to the bathroom or getting food for either herself or Duchess, she hadn't moved from this position for several days. She unburrowed her head to peek out. The knock at her door came again with more urgency.

"Who is it?" She tried to make her voice strong, disguising any trace she'd been experiencing long bouts of tears in the recent days. Her hair was a rat's nest of tangles, and her skin was an interesting combination of both pale and splotchy red.

"Ross," came the voice outside.

"I can't come into work today," she shouted from the couch. Luna had sent texts the last three days. It was hard to work when one was considering planning an escape route.

"Luna, come to the door or the door is coming off."

"You can't do that! It's a rental. I'll lose my deposit." She crawled from the comforter, unlocked the door, and cracked it. "I told you I couldn't come into work. Do you believe me now?"

Ross's face was filled with concern. "What's wrong?"

"I don't want to talk about it."

Her cousin pushed his way into the home.

"I'll be at work in a few days. I just want to be left alone right now."

He pulled her into a hug, which did a great job cracking the dam on her emotions. "Why didn't you call me? Or Mia? I've been worried about you."

Luna sniffed in between tears as she clutched his jacket. "You already have one crying baby at home. I didn't want you to have to deal with another one."

"Luna."

"What?"

Ross sighed as he smoothed her messy hair. "I can manage more than one thing. You're still my family. You can talk to me."

He led her to the couch, kicking discarded tissues away like snot-filled soccer balls. "Take a seat. You want me to make you some tea or coffee? What do you need?"

"Can you make me an omelet or a grilled cheese sandwich or something?"

"Sure." He kissed her head before strolling to her kitchen. "Oh God. What happened in here? Has Mia been by?"

Luna hadn't been doing dishes or throwing away delivery food or much of any household chores these days. Her place wasn't worthy of any Instagram photos. If she did take some, most of them would consist of ceiling shots. #NotBlessed #Cursed #SadNapping

"Where are your pans? I don't know where anything is in this kitchen," he called from the other room.

She stopped crying enough to groan, dragging herself to the kitchen. "You're supposed to be taking care of me. How are you doing that if I have to do everything?"

"It's either that or I'll dump some of this old Chinese food on a plate and nuke it for you."

Luna set a clean pan onto a burner while Ross perused the ingredients in her fridge. She leaned against a wall, watching him as he put cheese between slices of bread and spread mayo on the outside of the sandwich. He dropped it into the skillet, before grabbing the trash can and discarding the garbage on her countertop.

"I'm assuming this disgusting mess has something to do with your love life. It must be bad. This is worse than the last bastard. You haven't even created a makeshift dartboard yet." Luna appreciated having someone take the mantle of hate on her behalf, but she wasn't ready to make Sam the villain yet.

"I know. It's ridiculous. It was just Sam. It's not like I was going to marry the guy or anything. I-I shouldn't be upset at all." The last part of the sentence came out as a warble as she covered her eyes and cried against the wall.

He flipped the sandwich in the pan, studying her. "What happened?"

"The usual thing. I was being a brat about my birthday coming up. I think he'd just had enough of everything. He left." She couldn't tell Ross the whole truth because, after considering their last conversation, maybe Sam was right to protect his mother from her. If Luna could say horrible things to her own mother, it would be safe to assume she'd have no problems doing the same to someone else's parents.

"Can you get a plate?" He slid the sandwich onto the dish she retrieved. They returned to the couch, and he put his arm around her shoulder as she nibbled on her lunch.

"So, you really like this guy, huh?"

"Or I hate him. I haven't really made up my mind yet."

"I don't believe that. I haven't gotten a list of everything that's wrong with him."

"Maybe there's so much I'm overwhelmed."

"Except I remember what it was like when Mia left, and you look as miserable as I felt back then."

"Yeah, well, it seemed pretty clear that you guys were going to work out and you were in love with each other."

"Clear to who? It definitely doesn't feel that way when you're inside the bubble. Figuring everything out is work, Lu. It's never going to be easy. But when not having the person is worse, then you find you'll do almost anything, even the hard stuff."

Luna lifted her eyes to him. "I'm not sure anyone will ever feel that way about me. I'm not sure I've ever been a good person. Maybe I'm more like my mom than I thought."

"Stop it. You're a good person. You shouldn't hold back so much of yourself."

Her gaze dropped and she picked at what remained of her sandwich. "When have I ever held anything back?"

"Harsh truths are easy. Telling someone how much you really care, that's the scary part."

Honesty: Luna Lanza never had a problem telling the absolute truth.

Brutal honesty: Luna Lanza never had a problem telling the absolute truth unless the cost was revealing her own vulnerability.

Ross was right, of course. Her whole life's motto was all

about never giving too much of herself. Luna could never truly change as long as she kept giving in to her fears, kept from showing how much she cared. Maybe all this time she'd been holding the wrong part of herself back from the people she cared about the most.

Her cousin reached into his pocket, retrieving a scrap of paper. "This was lodged in the door."

Luna unfolded the tiny slip to find a handwritten message.

Please talk to me,
Sam

"I don't think he was the one who left this time," Ross said. He stood and made his way to the door. "I better get back to the shop. Aanya might start wondering where I've disappeared to. Take it easy the rest of the day, but you're coming back tomorrow."

"Ross," she called. He stopped and waited as she approached. "You—you know I love you, right? You've done so much for me, and I appreciate everything. I couldn't have had a better big brother."

He pulled her into another hug. "You're my Lulu. Always. I love you too."

For Ross, Luna forced herself to go to work the following day. And the same for the next day. And the day after that. She could do this. Mia appeared at one point and took her to lunch. Luna got to hold the baby as much as she wanted. It was great to focus on something requiring her full attention.

"You can come over and see the baby whenever you want, Luna. Just send me a text first. I've been too tired to get out as much these days, but I love your company, so you're always welcome to visit. I think I went a whole week without leaving the house and I'm not sure I liked it. And I have to get a haircut at some point. I'm considering shaving my head. I'm sick of the whole thing."

There was no doubt Ross had talked to Mia about the depressing sights he'd witnessed inside the bungalow a few days prior. Surprisingly, Luna wasn't angry about it. Mia had always been nice to her and treated her like a welcomed friend from the start. She was glad Ross had married her and brought her into Luna's life as well.

When she returned to her office, Luna retrieved her phone. She found her previous message sent to Tessa, still unanswered. She typed a new one. *"You were right. I was a horrible friend and I'm sorry I hurt you. I don't blame you for being angry and not wanting to be friends with me anymore. I should have appreciated your friendship more. I know you're probably done with me, but I really need your help."*

When her phone buzzed a few moments later, Luna jumped. With shaky fingers she unlocked her phone to find the message: *"What do you want?"*

She could have answered the question many different ways because she was a woman who had many selfish wants, but this time was going to be different. *"Ross's wife just had a baby and really needs a haircut. I want to book a house call appointment (Grandpa Victor's house). I don't live there anymore so you won't have to see me. She's really sweet, the complete opposite of me. I'll pay anything, just send me your bill."*

The follow-up text was Tessa's Venmo request and nothing else, not that Luna could expect much. She paid the bill, which was much higher than the salon discounts she used to enjoy, but the price was worth it. Luna was doing something good for someone who deserved it and perhaps Tessa would soften with time.

"YOU DOING OKAY?" Ross asked her a few days later inside her office.

"Hanging in there." If Luna assumed getting over Sam would be fast and easy, she would have found herself disappointed. For God's sake, she was still crying in bed at night. Escaping might be the only way to put it all behind her. She was beyond exhausted and looked the part too.

"You should come over for dinner tonight."

"Yeah, maybe."

Ross stood and walked from the office, but her heart froze when she heard him say, "Amy?"

"Is Luna here?"

Anxiety hit her.

"Uh," he said. "Did you tell her you were coming?"

Luna straightened her spine, lifted her chin, and pushed herself to be brave. She stood, walking to the doorway behind Ross. Luna didn't know what she had expected but she remembered her mom being quite vivacious, plus she was familiar with the old photos her grandfather had kept. The reality was her mom was smaller than she imagined, her dark shoulder-length hair frizzy, thin, and mixed with gray strands, her face gaunt. Her mother returned Luna's gaze of shock with her own.

"Luna," her mother said on a breath.

She didn't know what to say, crossing her shaking arms and replying, "Can I help you?" as though Amy was a regular customer.

Amy stood there, watching her carefully. "I was hoping we could talk. I know our last call didn't go well, but it might be better in person. All I'm asking for is the time it takes to drink a cup of coffee. Please."

Ross's face was full of silent questions directed at Luna. She didn't need him fighting her battles. She could handle the woman who stood before her. "Fine. We can go next door and grab a coffee."

"You're really pretty," her mother said after they took a table with their drinks. "You kind of remind me of Skylar."

After all this time, flattery wasn't going to move Luna's heart. "Why are you here? Is this about easing your conscience or something?"

"You're very blunt. I'm sure your grandfather loved that. I'm in remission. I'm not going anywhere yet. I would have contacted you sooner, but I thought it would be better if I reached out again after getting a clean bill of health. This way you know I'm here because I want to be, not because I need to make amends before I die."

"Congratulations."

"I get that you must feel a lot of anger toward me—"

"You're damn right I'm angry. How'd you expect me to feel? You've been gone over twenty years. You clearly didn't care about me. How many times have we been here, where you tell me promises that go nowhere? You know what I learned in that twenty years? That I was too much effort to pick up a phone, send an email, write a letter. That I was nothing to you." Frustration, hurt, and anger were working their way up Luna's throat.

"It's easy for you to sit there in judgment of me when you don't know what it's like. I thought maybe it would be fun to have a baby around, especially a little girl. But you were so difficult, you made everything so hard, and I was pretty much a kid myself. And then you hurt me. So, yeah, I made a lot of mistakes, but I was young, Luna."

Luna was too tired for this. "What exactly do you want? Why are you here? Because so far none of this is making me feel any better."

Her mother's face softened. "I want things to be different. I really do. You're right, I should have made more of an effort with you. I'm sorry I was a terrible mother. I want to be better. I have the time to be better. I'm just waiting for you to tell me whether it's too late or not. What do you want?"

"I don't know," she responded, and she truly didn't. She'd gotten the apology she'd always wanted but the surety she assumed that would come with it wasn't there. This wasn't going to be some happy reunion where she'd fling herself into her mom's arms and they'd have the relationship young Luna had always dreamed about. The reason was because Luna was still Luna, with the same history—the same everything. "All I've ever wanted, for as long as I can remember, was having a whole family."

Her mom leaned closer. "You can still have it. Come to South Carolina and stay with us, meet your sisters. Skylar is out of the house because she's studying to be a fashion designer, but Sunny is still home, and you can meet my husband, Hank. He's a really great dad. You can stay for as long as you want, make our house your home."

Here was Luna's chance to escape, maybe her chance to reclaim the family she missed out on because, all those years ago, she had told her mother she'd loved her grandfather more than Amy.

In spite of having the opportunity to start over, Luna hesitated. South Carolina was almost as far away as she could get. It was clear across the country, away from everything she'd ever known. And what was she running toward? Running away and running toward something were completely different, and she could no longer think of a reason to justify either one of these. Maybe she wasn't exactly like her mother after all.

"I can't," she said.

"Just try it. What do you have here that you can't find someplace new? Sometimes starting new can be freeing."

Luna looked at her mother flatly, not sure Amy realized how the comment reminded her of her mother's abandonment. But instead of swiping back, she decided to take a more practical approach. "For one thing, there's our store. I have responsibilities to my family here. Ross is married. I'm friends with his wife and they have a baby. I don't want to miss out on that."

"That's what social media is for. Do you think I haven't looked at your photos?"

Luna had put her whole life on social media not caring if strangers viewed her posts, but thinking about her mom spying on her life over the years was weird. She shook her head. "It's not the same. It doesn't give you the whole truth.

My posts tell you nothing about what I'm like or how I'm feeling. There's this guy…" Sam hadn't appeared in any of her social media posts and now it seemed wrong. If Luna ran away she'd never get the chance to show him something different.

Sometimes she swore his motorcycle would travel her street in the middle of the night or she'd find a small message lodged in her door.

I miss you,

Sam

Luna decided to give her mother the brutal truth. Not her typical type meant to strike a person down but one that struck herself straight in the heart. Staring her mother in the eye, she said, "What am I worth? Because I'm still difficult and I still mess up and say things that hurt people. And even though I don't always deserve it, I'm lucky enough to have people here who stick with me and make me feel valued in spite of my deficiencies. And if you don't think you can handle that, then let me go."

Amy sat there for a moment before leaning forward on the table. "I want to try, Luna."

"I don't want to hear words. I need you to show me."

Chapter Thirty-Two

"I WAS TALKING to Benedict, you know the new kid in apartment number seven, and he said he's never lived in a place with a pool either, and maybe we'll save money on air conditioning because if it's really hot, you can just jump in the pool and cool off. I can also help clean it if it gets things like leaves in it, just like I helped you water your plants. So can we get a pool, Sam, when the weather turns nice again?"

"Uh-huh."

Zabe stopped organizing the items in Sam's toolbox. "What? Really?"

He glanced at her from his job of moving the dryer out of the laundry room so he could finally give the area a good sweep. "What?"

The kid tilted her head, studying him. "Are you okay, Sam?"

He wiped a tired hand across his face. "I don't know."

"You can swear if you want. I won't tell my dad."

"Oh, thank you. Why aren't you in school?"

"We got out early today. Tomorrow's Thanksgiving."

It was? How had the weeks come and gone already?

The rule was, the more time that passed, the easier things

were supposed to get. Life continued to chug along no matter how much Sam wanted it to stand still. When he was first released from the hospital all those years ago, he had been struck by how much his world had changed, but the rest of the world continued forward as if nothing had changed at all. There were still kids having birthday parties in the park. The couple argued in the grocery store over what to eat for dinner. Cars raced along Highway 50 to spend a weekend gambling at the state line. Slowly, Sam established a new normal until he slipped in step with the rest of the world once again.

He was waiting for the same thing to happen again. But it got worse. The longer they were apart, the more he missed her. His whole body yearned for her.

Sam had finally established this amazing connection with a beautiful woman, who tasted of watermelons, smelled like flowers and cotton candy, and was creative and funny and honest. How was he supposed to forget all of that and go back to normal?

Perhaps he was wasting his time. Maybe the world was again trying to push him into a new normal, to let him know it was moving on whether he was ready or not. This could be one more time where he didn't know it was too late until it was.

The following day Sam went to his mother's house for their annual Thanksgiving meal. They heated the rotisserie chicken his mother had purchased the day before to eat along with deli macaroni salad, buttered corn, and some fruit Jell-O marshmallow thing. The sickly sweet fruit salad dish had maraschino cherries in it. Luna would have hated it.

"This is nice, right, Sammy?" his mother asked as they cleared a corner in the kitchen for a small foldable card table and chairs.

"Sure, Mom," Sam replied. "Maybe for Christmas, you can come to my place and I'll pick up Chinese food or something."

It was then he noticed a couple plastic Tupperware containers that he recognized because of the purple lids and severe discoloration. They were garbage and he had negotiated with his mom for two hours to toss them. Now they were back on her overcrowded dining room table.

He did his best to push down the frustration that threatened to bubble up. Leaning over, he grabbed the top one and held it up, looking at his mother expectantly.

His mother released a sob, covering her face.

Sam's heart stopped. While he wasn't happy, the last thing he wanted was to make his mother cry.

"I'm sorry, Sammy. I'm really trying. Please don't be mad at me."

He wanted to reassure her, but he was so damn tired. "I know. It's not your fault, okay?"

"I don't want to make you unhappy."

Sam rubbed his jawline with his knuckles. "I'm unhappy because I...I was seeing someone, and I screwed up. I really hurt her instead of telling her I loved her. I feel like I'm caught in this slow-moving avalanche and no matter how much I want to escape, I can't. And I caused the avalanche in the first place. I want to protect her, and I want to protect you, but the truth of the matter is I can't protect anyone. The avalanche is larger than any of us. I can't do this anymore, Mom."

His mother's eyes grew wide. "You're not going to help me?"

"This isn't something that you and I are going to be able to manage—because we're both stuck. I love you. I will do anything for you, but I need you to do something for me. Come with me to therapy. I need it because I can't stop feeling guilty about everything and how can I help you when I can't even help myself?"

"I don't know—"

"If you want to keep all of this, if this place works for you, then fine. I just want you to be happy. But if it doesn't work anymore, if you want it to change, please come with me."

His mother sighed. "Okay. I'll go."

And there it was.

The smallest glimmer of hope.

Chapter Thirty-Three

LUNA SAT NEAR the large dog bed, stroking the ears of Hermes the dog. She'd gotten into the habit of spending time in the jewelry workshop, Ross's domain, to chat about things happening in their life. He usually didn't say much, but it was nice to have someone to talk to.

"Oh, I got another email from Amy." It was the second one from her. Luna was surprised to get one email, let alone a second one.

"She say anything interesting?"

"She spends a lot of time bragging about her kids. I know they're technically my sisters, but it still feels like I'm getting stats on strangers. I read it more out of curiosity and the hope she might drop something really interesting, but so far the emails have been pretty generic, like she doesn't know how to talk to me."

"At least it's something," Ross said as he hunched over his workbench and focused on repairing a watch.

"I guess. My sisters are just doing so much and they're younger than I am. And here I am doing the books at a small jewelry store. It's not really much to brag about in return. I wonder if it's because they had more than what I had."

Her cousin stopped, lifting his head. "We had Grandpa.

They didn't. I think, considering the circumstances, it was still pretty good. And don't knock your accomplishments. What you've done, you did on your own. You went to college, and you're helping me continue the family legacy here."

"I didn't do it on my own. I had you."

"And I have to be worth at least a whole houseful of sisters. Why would you ever want to miss out on this?"

"You're right. I'm glad I'm here with you. Do you think you'll teach Victoria how to make jewelry?"

He returned to his work. "If she wants. I want more kids and one of them is bound to have some interest, hopefully. But, if not, there's always your future kids."

"Or maybe I want to learn. I don't know. I just have always had an itch to do something more. You wouldn't be mad at me if I wanted to do something else besides accounting, would you?"

"Why would I be mad? Is that what you want?"

"I don't know. It's just I really like doing the designing thing, but I know going to college cost a lot and—"

"Stop." He lifted his head. "Don't ever think you're stuck in one thing and can't do something else. We'll figure it out."

Her cousin's support made her want to cry with gratitude. He was right. She wouldn't give him up for a houseful of sisters because he was the best. She wished there was more she could do for him and Mia. Oh! There was one thing.

"If you ever want me to babysit so you guys can do a date night or something, I totally will. You need to take Mia out. Or you stay home and let me take her out. It doesn't matter as long as someone gives the woman the break she deserves. Oh, and I told Aanya I'd cover for her in January so she could take that cruise with her family for her anniversary. I think you and I should pool our money together to get her a nice gift basket or something for the holidays. She's earned it by putting up with us."

"Yeah, that sounds good to me." He slid a glance at her and smiled. "I'm really glad you're here to keep things on track."

"Of course. We're in this together, even if I'm out doing other things and not working forever in the office."

"Agreed. Anything else from your mom?"

"She asked me a list of questions, like the last email."

"Are you going to answer her this time?" Ross asked.

"Maybe. I don't know. I'm just waiting for her to lose interest in me again. But, yeah, maybe I'll answer this time and see how it goes."

"That's good."

"She did ask about you."

"Me?" He acted surprised.

"She is your aunt after all."

"I'm just used to being forgotten, I guess." The shop doorbell jingled, and he lifted his magnifying glasses onto his forehead, peering through the security window between the workshop and the main store. "Who's this hottie with the baby?"

"You better be talking about Mia or I'm snitching."

Sure enough, Mia popped through the workshop door with baby Victoria in her arms, a huge smile lighting her face. "Hey, Victoria, look who we have here. It's Daddy and

Auntie Luna."

Ross stood and claimed his baby, pressing kisses to chubby cheeks.

"Look at this sexy lady with the sexy hair," Luna said.

Mia sported a cute shaggy bob, pulling her into the biggest hug. "Thank you so much, Luna. You're so sweet. And I loved Tessa. She's amazing and gave me a hand massage and everything. I almost started crying. Also, I may have convinced her to start a new side business offering in-home haircuts for new moms or other people who are homebound. We're still working out the details, but I might help her do a new website and get some new pictures. And you should text her. I think she misses you."

"Me?" Luna couldn't believe it.

Mia laughed. "Of course, you're fun and funny and really the best person to be friends with. Good Lord, this family. I don't know why I always have to work so hard to convince you guys that you're wonderful. I guess some people just need a little extra persuading."

Ross took one of her hands, pulling her toward him and kissed Mia on the lips as he gently swayed the baby in his arms. "You can work some of your magic over here now."

"I gave you a baby. That should be magic enough." But she leaned into him, and Luna had an inkling this was the beginning of things getting sappy and so she snuck onto the sales floor.

She was happy for them, but she didn't need to get sticky, especially when Luna was still fairly miserable and missed Sam. She hadn't gotten a new note from him in a couple weeks and something about that made her heart drop into the depths of her stomach. Maybe she could reach out to both Tessa and him. So far, being brave was paying off for her and these days she felt strong enough to take the chance.

On the shop floor, Aanya was helping a customer, but there was another older woman perusing the glass cabinets. Luna approached her. "Is there something I can help you with?"

Gray eyes lifted to hers and then glittered. "I can see why he likes you. You're very pretty."

Her expression shifted to befuddlement. "I'm sorry?"

"You're Luna, right?"

"Yeah."

The woman gave a warm smile. "I'm Mattie Sunderland. I'm Sam's mom."

Luna had a moment of panic. She didn't want to mess up this opportunity. She should compliment the other woman's purse. Or her shoes. But she didn't like either one. Luna decided to go with something she did find to be true. "You both have the same smile. It's really nice." This must have been the correct answer because the woman's smile grew larger.

"Are you just browsing or are you looking for anything in particular? My cousin makes all the jewelry in our shop."

"I'm actually here to see you."

"Me?" Luna said for the second time that afternoon.

"Sam said you wanted to meet me and, of course, I couldn't wait to see what you were like for myself."

Over Mattie's shoulder, Luna spotted Sam walking past the shop, who did a quick glance before it turned into a double take. He jerked to a halt. He walked through the door, holding his motorcycle helmet in one hand and a coffee in the other.

"Mom, you told me you wanted a coffee, but I turned around and you were g—" As soon as he made eye contact with Luna, everything stopped.

Sam was very much the same as he had always been. He was still second-hand Levi's, but the River Cats hat was missing. He'd gotten a decent haircut and shaved. Her knees weakened and she had to grab the end of the cabinet to keep standing.

His mom pried the coffee from his hand. "You said you were going to talk to her, Sammy. I was just making sure it actually happened this time."

"You were coming for me?"

He swallowed and nodded. "Is there someplace we can talk?"

She tipped her head in the direction of her office and, in a miracle, was able to make her way on her own two legs. Sam shut the door behind him. Neither one said anything for a moment.

Luna pushed her courage forward. "I'm really trying to be less of a selfish—"

But she wasn't able to release another word because, in a single graceful motion, Sam dropped the motorcycle helmet on the desk and pulled her into his arms, wrapping her in a tight hug. "I'm so sorry, Lu. I'm sorry I hurt you."

"You were just worried about your mom. I get it." Tears came to her eyes, she couldn't help it.

"Listen to me. What I said that night didn't really have anything to do with you. You didn't do anything wrong. It's about me and my issues that I need to work through. Getting to be with you had always felt like a dream but once things started getting serious, I freaked out."

"You don't want anything serious?"

Sam held her face between his hands. "No, I'm saying that I'm currently getting help and putting in the work so I can have something serious with you. I love you."

She sucked in a breath, could hardly believe this was all real. "You love me?"

"Yeah." He smiled, using his thumb to wipe a tear from her cheek. "If you can see potential in a crap-shack apartment, maybe you can see potential in a crap-shack guy."

"Ask me what I want?" she whispered.

"What do you want, Luna?"

"I want you to have a place to grow your garden. To have someone who'd help you carry your toolbox. To always have a cat to cuddle with so you can feel warm and safe. But mostly I want you to be happy because I love you. You're not a crap-shack guy, Sam. You're my red door, my safe harbor."

With tears in his own eyes, he pressed his lips to hers. Kissing him was the same as coming home. Familiarity in this case gave her exactly what she needed. Him.

"What happens now?" Luna asked when they took a breath.

"Maybe you want to join my mom and I for lunch. We've been going to lunch after our therapy session and would love for you to join. You can get to know each other."

She grinned, her heart lifting as if the weights had finally been cut free. "Really?"

"Mm-hmm." He brushed a strand of hair from her face.

"Oh, I got you something." Sam lifted the black motor-cycle helmet from the desk. "Sorry, I missed your birthday. Maybe this can be an early Christmas gift."

With the item in her hand, she could see it wasn't Sam's regular black helmet. This one was shiny and new and one side was custom painted with the words *Queenie* in purple swirly font and a tiny crown. Luna laughed because she was so overwhelmed she didn't trust herself to react any other way. "Oh my God. You got me a helmet. It's perfect."

"Now you can take a ride with me."

"Maybe I can get my own motorcycle."

"Come on, Luna. I'm still scared as shit just to have you on the bike with me, and we'll probably never hear the end of it from my mother. Let's take it slow so my heart doesn't give out completely before its time."

"Hey, Sam?"

"Yeah?"

"I love you."

"You can have whatever you want, Queenie."

She laughed. "So, are we doing lunch then?"

He grabbed her hand, and they departed the office.

"Oh, good. She's coming with us?" Mattie said with a huge smile.

"Yes, I'd love to."

Luna had always seen the events that happened to her through the lens of bad luck. Accidentally kissing a random man in the park. Not getting her dream duplex. Running out of gas on Highway 50. But she'd begun to wonder if she'd been struck by luck the whole time. The realization glittered down on her heart until it sparkled.

As they walked out, she leaned toward her love, who was her perfect everything, and said, "You were mine as soon as you gave me your hoodie."

And then their lips met.

Epilogue

"It can't be that much of a disaster," Luna texted to Tessa.

"No, it is. I don't know when the salon was last given an updated look. Why would people come into our place for a new hairstyle when our place looks outdated? I told my mom that it was your new business, and she is all excited to hire you."

"It's not technically my official new business yet."

"Girl, yes it is! If you believe it, then it is. Say it!"

Luna's cheeks hurt from grinning so much. Having Tessa back in her life made her happy life feel even more complete. *"Okay. It's my business. At least my part-time business. I still have to help Ross, and Sam is building a community garden area at Schnell Ridge, so I want to help him with that."*

"Busy, busy," Tessa replied. *"You still have time to meet tomorrow for lunch, right?"*

"Yes! Lunch with you will always take priority in my schedule. We can talk more about what you're looking for at the salon."

The sound of a motorcycle pulling to the curb caught Luna's attention. *Shit!* She had planned to make dinner and surprise Sam, but she may have gotten sidetracked talking to her best friend. He would walk in and find her sprawled on the couch. She scooted to the kitchen and tossed a pan on the stove before grabbing an onion.

"Hey, babe. You're home earlier than I expected. I was just throwing something together for dinner and…" She stopped when Sam entered the kitchen. He had a funny expression on his face, as though in a daze. "What's wrong?"

"We need to talk."

The phrase still had the ability to make her heart leap into her throat. She quickly ran through every recent situation they had experienced over the last few days, trying to figure out what she may have said that could possibly get her into trouble. Had she said anything to his mother recently? If anything, Sam had made the comment that they were getting too close and he felt they sometimes ganged up on him which *wasn't fair and what's wrong with my clothes anyway? They're still good.*

Mattie was so sweet and was trying hard to make Sam proud of her. She still struggled letting things go in her house, but she was working with a professional and Luna got her into the world of Pinterest. Sam's mom started a raccoon board so she could safely pin as many raccoon items as she wanted. While before Mattie had talked a lot about moving to some cabin, lately she'd been saying that she might stick around, and after the house got cleaned up, they could have holidays with her there. Luna couldn't think of anything better, her heart becoming completely full when Mattie would introduce her to people and referred to Luna as her adopted daughter.

But now the words "we need to talk" had been spoken inside the kitchen, and Luna wasn't sure what happened next—if everything she had fought for was suddenly going to disappear. Didn't Sam know she hated to be held in suspense?

"Is it bad news? You do realize I have a huge chef's knife

in my hand."

He shook his head, leaning against a wall as he pushed his hands into his pockets. After a big sigh, he said, "Leslie's retiring."

She breathed easier. "Dammit, Sam. I thought it was something big. Don't do that to me."

"I talked to my dad and there's going to be some changes happening at Sunderland Properties."

"Okay." Luna returned to chopping her onion.

"Ponderosa bungalow has a new owner."

"What!" Her attention returned. "Your dad sold it? Nooooo. Do I have to leave? Will the new owners let me stay?"

He scratched his neck. "Well, it's not going to be a rental anymore. I'm taking over Leslie's position. In the deal, my father agreed to let me run Schnell Ridge as part of the Second Chances non-profit division of the company and give me the bungalow."

Luna gasped, tossing the knife on the cutting board in order to come closer and whack him on the shoulder. "Shut. Up. Ugh! I hate you so much! But also I love you! But why would you make me go through a moment of agony like that? You are the worst! But also you're the best boyfriend in the world."

Sam cleared his throat after her scattered declaration. "What if I don't want to be your boyfriend anymore?"

Her hand locked on to a hip. "Excuse me? You know, it's not nice to break up with someone right before the holidays."

His face scrunched in an expression of befuddlement. "It's June."

Luna's mouth dropped. "So, you *are* trying to break up with me?"

The arrogant prick released an amused scoff. "Luna, I'm trying to propose."

"You're doing it very badly. I should say no just to teach you a lesson, and then spite you by never leaving the bungalow so you can never really enjoy it."

He slipped his arms around her waist, pressing kisses to her jawline. "Good. I don't want you to leave. I want to marry you. And we can stay here for as long as you want, or until we outgrow the place. I'm not living in this tiny-ass house with a bunch of kids."

"Will you promise me our future place will have a red door too?"

"We can paint whatever color door you want. But I thought you eventually wanted a green one."

"You don't get to tell me what I want. I only want red doors from now on."

"Are you going to marry me or not? That's all I care about."

Luna wrapped her arms around his neck. "I am. I love you even when you make me mad."

"I can't promise to never make you mad. You seem to forget that I'm not a nice person, Queenie."

"What a lucky coincidence, neither am I."

The two *not nice* people decided that the kitchen was an ideal place to make out. And they agreed to get delivery for dinner because all happy endings should include pizza. #Luna&Sam4eva #pizzaphilosphy #RedDoorLiving

The End

Acknowledgments

With every book written, I find that I'm continually cracking myself open to extract feelings and experiences in order to give my characters life. While this makes for a more interesting story, I realize I'm more like Luna than any of my other characters. Neither one of us wants to feel too much and both of us tend to be mischievous brats for our own amusement. So when we do find our people, we'll latch on tight. I'm fortunate many of them helped me in the creation of this book.

First, I'm so appreciative of all the support I've received from my agents, Ashley and Kelly. Being able to bring my words to the world has been a dream come true, and both of you made that happen for me. I will adore both of you forever.

Thanks again to my publisher, Tule, for taking a chance on me. It's been amazing working with the team to see my story as nothing more than words in a document being transformed into a beautiful real book. I appreciate all the work and effort done by Sinclair, Meghan, Nikki, Voule, Lee and the rest of the team. Thank you for everything.

I always feel bad making people read those earlier rough drafts of a story. Luckily, I've had great people willing to do it in order to give me much needed feedback. Thank you (and I'm also extremely sorry) to Frank, Starla, Kristen, and Sonia. And to my friend, Sarah Smith, thanks for eating cupcakes with me and allowing me to vent about how hard writing is.

Special thanks to a group that kept me laughing when I felt like crying and ripping my hair out. To Romance Fight Club: Denise, Beth, Allie, and Janel, thanks for always giving me the best advice and reading sections that I'm panicking over. You're all such badasses that I'm grateful I don't have to fight you for real, although we'll always disagree on whether real heroes should know anything about proper bed sheets.

To my fellow Tule sisters, Mia, Denise, Lisa, Kelly, Heather, Stacey, and Rebecca, I'm so happy you welcomed me into your group and are willing to hold my hand through this wild journey and gifting me with your wisdom and experience.

Also, I want to thank all the writing friends I've met through social media. All the encouragement and love shown to me and my books have been amazing and kept me going even on the hard days.

As always, I have to give thanks to my Gemini husband who has always given my writing lots of support. Being able to pick your brain and getting help when I find myself in a story dilemma has been the best kind of help. You still will never be able to tell me what to do, because you're not the boss of me, but I love and appreciate your creative thinking.

And, lastly, I'd like to thank friends, family, and readers who have come along on this journey with me. While having my words read is always a scary prospect, I feel fortunate whenever my stories find a new home in people's hearts. Anytime I hear that my writing has touched a reader, it's the best encouragement to write more. I hope I write forever.

Love in El Dorado series

Book 1: *Striking Gold*

Book 2: *A Poinsettia Paradise Christmas*

Book 3: *Lucky Strike*

Available now at your favorite online retailer!

About the Author

Janine Amesta is a California girl who now lives in the high desert of Oregon with her husband and their cat, Hitchcock. She studied screenwriting in college, but her moody thrillers always had way too much flirty banter. She's a master at jigsaw puzzles, skilled at embroidery, and critiques bad movies on Twitter.

Thank you for reading

Lucky Strike

If you enjoyed this book, you can find more from all our great authors at TulePublishing.com, or from your favorite online retailer.

TULE
PUBLISHING

Printed in the USA
CPSIA information can be obtained
at www.ICGtesting.com
LVHW090542280124
770020LV00003B/308

9 781961 544442